Me

Regina could remember all too clearly Charles Swinburn's godlike handsome face swimming in her dazzled gaze . . . the feel of his supremely seductive lips on hers . . . until they moved downward, trailing kisses on the nape of her neck, then lower still to the bare expanse of skin above her half-exposed bosom . . . while his hand on the curve of her breast roused feelings within her she had never dreamed possible.

She could still recall that past passion pulsing through her very core as she yielded up her lips again.

But it was not Charles' almost indecently blond male beauty that confronted her, but the stern and dark features of his rigidly righteous brother, Richard.

It was not Charles' warm words of endearment she heard, but Richard's chill silence.

She had married Richard for better or for worse.

And now as she compared his amorous effect on her with his brother's, she feared what the answer would be. . . .

The Colonel's Lady

by
Patricia Oliver

A SIGNET BOOK

SIGNET
Published by the Penguin Group
Penguin Books USA Inc., 375 Hudson Street,
New York, New York 10014, U.S.A.
Penguin Books Ltd, 27 Wrights Lane,
London W8 5TZ, England
Penguin Books Australia Ltd, Ringwood,
Victoria, Australia
Penguin Books Canada Ltd, 10 Alcorn Avenue,
Toronto, Ontario, Canada M4V 3B2
Penguin Books (N.Z.) Ltd, 182–190 Wairau Road,
Auckland 10, New Zealand

Penguin Books Ltd, Registered Offices:
Harmondsworth, Middlesex, England

First published by Signet, an imprint of Dutton Signet,
a division of Penguin Books USA Inc.

First Printing, May, 1996
10 9 8 7 6 5 4 3 2 1

For Albert,
whose support and encouragement
mean so much to me

Prologue

"Oh, Charles"—a breathless female voice whispered out of the semidarkness of the old summer house—"do you think you ought?"

The summer air was deliciously warm and redolent with the perfume of roses and honeysuckle. Lady Regina Heathercott sighed in ecstasy as she felt the gentleman's lips trace their slow, tantalizing path down her neck and into the hollow at the base of her throat. They seemed to nestle there as though they belonged, and Lady Regina felt them stretch into a smile against her sensitive skin.

She had never imagined it possible to be so deliriously happy.

The gentleman's hand, which had settled so lightly, so naturally upon the curve of her left breast, increased its pressure until Regina, heady with longings she could not explain, felt impelled by modesty to utter her whispered protest.

The gentleman laughed softly. "And why ought we not, my dearest Regina? Do I not please you, love?"

The warmth of his breath on the bare expanse of her bosom exposed above the spangled silk of her bodice caused a tremor of delight to run through Regina's whole body.

"Oh, yes, Charles," she murmured, putting her whole heart and soul into this artless confession. "Oh, yes, of course you do, but—"

His lips swooped up to stop her mouth with a flurry of butterfly kisses that quite made Regina forget the argument she had been about to use to restrain the gentleman's impetuous advances. If truth be told, she admitted, she had no wish to restrain him, although she knew she ought.

At twenty-two, Regina had been kissed before. Her pale golden beauty and startling green eyes, no less than her indecently large fortune, had attracted a swarm of suitors in the two Seasons she had spent on the Town. And some of the titled young aristocrats her father had carefully selected for her had kissed her. But not one of them had made her see stars in the daytime and hear music where there were no musicians, or turn her bones to molten fire and her mind to mush, before Captain Charles Swinburn, the younger brother of a mere baronet, came to the ducal estate in the summer of 1813.

Her whole world had exploded in that awesome moment a month ago when she had first laid eyes on the glorious, golden figure of Captain Swinburn. On that memorable evening Lady Regina came as close as she had ever come to dissolving into a swoon. She did not actually do so, of course. Such die-away airs and missish starts were not her style. But something inside her had dissolved, or so it seemed to her at the time. Her longstanding contempt of gentlemen in general and of prospective husbands in particular had dissipated into stardust and blown away, leaving her vulnerable—oh, so unexpectedly vulnerable—to the captain's charming smile and laughing eyes.

So Lady Regina had found herself entranced, vanquished, and utterly seduced by that first glance from a pair of teasing blue eyes. This overwhelming sense of joy and delirium had to be love, she told herself in a vain attempt to explain the indescribable rapture the mere sight of this stranger had brought into her heart. For the first time in her life, Regina understood what it meant to be swept off her feet. Just like those impossible heroines in the romantic novels she used to read as a very young girl. Perhaps those delicate, ethereal creatures knew what they were about after all.

Yes, she mused, as Captain Swinburn deepened his kiss and her argument against such improper intimacies faded into a blur of happiness and awakening desire: she must be in love.

And this impossibly dashing gentleman loved her, too. Had he not whispered as much yesterday afternoon when he had discovered her in her father's hothouse among the orchids? Had he not vowed it the morning before that when he came upon her in the garden gathering roses for the ducal drawing rooms? And two days ago at her mother's intimate little soirée, had he not hinted at it in his laughing eyes as he swung her improperly close to his broad chest as the strains of a romantic waltz turned her into a blancmange? Was he not confirming it now with kisses Regina was sure no gentleman would dream of bestowing on any lady but the one who had stolen his heart away?

And if he loved her, she mused, reveling in the erotic sensation of the captain's hand caressing her back, surely he would not delay much longer in offering for her? And surely her darling papa—who had hinted several times of late in that stern manner of his, that the two Swinburn brothers were not for a moment to be considered as acceptable for a duke's daughter—would not deny her this ultimate happiness?

Or would he?

Lady Regina brushed this annoying doubt into a dark recess of her mind. The Duke of Wexley was a stern and demanding parent, stiff and unrelenting in matters of pride and family honor, and Regina was well aware that her four brothers held him in respectful awe mingled with a healthy dose of fear. Even Robert, his heir, known by the duke's lesser title of Marquess of Gresham, and who had long ago deserted the ancestral estate for the pleasures of London, rarely crossed their father if it could be avoided.

Regina did not especially relish crossing her father herself, but she never hesitated when she had set her heart on something. And Papa rarely if ever held out long against her when she brought her wiles to bear upon him. Everyone at Wexley Abbey knew that the duke doted on his daughter. After siring four healthy sons, and expecting a fifth to follow in due course, he had been completely captivated by the tiny golden girl-child the duchess had unexpectedly produced. Times without number her mother had told Regina the story of her father's sudden and lasting infatuation with the sunny-tempered cherub who had entered his life and changed it radically. And now that she had passed her twenty-second birthday this past June, Regina still held that privileged place in the duke's heart.

So Lady Regina blithely discarded any misgivings she might have had about the duke's hints concerning the eligibility of the Swinburn brothers. Papa need have no fear regarding the elder Swinburn, of course, who was too tall, and too dark, too stern, and decidedly too old and humorless for Regina's taste. No, the beautiful, wealthy, and highly temperamental duke's daughter was in no danger of losing her heart to such a curmudgeon. There had been no admiration for the undisputed Toast of London in Colonel Sir Richard Swinburn's dark eyes when they met, and he had refused to flirt with her during the one and only dance she had granted him during his brief stay. He had not requested a second, Regina had to admit, but had he done so, she would have given him the set-down he deserved for refusing to pay homage to her beauty and wit.

No, she thought dreamily, there had been no danger from that quarter. But the younger Swinburn had been an entirely different matter. Charles was everything his taciturn brother was not, and it did not take Regina long to realize that she wanted this dashing, amusing, gallant gentleman for her very own. She, who had refused adamantly and with occasional bouts of tears, to allow her parents to take her up to London for the glittering come-out they had planned for her after her eighteenth birthday, and had only under duress agreed to attend the past two Seasons, had—quite unexpectedly and without hesitation—decided she was now ready to take a husband. Provided, naturally, that the husband she took was Captain Charles Swinburn.

And now such joy was undoubtedly within her grasp, Regina thought, her body growing warm and flushed under the enticingly improper caresses of the young captain. Indeed, it was almost as though they were married already, she mused, returning Charles's kisses with growing abandon. Throwing modesty to the winds, Regina pressed herself more intimately against the captain's tall frame and was gratified to hear him groan with repressed passion. If they were married, there would be no need for restraint a wanton little voice whispered incitingly, shocking her so much that she shivered.

Instantly the captain raised his head. "Cold, sweetheart?" he said tenderly. When Regina shook her head, he laughed softly and nuzzled her throat. "You naughty minx," he murmured against the curve of her neck. "I wager you are wishing you were mine tonight. Am I right, love?" And then after a slight pause, he whispered in her ear, "You *can* be, you know."

This scandalous suggestion made Regina start guiltily. She could hardly deny that she had been dreaming of just such a sensuous finale to their romantic rendezvous in the summer house, but the notion of admitting her desires so openly gave her gooseflesh. Did she dare? she wondered. Would her surrender merely hasten what was already inevitable anyway? Would it push the captain to claim her for his very own?

"No," she whispered in reply, opting at the last moment for propriety over wantonness, "I was wondering when you are going to speak to Papa about us, Charles."

A distinct silence followed this leading question, during which Lady Regina held her breath. Could she have been mistaken in the captain's intentions? she wondered, suddenly feeling the cold wind of apprehension dampening her overheated imagination.

And then the captain laughed his soft, caressing laugh, and Regina's stomach unknotted. "You silly puss," he teased, feathering light kisses on her upturned lips. "So impatient, are we? It is much too soon to speak to the duke, love. We must work on softening him up first."

"Oh, no!" Regina exclaimed happily. "Papa will not deny me anything. Do promise you will speak to him first thing tomorrow, Charles," she begged, flashing him her most seductive smile. "Do say you will."

"His Grace does not regard me as an eligible candidate for your hand, my pet. We would do well to let him get used to the idea."

"That is nonsense," Regina said impatiently. "Papa would never deny me, I promise you. Now tell me you will do so tomorrow."

"Are you quite sure about this, Regina?" the captain asked, his face for once entirely serious.

"Of course, silly!" she exclaimed, her spirits faltering at the notion that he could doubt her. "Of course I am sure." And then a disturbing thought struck her. "Can it be that you are not, Charles."

The captain laughed again, but to Regina's overwrought sensibilities it seemed that his laugh did not quite ring true. "How can you ask, my love?" he murmured, pulling her against him again and bending to claim her lips.

Lady Regina turned her head aside and his mouth brushed her ear instead. "Then how can you talk of waiting?" she demanded with a hint of exasperation. Having disposed of all possible obstacles to her desires, Regina could neither understand nor tolerate the delay.

"What little faith you have in me, my love," he teased. "I will promise to consider the matter, how will that suit you?"

"Not at all," Regina responded sharply, breaking free of his encircling arms. "I wish the matter settled by tomorrow."

The captain regarded her enigmatically for several moments, his blue eyes no longer smiling. "We must be patient, my little love," he said at last, running his knuckles gently down her cheek.

"*Why* must we?" Regina replied, hearing the telltale note of peevishness in her voice.

"Because I say so, Regina," the captain said in a firmer voice than she had yet heard him use. "But I tell you what, my love," he added, rummaging in one of his waistcoat pockets. "Let me give you this small token of my love, my pet. Wear it for me until I can get you a real betrothal ring, and we can get your father's permission to send the notices to the newspapers. What do you say, love?"

Regina looked down at the ring the captain placed in her palm, a slender band of gold with a very modest garnet in a plain setting. Not at all the kind of ring she had dreamed of one day receiving as a betrothal gift, but it suddenly occurred to her that the captain might not be plump in the pocket at the moment. Gentlemen were often short of funds, she knew from her brothers, who had applied to her for loans when their quarterly allowances failed to stretch for some article or other they simply had to have. Regina had no idea how deep Colonel Sir Richard Swinburn's pockets were, but she doubted he would countenance a loan to his brother for so frivolous a purchase as a betrothal ring for a duke's daughter.

She sighed and slipped the ring onto her finger. At least this clandestine gift would signify that their betrothal was real if only temporarily secret. She glanced up at the captain, her apprehensions momentarily assuaged and was rewarded by a glittering smile.

"Now that we have settled that," the captain murmured in his most seductive voice, "perhaps we can proceed to satisfy some of those naughty thoughts I know you harbor in that pretty head of yours, Regina. Come here, love," he muttered hoarsely, catching her roughly in his arms and running his hand boldly down her back to cup her derrière and press her against his thighs until there was no longer any doubt in Regina's mind what the captain had in his.

Her head swam dizzily, and she felt the warmth and tingle of desire invade her limbs. But something he had said disturbed her, and she pulled abruptly out of his grasp, retreating to the entrance to the summer house. Everything was *not* settled, she thought, half regretting this sensible side of her mind that demanded truth, and honesty, and plain speaking. And at the most inconvenient moments, too.

"No, Charles," she said sharply. "We have not settled anything really. And it will not be settled until you speak to Papa." She regarded him anxiously, half wishing that she were back in his arms. She saw a smile curve his well-shaped lips and felt her resolution waver, yet something in the depths of his eyes warned her that, like all other men, the charming captain was not to be trusted too far.

He took a step toward her, and Regina whirled and ran down the steps. "Tomorrow"—she threw over her shoulder with a lilting laugh—"tomorrow it could all be settled. Just as soon as you speak to Papa."

Without waiting for a reply, Regina lifted her skirts and ran across the narrow stretch of lawn and up onto the terrace. One hand on the handle of the French doors, she paused to stare back into the twilight. The captain stood where she had left him, one hand resting negligently against the lintel of the summer house, a dashing, romantic, vaguely mysterious figure. Regina's heart gave a painful lurch as she imagined she saw the flash of his smile in the semidarkness.

And this fascinating creature was soon to be all hers. Tomorrow, she thought joyously as she made her way up to her chamber, where her abigail waited to help her into her night things. Tomorrow she might be betrothed to the handsomest rogue in Christendom.

But nothing had happened as she had wished.

The following morning brought an urgent summons from the War Office for the Earl of Uxbridge, Colonel Swinburn's commanding officer, in whose retinue both Swinburns had traveled to Wexley Abbey. The departure of the earl's party was precipitous, and Regina had to be content with the briefest of exchanges with the captain before he joined his brother in riding beside the earl's carriage.

"I shall be back to claim you, little one," the captain, dazzling in his red-and-gold uniform, had assured Regina between furtive kisses behind a potted palm. "Do not forget your Charles, my love," he had said, his blue eyes dancing with excitement. "By Christmas the blockade of Salamanca will be over and Wellington will probably return to France. Expect me then, sweetheart," he had whispered confidently, and strode out of the door with a wave of his gloved hand.

Those were the last words Lady Regina was to hear from her betrothed for a very long time.

CHAPTER ONE

Daring Decision

Hampshire and London, Spring 1815

"I trust you are not writing yet another letter to that heartless rogue, Regina." Lady Egermont's usually sweet voice betrayed her exasperation, and Lady Regina turned from the delicate French escritoire where she had been scratching away for the past half hour and smiled affectionately at her aunt, who stood in the doorway, eyeing her niece suspiciously. "Particularly when he has left you kicking your heels for so long without a sign that he is alive or dead."

"Do not tease yourself, Aunt Phoebe," Regina replied lightly. "No doubt Captain Swinburn is so busy with his military duties, especially now that Napoleon is back in Paris since March, that he cannot spare the time to sit down and write to me."

"Fiddlesticks!" her ladyship retorted sharply. "Your brothers seem to find time to write. Infrequently, it is true; but letters do get through in spite of the recent upheaval the emperor has caused with his return to France."

"Have you considered that perhaps Charles lacks the utensils to write as well as the time?" Regina suggested, anxious to stave off yet another brangle with her aunt over the disturbing lack of even the briefest communication from her betrothed.

"Pooh!" her ladyship exclaimed tartly. "You are a lack-wit of the worst kind if you believe such rot, Regina," she said. "You are clutching at straws, my dear."

Regina sighed. Of course she was clutching at straws, she thought crossly, but what other option did she have? It was almost two years since she had watched Captain Charles Swinburn ride off down the wide avenue of ancient oaks at Wexley Abbey that summer morning, feeling her heart being torn from her breast as the captain's white horse bore him inexorably away from her. He had not looked back, not even once, and Regina was left with the disturbing suspicion that Charles had been relieved at that sudden call back to duty. She brushed the disloyal thought aside.

"I know little of military life," she said, forcing her mind back to the present, "but from what Geoffrey tells me in those infrequent letters of his, the poor men are forever looking for places to bivouac, or foraging for food, or riding on patrols, or any number of activities that take up their time and energy. No doubt Charles spends what little free time he has in bed sleeping."

"I do not doubt it for a moment, my dear," Lady Egermont retorted caustically. "That the rogue spends a good deal of his time in bed, I mean. But from what I remember of that dashing scoundrel, I am willing to wager he does not waste much time sleeping."

Regina turned a shocked face to her aunt. Like her niece, Lady Egermont had a reputation for plain speaking, but this indecorous reference to a gentleman's sleeping habits struck Regina as beyond the pale. Besides, the very thought of another female enjoying the captain's attentions—although her more practical self recognized the futility of expecting celibacy from a gentleman as handsome and virile as her betrothed—gave Regina a severe case of the mopes.

Her finger flew to the modest garnet ring that she wore on a chain around her neck, and that had never left her from the moment the captain had given it to her that memorable night in the summer house. It suddenly occurred to Regina that Charles had made no move to place the ring on her finger himself, but had merely dropped it into her palm. But he had said, and quite distinctly she recalled, that the bauble was a token of his love. Would he have said so had it not been true? She had asked herself the same question innumerable times over the intervening months, and had spent many a solitary hour sitting in that same summer house, reliving that magical, enchanted evening when Charles had held her in his arms, making her head spin and her heart flutter with his whispered endearments. No, she chided herself sternly, closing her mind to that impish voice which had of late become ever more insistent in suggesting that the beautiful Lady Regina Heathercott, pampered daughter of the Duke of Wexley, had been led down the garden path, expertly and with cynical deliberation, by the most fickle and inconstant rogue in England.

Regina raised her eyes to meet her aunt's astute gaze. Had Charles flirted with her and deceived her into losing her rebellious heart merely for his own amusement? she wondered. Instead of brushing this heresy aside, as she had so often in the past year, Regina allowed the notion to swirl about painfully in her mind. Her aunt's words only strengthened the suspicions she had repressed until now.

"Do you believe he would, Aunt?" she murmured, her voice unsteady.

Lady Egermont crossed the room and laid a dainty hand on her niece's shoulder. "Yes, my love," she said gently, "I do. But do not tease yourself over things we cannot change, Regina. Gentlemen being what they are, we must be content with what little loyalty they choose to give us, dear. Some are much worse than others, naturally, but in general they are a feckless lot. Only consider my own dear Egermont's interminable string of ladybirds, flaunted so blatantly before the *ton* that I hardly dared show my face in Town for fear of hearing that some new Cyprian had been added to the list. It came as no surprise to me when he gave up the ghost in bed with one of them—I forget which one, dear, but it does not signify now. Much as I hate to say so, it was a relief to be free of the constant heartache of knowing he frequented other females."

Lady Egermont paused for a moment, absently stroking her niece's shoulder, and Regina, who had heard much of her aunt's story before, captured the countess's fragile hand in both hers.

"Do not repine on the past, dearest," she murmured, her own troubles receding in the face of Lady Egermont's tale of marital misery. "Just think of the hordes of beaux who are eagerly awaiting your arrival in London to sweep you off your feet."

The countess laughed sadly. "They are wasting their time, my dear. It will be a cold day in hell before I venture on the torturous seas of matrimony again."

It was Regina's turn to smile. "I fancy you have seriously mixed your metaphors, Aunt. And do not try to convince me that you do not look with favor on any of your suitors. Lud, Aunt, I swear you have more gentlemen dancing attendance upon you than I do."

"What a bouncer!" Lady Egermont exclaimed. "But even if that were true, I would not change my mind. I cannot forgive Gerald, you see." She paused, her wide blue eyes growing misty. "But neither can I forget him, dear. Such a handsome rogue, he was. I only wish some kind soul had warned me what to expect from a man whose smile was quite as charming for every other female as it was for me. But even then I probably would not have heeded the warning. I loved him most desperately, my dear Regina, but I was deceived by a handsome face."

It was impossible for Regina to ignore the parallel her aunt had drawn between the no longer philandering Earl of Egermont and her own charming Captain Swinburn. Yet in spite of the countess's unhappy experience, Regina could not quite bring herself to believe that Charles would ever play her so false.

As if to prove this to herself, she signed her name with a flourish and folded the letter, sealing it with a wafer and placing it on the silver tray ready to be sent off.

She sighed and rose to join her aunt, who had moved to the library window and was gazing pensively out at the April rain which fell lightly but relentlessly on the budding chestnut trees scattered over the ducal park.

"Your papa is growing impatient, love," Lady Egermont said presently, all trace of sadness gone from her voice. "In his letter this morning he demands to know why we have not already removed to London. We should have left two weeks ago, dear, and if we delay much longer, I do not doubt we will have my brother traveling down to Wexley Abbey himself to drag us both up to Town for the Season."

Regina made a gesture of impatience. "I have no liking for the frivolities of London, Aunt. How many times must I tell Papa before he realizes that I cannot enjoy such pleasures when Charles is over there risking his life for his country? Perhaps even already dead," she added, giving voice to another of her deepest fears.

"Fiddlesticks!" her aunt exclaimed mildly. "I have been expressly commanded to escort you up to London with all possible speed, my dear. I have already instructed Claudette to pack your trunks, and the carriages are ordered for tomorrow morning at nine of the clock. No more procrastination, love. Just think of all those suitors of mine languishing in my prolonged absence from the many select *ton* gatherings we have already missed on account of dawdling here in Hampshire."

Regina saw that her aunt had set her mind on their immediate removal from Wexley Abbey and sighed. She had managed to delay their departure three times already, but she knew that ultimately her father would not be denied. The duke had tried unsuccessfully for several Seasons to interest his daughter in marriage, and had waved aside Regina's repeated assurances that she would be wed just as soon as a gentleman won her heart. He knew nothing of the garnet ring she had worn religiously on a chain around her neck since the captain's departure, but would doubtless have declared it a worthless gewgaw, as unworthy of her hand as that insolent puppy Swinburn.

Undaunted by this unexpected parental obstinacy, Regina had already refused the offers from a marquess, two earls, and four viscounts, as well as sundry lesser mortals, driving the duke to express himself more forcibly than she had yet had occasion to hear on the dire fate awaiting disobedient daughters who refused to do their father's bidding. Regina had put her arms about the duke's neck and nuzzled his cheek, but this affectionate demonstration seemed to have lost its power to move him, for her father gently put her aside and warned her, in the voice he normally reserved for his sons when they had behaved particularly badly, that if Regina did not wish to wind up irrevocably on the shelf, she would do as she was told.

Lady Regina had no intention of doing what she was told unless it suited her. In June she would be four-and-twenty, for all intents and purposes already on the shelf, but she had vowed to lead apes in hell before she would agree to wed one of the highly eligible offsprings of her father's political cronies. As yet the duke had not put his foot down and made her selection for her, but Regina sensed that she would be fortunate indeed if she saw the end of this London Season unwed. If Charles did not return to claim her in the next month or two, it would be too late, she thought, and she could not let that happen.

"Very well, Aunt," she said brightly, linking her arm in Lady Egermont's and escorting her out into the hall. "Let us dawdle no longer, dear. By all means, let us go up to London and see what prospective suitors His Grace has marshaled for my inspection."

"You would do well to heed your father, Regina," Lady Egermont remarked soberly as the two ladies made their way to the drawing room for tea. "He only wishes what is best for you, dear."

"Oh, I am well aware of that, Aunt. And I do heed him. At least most of the time. But I do believe I should be allowed to choose the man with whom I must spend the rest of my life. And as you know, I have already made my choice, Aunt. Why cannot Papa accept that?"

"Captain Swinburn is about as ineligible as a gentleman can get and still be received, my love. Poor Roger had such high hopes for you, Regina. You were always the apple of his eye, you know, and if he could, he would give you to the captain. But he cannot, dear. The Wexley pride forbids it, and besides, no Heathercott has ever married lower than an earl, as well you know. You will break his heart if you persist in this mad infatuation with a penniless soldier who cares so little for you that he does not even bother to write."

Her aunt's blunt words struck sudden dread in Regina's heart.

Could it be that her dream of love was indeed built on the sands of illusion?

Later that night, after all her trunks had been packed and taken down to the front hall, her traveling dress laid out ready for the morrow, and her silvery curls brushed with Claudette's strong strokes until they glinted in the candlelight, Regina lay in her bed and pondered her options. At no time did she ever contemplate bowing to her father's demands. She knew that Aunt Phoebe had spoken nothing but the truth when she pointed out that the duke wished only the best for his daughter. Regina had known that all her life. What puzzled and frustrated her was that her father had chosen to gainsay her in this, the most important step she had yet to take.

She was determined to marry Charles; in that Regina would not waver. But it would have to be soon, or her father would find a way to thwart her. Captain Swinburn must be informed of the urgency of their case, and persuaded to return to London to claim her as he had promised. If he did not . . . But Regina refused to consider the alternatives. He *must* return to London. And if his duties did not permit his coming, then she must find some other way.

The notion was a novel one, but it gave Regina's tormented mind a new direction. Yes, she mused drowsily, why had she not thought of it before? If Charles could not come to her, perhaps she could find a way to go to him.

By the second week after her arrival in London, Regina could not fail to notice that her father had once again mustered the bluest of England's blue bloods to pay court to his daughter. No sooner had the announcement of her arrival in Town appeared in *The Gazette*, than invitations began to accumulate on the hall table in alarming numbers. Accustomed as she was to causing a stir wherever she put in an appearance, Regina was not so vain as to imagine that the invitations she received daily from London's reigning hostesses owed as much to her own popularity as to the duke's determined efforts to mobilize the *haut monde* in his personal campaign to see his daughter wed.

"This is becoming ridiculous, Mama," she complained to the duchess one morning over the breakfast table. "Are you aware that Papa has actually countenanced my driving in the park with that wastrel Wolverton? Why, it is common knowledge that he runs tame in half the boudoirs of London."

"Regina!" the Duchess of Wexley exclaimed reprovingly.

"Wherever do you get these unsavory *on dits,* dear? I swear you have never heard such scandal-broth from me."

"Aunt Phoebe told me," Regina admitted blithely, throwing a teasing glance at Lady Egermont, who had that moment drifted into the breakfast room, a vision in vivid blue-and-white striped muslin and a trailing shawl of Norwich silk around her slender shoulders.

Lady Egermont took her place at the breakfast table and motioned to Hobbs to fill her teacup. "What is this I am supposed to have told you, my love?" she inquired, accepting a slice of toast from the butler and reaching for the pot of strawberry jam. "Nothing wicked, I trust?"

"No, not exactly wicked, Aunt," Regina replied with a smile. "I was just telling Mama that I am to drive in the park with Guy Hawkhurst this afternoon. Can you credit Papa entrusting my reputation to such a notorious rakehell?"

"He is a duke, my dear Regina," her mother put in mildly. "Your father was up at Oxford with the former duke, Hawkhurst's father, and you have been acquainted with Guy Hawkhurst any time these ten years, child. A most suitable match, I would say."

"He may be a duke of the realm, and a friend of Robert's," Regina retorted scathingly, "but he is also the world's worst libertine. Even worse than Robert. Or so Aunt Phoebe says," she added slyly, to forestall the duchess's objections.

"Aye, he is that to be sure," Lady Egermont agreed. "A charming rogue, of course, like so many of them, but wholly given over to debauchery and lewdness. Sally Jersey told me just the other evening that Wolverton seems bent on self-destruction. In truth, he was so obviously in his cups the night of Lady Berkford's ball that he had to be escorted out by two footmen. I feel for his poor mother, who cannot be ignorant of her son's reprehensible conduct."

"And this is the sorry creature Papa wishes me to encourage?" Regina inquired with thinly veiled sarcasm. "And if the bosky duke does not come up to scratch, there is always that other notorious womanizer, the Marquess of Monroyal, who, if gossipmongers can be believed, has sworn off marriage entirely. How Papa expects me to change his lordship's mind is beyond me."

"Your father informs me that the marquess is of an age to start thinking seriously of his nursery, dear, as all men must sooner or later, regardless of their natural tendencies to avoid parson's mousetrap. It is not every day that a man is presented with the opportunity to snare a duke's daughter, dear. No doubt he will realize how fortunate he is if you were to give him a little encouragement, Regina."

"Snare?" Regina repeated caustically. "You overrate my attractions, Mama dear. I doubt that Wolverton is overly anxious to snare anyone, except perhaps another opera dancer or two. I hear he is addicted to them."

"Regina!" her mother exclaimed in scandalized tones. "You will keep your mind out of the gutter if you please. I tremble to think what your father would say if he could hear you." The duchess cast an accusing glance at her sister-in-law, who appeared to be engrossed in slathering strawberry jam on a second piece of toast.

"What a lucky coincidence that the Marquess of Carrington has recently leg-shackled himself to Lady Samantha Ashley," Regina remarked sarcastically, helping herself to a second cup of tea, "otherwise, Papa would undoubtedly have coerced him into paying court to me as well."

"Carrington's father was in trade," her aunt remarked dryly. "And from what I hear, the late marquess tripled his already indecent fortune in India. But if I know anything about my dear brother, child, he would never countenance an alliance with anyone who would bring the smell of the marketplace into the sacred precincts of the Heathercotts."

Lady Regina grimaced. What her aunt said was all too true, she knew. The Duke of Wexley was as stiff-rumped as they came in matters concerning the reputation and prestige of the Heathercott line. In large part, this unbending pride had helped to create the longstanding friction between her father and her eldest brother Robert. The Marquess of Gresham was taking his own sweet time in selecting a suitable bride and presenting his parents with a male heir to assure the continuation of that illustrious line. And if Robert was in Papa's bad books for not living up to the duke's expectations, Regina mused unhappily, how could she hope to escape the same fate unless she consented to be guided by him?

The mere notion of falling permanently out of favor with Papa made Regina's spirits sink. But if what her aunt had said about Carrington's tarnished image was true—and she had no reason to doubt it—then her own dream of introducing a lowly soldier, and a commoner to boot, into the family was doomed to fail.

For the first time since that glorious, balmy evening in the summer house at Wexley Abbey when she had discovered, quite suddenly and with shattering clarity, the power of love, Regina faced the unpleasant realization that her dream of happiness could not withstand the weight of generations of Heathercott tradition.

She would not be allowed to wed Captain Swinburn.

The thought lay like a stone in her stomach, and Regina found she no longer had an appetite for the plate of coddled eggs and ham Hobbs had placed before her. She waved it away and excused herself, ignoring the sidelong glances from her aunt and her mother's mild protest.

Twenty minutes later, mounted on her favorite mare, Medea, and followed closely by one of her father's grooms, Lady Regina entered the gates of Hyde Park. At that early hour the park was practically deserted except for a bevy of nursemaids with their boisterous charges, and the solitary ride gave Regina a chance to collect her shattered thoughts and begin to consider various ways of thwarting her father's machinations to force her into matrimony against her will. If Robert had managed to ignore the duke's wishes all these years, surely she had enough wit to devise a way of achieving her own ends, she thought, reining her mare down to a walk and glancing over her shoulder at the brawny groom who rode a discreet distance behind her.

Dodson could be trusted implicitly, Regina knew. Having been instrumental in placing her on her first pony, the stolid, country-born groom had known her all her life and had often covered up her youthful indiscretions at Wexley Abbey, besides teaching her everything she knew about horses. Dodson was the epitome of the devoted English servant, and, like her French abigail Claudette, might be trusted with her very life. With these two on her side, Regina mused, turning Medea's head toward home, and with a little assistance from Lady Luck, she might be able to risk embarking on the daring plan that was taking shape in her head.

When she arrived back at Wexley Court on St. James's Square, Regina felt her spirits soar with anticipation. If she could but devise a suitable means of traveling to Brussels without being detected, she would soon be in her beloved Charles's arms again.

The delicious sense of being within reach of her most cherished desire made her heart sing again.

The opportunity Lady Regina had been waiting for did not occur until the end of May, when the duke expressed his impatience that Wolverton was taking such an inordinate time to declare himself. Regina wisely refrained from informing His Grace that, in spite of having become her most assiduous escort over the past weeks, Guy Hawkhurst, the Duke of Wolverton, whom she had taken into her confidence, had no intention of offering for her or for any other female in the near future. She did, however, feel compelled to inform Wolverton of her father's intention of broaching the subject to him directly.

"Papa is quite capable of forcing the issue, Guy," Regina said bluntly one afternoon as Wolverton drove her in Hyde Park at the fashionable hour of five. "Perhaps it would be wise for you to play least-in-sight until I can arrange to leave town. I should not wish Papa to discover that you are not truly dangling after me at all. He would be most annoyed, and when Papa is annoyed, the whole house quakes."

"Including you, my dear?" Wolverton drawled, a smile lurking in his gray eyes.

Regina glanced at her companion impatiently. "This is not a matter to be taken lightly, Guy," she protested. "We are in serious danger of finding ourselves riveted to each other if Papa suspects there is anything havey-cavey about our budding romance. And that would be a disaster, let me tell you."

The duke let out a crack of laughter which made the Dowager Countess of Mansfield, passing at that moment in her crested landau with her daughter-in-law Cassandra Ravenville, glance curiously in their direction.

Regina smiled and waved a lilac-gloved hand at Cassandra, the Countess of Mansfield, who was one of the few females in London circles who did not bore her with frivolous chatter.

"You are making a spectacle of yourself, Guy," she chided. "And I am surprised you find the prospect amusing, for I certainly do not. Perhaps I should have taken Monroyal into my confidence instead of you," she added, knowing that this would raise her companion's hackle as nothing else could. "I have it on reliable information that he prefers widows and actresses to innocents."

"In that he is not alone, my pet," Wolverton drawled, his eyes still full of amusement. "I rather like actresses myself, but I prefer bored wives to widows, who can become rather rapacious and demanding if one is not careful. Monroyal will find himself trapped one of these days, mark my words."

Despite her own predilection for plain speaking, Lady Regina felt the need to reprimand her companion's unexpected frankness. "You are lucky that Mama is not here to listen to such scandalous talk, Guy," she pointed out. "She would insist upon your immediate elimination from Papa's list of eligible *partis*. And I cannot say I blame her. You are trying to shock me, I see, but you forget that I have four brothers, one of whom is Gresham, whose reputation is quite as infamous as yours, Guy, perhaps even worse."

At her words, Wolverton looked at her sharply. "Does Gresham know what Banbury trick you are planning, Regina?" When Regina shook her head, the duke relaxed. "I would not like it bruited about that I am a party to this addlepated start of yours, my dear. Your brother can be mighty unpleasant when he is rattled, as I am sure you know. Too handy with his fives by half."

"Unpleasant, indeed?" Regina laughed. "Robert can be a good deal worse than unpleasant when the mood strikes him, Guy. But enough talk of my family. Let us go over the plan once more to make sure nothing can go wrong."

Wolverton grinned cynically. "Never think that things cannot go wrong, my dear Regina," he drawled. "That is the first rule of a successful campaign. Believe me, my years in the Army have taught me that." He paused to raise his curly beaver to a stately female who was regarding him pointedly from an approaching barouche.

"Sally Jersey is about to stop to exchange gossip unless I am mistaken," he whispered under his breath. And he was correct, for hardly had Regina acknowledged the lady's salutation than the elegant barouche came to a halt beside them, effectively blocking traffic in both directions.

"My dear Wolverton," Lady Jersey simpered, her eyes ranging keenly over the occupants of the duke's curricle. "And our dear Lady Regina," she added in feigned surprise, as though she had not noticed the Duke of Wexley's daughter until that very moment. "How naughty of you to steal a march with our darling Wolverton over all the belles in London, my dear." Her glance darted speakingly to the duke. "And you, you sly creature, when are we to wish you happy, my dear boy?"

Regina felt a familiar revulsion for the silly games played by the *haut monde* to worm information out of the unwary, which would later be bruited about shamelessly in every London drawing room. She forced herself to smile coyly up at Wolverton.

"That is for Lady Regina to say, my lady," he replied with practiced smoothness, returning Regina's simpering smile with one equally as false.

"You will have the old gel thinking there is a match in the wind, Guy," Regina hissed as soon as the barouche had pulled away with its inquisitive occupant.

"Let her think what she may," Wolverton growled. "They are all in for a rude awakening I fear. Now, tell me, Regina"—he continued in a serious voice—"I take it that you are still set on this harebrained scheme of yours, and that the great escape is still set for Tuesday evening while your parents attend Lady Richmond's dinner and then go on to the opera?"

Now that the time for action was almost upon her, Regina felt a tremor of anxiety at the daring deception she was about to practice on her family. "That is correct, Guy," she replied in a hushed voice. "And all I require of you is that you let it be known that you will be escorting me to your mother's musicale that evening. In actual fact, you will escort me as far as Rochester—"

"I shall escort you all the way to Dover," the duke put in. "It is hardly the thing for you to go traipsing about the countryside unescorted, Regina. And I do not wish to hear any arguments, if you please."

In truth, Regina was only too glad of Wolverton's escort, although the Dover Road was supposed to be fairly free of highwaymen and other brigands.

"Very well," she said meekly. "And since you will not be in Town when Papa realizes I have fled, everyone will assume that we have run off together—"

"Now, that is the part that I do not like above half," Wolverton interrupted again. "Why in Jupiter's name would I elope with you when it must be obvious to anybody with half an ounce of wit that we have your father's blessing? It will make me seem like the merest rattle, my dear," he added plaintively. "I cannot like it, Regina."

"Pooh!" Regina answered cavalierly. She was not about to confess that she had not given that aspect of their plan much thought, but she rallied quickly. "I shall leave a besotted note rambling on about romantic trysts and other rot to throw them off the scent," she said resolutely. "And when you eventually return to Town, you will claim to know nothing at all of the affair, and furthermore, you will produce a note from me pleading a megrim as an excuse not to attend the musicale. You will not have seen me at all that evening. It cannot fail, Guy," she added, seeing that the duke still looked dubious.

"Very well," he finally agreed, rather reluctantly. "But if anything goes wrong, I shall tell your father the whole, Regina, and let the cards fall where they may."

"Agreed," Regina replied, thankful that he had actually agreed to go along with her madcap scheme.

Of course, she could probably have managed very well without Wolverton's help, she thought on Tuesday evening as her well-

sprung traveling chaise bowled over Westminster Bridge and out
of London onto the Rochester road. His presence was comforting,
naturally, but the burly Dodson, who rode up with her trusted
coachman, was fully armed and prepared for anything. She herself carried a slim dueling pistol belonging to her brother Geoffrey, which she had secretly filched from his room ten days ago,
in the pocket of her voluminous cloak, so Regina felt confident
that even without the looming presence of the duke riding beside
the chaise, she would have reached Dover without incident.

Wolverton did come in handy at the posting inns where they
stopped to change horses. He seemed to be well-known along the
Dover road, Regina soon discovered, and his presence guaranteed
that service was swift and that the horses were the pick of the stables.

Upon their arrival in Dover in the early hours of Wednesday
morning, Regina was touched to find that Wolverton had placed
his own yacht at her disposal, with orders to convey her to Ostend
with all possible speed and comfort. Since her destination was
Brussels, where Field Marshal Wellington had established his
headquarters in early April that year, a town Regina had never before visited, she was grateful for Wolverton's assurance that his
captain would take care of all the arrangements for the journey to
the capital.

"You are a true friend, Guy," she exclaimed rather tearfully as
she said her good-byes. "And I shall pray that you do not get into
trouble with my father for this night's work. If by chance you
do," she added with a mischievous twinkle, "I promise to swear
that it was all my idea."

"And so it was, my dear," Wolverton drawled in a bored voice.
"Nobody would dream of associating me with such an addlepated
scheme, I can tell you."

For a perilous moment, Regina was tempted to beg his company for the rest of the journey, but she resisted. It was quite
scandalous enough that they had traveled all through the night together; if they arrived together in Brussels, her father would undoubtedly insist that Wolverton had compromised her and force
them to wed. That eventuality did not fit into Regina's plans. She
had quite another husband in mind for the wedding she was looking forward to so anxiously.

So when Wolverton took his leave, placing a warm kiss on her
fingertips, Regina reached up impulsively to kiss his rough cheek,
and watched mutely as his tall figure strode down the gangway
and disappeared into the mist.

After he had gone, and the yacht slipped quietly through the waves away from shore, Regina turned her face resolutely toward France. Somewhere over there Charles was waiting, she thought, a lump suddenly forming in her throat. God willing, he would not wait much longer.

And neither would she, Regina thought, a smile of happy anticipation curving her lips.

CHAPTER TWO

Unwelcome Surprise

Brussels, June 1815

Although the Duke of Wolverton's private yacht made the crossing in excellent time, given the smooth seas and a favorable wind, Regina wasted little thought on her immediate surroundings. After the mists dissipated and the sun came out to warm the air, she took up a position in the bow of the ship, out of the way of the sailors, who went about their business as though she did not exist. From occasional surreptitious glances, however, Regina soon realized that the duke's crew might well have mistaken her for one of Hawkhurst's fancy pieces, and the notion amused her. Only Captain MacDougall, a huge Scotsman with a merry twinkle in his blue eyes, knew who she really was. Hawkhurst had considered it prudent not to divulge the exalted rank of his passenger to avoid undue comment.

When the coast of France came into view, Regina felt a rush of joy at the thought of the hoped-for reunion with her elusive captain. She glanced down at the inconspicuous shape of Charles's garnet ring under the bodice of her traveling gown. Although the small token could in no way compare to the expensive jewelry she was accustomed to wear, the ring had helped her to keep the flame of her love alive through the lonely months of separation, and Regina hoped that in the not too distant future, her betrothed would exchange it for a more fitting symbol of their future together: a wedding band.

As Regina's thoughts flew ahead to the happiness in store for her in Brussels, the *Gladiator* swung east along the coast and continued for several miles until the port of Ostend came into sight. The seaport appeared exceptionally busy as they weighed anchor in the bustling harbor, but Regina thought nothing of it until Captain MacDougall came to stand beside her at the railing with a frown on his jovial face.

"Is anything the matter?" she demanded, when it became evident that the captain was not about to reveal his thoughts.

The captain glanced down at her, his eyes serious. "I dinna like it a bit, milady, and that's a fact," MacDougall muttered, almost to himself. "I have been in and out of Ostend all my life, but never have I seen so many vessels vying to dock here."

It was then that Regina noticed that they were not the only ships waiting for space to dock. Several other yachts and fishing boats of various sizes and degrees of seaworthiness lay anchored around them and even Regina could see that it might be some time before they could find a berth.

The captain gave a snort of disgust and waved at the apparent chaos on the docks, where a host of ill-assorted vehicles, among them the fanciest of varnished chaises jostling the most dilapidated of hired coaches, clogged the wharf as they disgorged a host of travelers who seemed intent on boarding one or other of the vessels lining the wharf.

"Best stay on board until I can determine what all the bustle is about, milady," he said dourly and stalked off to give orders for a longboat to be lowered.

Seething with impatience, Regina stood at the rail with an anxious Claudette, who chattered distractedly under her breath in French about the foolhardiness of her ladyship's venture and the host of possible disasters that awaited them if they dared to set foot on soil contaminated by that brigand Napoleon.

"Oh, do be quiet, Claudette," Regina ordered, after this string of admonitions from her normally sensible abigail set her teeth an edge.

"You are making a mistake, milady, *vraiment* I tell you," Claudette muttered in response. "The English they underestimate *l'Empereur*, who has as they say, the cheek of old Nick and the daring of a madman."

"We are going to General Wellington's headquarters, you silly goose," Regina snapped. "Napoleon himself would not dare to touch us there, as you must know. We shall be quite safe."

"You do not know *l'Empereur*, milady," Claudette responded in her direct manner. "He is a wily one, and remember," she added sententiously, *"il n'y a qu'un saut de Paris à Bruxelles, ma petite."*

"Ah, but are you not forgetting our own illustrious Wellington, Claudette? The field marshall will never let Napoleon within sight of Brussels, so cease your babbling and fetch me a shawl if you please, the wind is becoming rather chilly."

Some considerable time later, Regina spied the yacht's longboat returning from the wharf and sought out Captain MacDougall to hear what news the captain had discovered.

"It is just as I thought, milady," the captain explained, his expression grave. "My bo'sun reports widespread rumors that Napoleon has quit Paris and is marching north to prevent the allied forces from striking at the capital. Many English visitors who have flocked to Brussels in the past few months seem to have panicked, as have many of the locals. The congestion you see before you," he added, sweeping the teeming wharves with one thickly muscled arm, "is in the nature of a civilian rout, milady. Everybody who has the means intends to embark for England before the anticipated confrontation between the allied forces and Boney's Army."

"Are you telling me that they have no confidence in Field Marshal Wellington?" she asked in surprise.

MacDougall grinned. "The world is full of fools, milady. But just to be on the safe side, I strongly recommend that you return with us to Dover. There is never any point in risking your neck unless you have to. If you will forgive me for saying so, milady."

Regina stared at him in dismay. "Oh! But I have to, Captain. I must get to Brussels. Now more than ever. You see"—she continued, seeing that the big man was not at all convinced—"there is someone I must see. If I wait, it might be too late," she added, hearing the catch in her voice.

"Please help me," she pleaded, throwing restraint to the winds.

After a moment's hesitation, the captain gave in. "As you wish, milady," he said reluctantly. "But it may be hours before we can get a berth to dock."

"Oh, that is easily resolved," Regina said happily. "I would be glad to go ashore in the longboat. I am not in the least squeamish, you know."

And so, after several futile attempts by the good captain to change her mind, Regina found herself standing on the dock surrounded by her abigail and groom, an assortment of luggage, and several burly sailors from the *Gladiator,* whose task it obviously was to protect her from the frenzied crowd.

There were carriages galore to be hired, but most drivers balked at the notion of returning to Brussels, which, from the wild rumors bruited about among the recent arrivals, appeared to be already under siege by the Corsican and his troops.

"That is nonsense, of course," Captain MacDougall assured Lady Regina when he was finally able to bribe a tough-looking driver with a staggering sum to see the English lady and her retinue safely deposited in Brussels. "Rumors are always exaggerated, milady, and from what I can gather, nobody has any proof at all that Napoleon has ever left Paris. On the contrary, I would offer you odds that the Frenchies will not venture north for an-other week or two."

Cheered by this optimistic evaluation of the probable state of affairs, Regina allowed the captain to assist her into the hired car-riage and, after heartfelt thanks to the good man for his efforts on her behalf, wished him a safe return to England.

"And I wish you the same, milady," the bluff seaman re-sponded. "Are you sure you would not like me to hold the *Gladi-ator* here in Ostend for a few days, just in case you change your mind and decide to return?"

Regina had to smile at the fatherly interest Captain Mac-Dougall had taken in her welfare, but she shook her head.

"I expect that when I come back this way, my husband will be with me," she confessed on the spur of the moment. "And since he is an officer in Wellington's Army, I am sure I will be quite safe."

She smiled at the captain's surprised expression, but as the coach rattled away, Regina wondered how she had dared to reveal her secret to a stranger. If she were of a superstitious nature, she thought wryly, she might not feel as joyfully sure of her future as she did.

She pushed the notion aside and laid her tired head back against the grubby squabs, a satisfied smile on her lips.

They passed numerous carriages on the road to Brussels, all traveling with varying degrees of haste in the opposite direction. Lady Regina paid little heed to the advice she received from En-glish travelers, encountered at the various posting inns where they stopped to change horses, to turn her carriage about and return to Ostend with all possible speed. Her thoughts were set on the im-minent and long-desired reunion with her beloved Charles, and as the hired coach made its ponderous way toward Brussels, almost eighty miles inland, she was thrown into a flutter of agitation quite unlike her usual confident self.

Much to her disgust they were obliged to rack up for the night at Ghent, beside the river Scheldt, and it was here that Lady Regina heard from the garrulous innkeeper that Captain Mac-Dougall may have been correct in his assessment of Napoleon's position. According to the latest rumors, Monsieur Gourmand as-sured her ladyship as he himself served her dinner in the only pri-vate parlor available at *La Poule Verte*, the *Empereur* had not yet departed Paris. But one never knew with Napoleon, the rotund innkeeper added lugubriously. Even as they spoke, he may be on his way north to join *l'armée du Nord.*

The following morning, Lady Regina woke early after a restless night, and insisted upon getting an early start. To her heightened senses, the coach appeared to crawl toward her destination, and as each one of the remaining forty miles that separated her from Charles slipped by, Regina's trepidation grew. What would she do, she asked herself a dozen times during the tedious journey, if Captain Swinburn was not actually stationed in Brussels as she had assumed?

As with most things that did not fit neatly into her plans, Lady Regina dismissed the notion as preposterous. Where else would an officer in Wellington's Army be posted, for goodness' sake? She was working herself into a pother quite without cause, she decided, and by the time the coach rattled into the cobblestoned streets of Brussels, Regina had convinced herself that the dashing Captain Swinburn would be there in the full glory of his uniform to hand her down from her carriage.

Such pleasant illusions dissipated quickly when the coach finally came to a rest before the uninspiring building the driver assured her, with a crooked smirk revealing a ragtag set of broken teeth, was *bien sûr le quartier général* of the great British leader.

Until now, Lady Regina had not given a thought to her reception by Field Marshal the Duke of Wellington, who had long been known to her father, but as she entered the main hall and saw the grim expressions of the officers who scurried about with official-looking dispatches, it suddenly occurred to her that her arrival might not be greeted with as much enthusiasm as she had imagined.

"I have important business with the His Grace the Duke of Wellington," she stated, with the hauteur that came naturally to her, when a junior officer approached her hesitantly.

Her request seemed to disconcert him, and Regina had to exert all her authority and not a little charm to persuade a nervous Lieutenant Jefferies to convey her message to his superior officer, who reluctantly agreed to pass it on to their commander-in-chief.

After kicking her heels for all of forty-five minutes, Lady Regina was relieved to hear the duke's jovial voice behind her.

"Lady Regina!" he called out in the hearty, unaffected manner she knew so well from his visits to Wexley Abbey. "I could not believe my ears when they told me you were here, my dear. Where is Wexley?" he continued, glancing around at the deserted hall.

Regina felt a sudden embarrassment at the awkwardness of her presence, unescorted, so far from home.

"Papa is not yet arrived, Your Grace," she said, stretching the truth a little. After all, it was not at all far-fetched to assume that if and when her father discovered her destination, she reasoned silently, he would waste no time in following her. "But he sends his sincere hopes for a successful campaign," she added with forced calm.

The Iron Duke looked nonplussed. "Who accompanies you then, child?" he demanded, his voice a shade sterner, as though he were reprimanding a junior officer. "And what brings you to Brussels in these unsettled times?" he added before she could find an adequate answer.

Regina gathered her courage in both hands. "I have come to be wed, Your Grace," she said firmly, blithely ignoring the duke's first question. "My fiancé is an officer on your staff, and since I have but this hour arrived, I came straight here, thinking you might help me find him."

Wellington stared at her in surprise, his bushy eyebrows twitching inquisitively. Then a slow smile began to soften his thin lips and spread to his eyes. "Ah! You little minx," he chortled, much to the astonishment of two officers passing through the hall at that moment. "You have become tired of waiting, I take it? Well, let me warn you, Lady Regina, that if you wed a soldier, you must accustom yourself to these long periods of separation, particularly when there is a war going on."

"Forgive me, Your Grace, but I have been waiting for almost two years," Regina replied, her natural confidence reasserting itself. "You will not deny that two years is enough to try the patience of a saint, which I have never claimed to be."

This witticism set off another burst of hearty laughter, and Regina began to feel that she had found an ally in the jovial duke.

"I agree that two years does appear rather excessive, my dear," the duke acknowledged, stroking his chin and gazing at her with sharp eyes that seemed to see right through her. "And who, may I ask, is the fortunate man who has provoked this flattering impatience? He must indeed be a paragon beyond price."

"Oh, *yes,* Your Grace," Regina purred, her voice betraying her emotions, as Charles's handsome, laughing face flashed before her mind's eye. For a magical moment she forgot where she was, forgot all about the *Gladiator,* the tiring journey to Brussels, even the presence of the imposing man who stood before her. In her mind Regina was once again in the summer house at Wexley

Abbey with Charles, his blue eyes laughing down at her, his warm lips teasing hers, his . . .

"Well?"

The duke's voice shattered her daydream, and Regina blinked around the unfamiliar drab hall and dragged her thoughts back into the present.

"Does this paragon have a name, my dear?" Wellington was smiling again, and Regina felt a rush of affection for the man who was about to reunite her with her beloved.

"Swinburn," she murmured softly, relishing the sound of his name on her lips. "He is Cap—"

"Swinburn?" the duke bellowed in astonishment, his eyebrows jumping alarmingly. "Impossible!" He peered at her more closely. "Did I hear you say Swinburn, child?" he demanded in less strident tones, staring at her intently.

Regina swallowed and stared back at the man glaring down at her ferociously. The duke's reaction had been so unexpected, she could not for the life of her think of an explanation for his agitation at the mere mention of Charles's name. Could it be that Charles was in some kind of trouble? she wondered, watching in fascination the conflicting emotions that flickered across Wellington's weathered face.

"Well?" the duke repeated sharply. "Did you say Swinburn?"

Regina nodded, her heart sinking down to the soles of her green leather half-boots. Charles must have done something quite dreadful to cause his commander to bellow at the sound of his name.

Wellington glared at her for a full minute before his face began to relax into a reluctant smile. "Well, well, well," he murmured under his breath, as though he were savoring a grand jest. "Swinburn? Who would have thought . . . Betrothed, you say? What a damned sly fox! Begging your pardon, my dear," he added quickly. "This comes as a bit of a shock, you see. Swinburn?" he repeated, as though not yet convinced he had heard aright. "And Wexley's daughter no less," he added, staring at her with odd fascination. Then to Regina's intense discomfort and annoyance, the Duke of Wellington burst out into one of his famous horselaughs that seemed to shake the very foundations of the building.

Regina found nothing remotely amusing in the duke's odd behavior, and stood, stony-faced, until His Grace had exhausted his unexplained humor and seemed to recall her presence.

"Forgive me, my dear lady," he said apologetically. "It is not often that anyone takes me by surprise, let me tell you." He glanced over his shoulder as if expecting the cause of his mirth to appear in the flesh. "I cannot tell you how delighted I am to welcome you to Brussels, my dear. Swinburn wed!" he muttered in an awed tone. "I cannot wait to congratulate him, Lady Regina," he said with a grin. "I shall send him in to you immediately."

"Is he *here?*" Regina asked breathlessly. Now that the moment was actually upon her, she felt shy and strangely reluctant.

"Of course, my dear," the duke said briskly. "Where else would he be at a time like this? One of my best officers is Swinburn. Now do not worry about a thing, my dear," he added, patting her hand in a fatherly manner. "Swinburn will see to everything for you. And please count on my home for the ceremony, Lady Regina. My staff will make the arrangements."

And with these kind words and a wave of his hand, the duke was gone, striding off down the hall as though his mind was already occupied with other things, which Regina could well imagine it might be.

She heard a polite cough, and turned to find Lieutenant Jefferies hovering at her elbow.

"The general has instructed me to escort you to a more comfortable room and bring you some refreshments, my lady," he said, indicating a door leading off the hall. "We do not usually entertain ladies here at headquarters," he added, his face pink with embarrassment, "but I can offer you a cup of tea if you wish."

Regina accepted his offer gladly, but after finishing her second cup, she began to feel her apprehension returning. For the first time since devising her brilliant plan to run Charles to ground in Brussels, she wondered if perhaps this had been the wisest choice to make. It was too late now to change her mind, Regina told herself firmly, disgusted at her sudden uncharacteristic missishness, and any doubts she might have had evaporated the instant she heard the door open and close behind her.

In the sudden stillness that followed, Regina held her breath for a heartbeat before she whirled and started across the room, a brilliant smile of welcome on her lips. When she recognized the man who had entered the room and stood regarding her with an odd expression—which in any other man might have been taken for admiration—on his harsh face, Regina froze.

"*You!*" she uttered in astonishment not unmixed with dislike. "What are *you* doing here?"

"I understand you are looking for me," Colonel Sir Richard

Swinburn replied brusquely, his dark features settling back into the uncompromising lines she remembered so well.

"You are mistaken, sir," Regina replied in her most arctic voice. "I am looking for your brother."

The colonel smiled humorlessly. "Then you have come on a fool's errand, my lady," he said with equal coldness. He bowed stiffly and turned toward the door.

Regina could not believe the man's rudeness, and it took a moment before she could find her voice.

"Wait!" she ordered sharply, anger at this cavalier treatment bubbling up inside her.

With obvious reluctance, the colonel turned to face her, and as Regina gazed into the cold, hard face of Colonel Swinburn, she began to understand Wellington's amazement when he learned that the Duke of Wexley's daughter had traveled all the way from England to wed one of his best officers.

Only of course she had done no such thing, she corrected herself instantly. Never in a hundred years would she be tempted to contemplate marriage to this offensive, unappealing, taciturn man.

The incongruity of her situation suddenly hit her, and Regina had the insane urge to laugh.

"A lady to see *me*, Your Grace?"

Sir Richard Swinburn, adjunct to Lieutenant-General, the Earl of Uxbridge, Commander of the Cavalry Corp., stared at his commander-in-chief in disbelief. Had it not been Wellington himself who brought this astounding piece of news into the map room, where the duke and his senior officers had been conducting a planning session for the inevitable confrontation with the French forces, Swinburn would have suspected a hoax. He discarded the notion instantly. This was neither the time nor place for such horseplay, and the duke was not given to concocting hoaxes in the middle of serious deliberations affecting the future of the entire Continent.

"Oh, yes indeed, Swinburn," the duke replied with a wide grin, returning to his place at the head of the table cluttered with maps and glancing around at the stunned faces of his staff. "And if I am any judge of females, Colonel, I would not keep the lady waiting if I were you."

This advice was accompanied by a loud bray of laughter from the duke and several salacious grins from Swinburn's fellow officers.

"There must be some mistake, Your Grace," Richard said stiffly. "I do not know any ladies in Brussels who would come looking for me *here*, sir."

This remark caused an outburst of hilarity among his comrades, who seemed to think the notion of one of the numerous Cyprians frequented by the single officers daring to enter the precincts of the duke's headquarters vastly amusing.

"Not a chance, Swinburn," the duke retorted jovially. "You have been found out, you rogue. And I fancy you know perfectly well who this nonpareil is. So get along with you and do not keep the lady waiting any longer." Wellington waved imperiously toward the door, and Richard had no option but to leave, conscious of the murmurs and speculations he left in his wake.

Who could this mysterious female be? he wondered as he strode along, his booted steps echoing loudly in the arched corridors. Although always welcome at the numerous festivities that seemed to fill the social calendar of every eligible officer stationed in Brussels, Richard knew himself to be far less acceptable to the female population than his younger brother Charles, whose blond good looks and charming, flirtatious ways had always attracted the ladies like bees to honey. Unlike Charles, who openly reveled in his popularity, Richard did not consider himself a ladies' man and rarely went out of his way to be more than strictly polite to his female acquaintances.

Lady Helen Dalton, or the Countess of Middlemarch as she was now, had cured him of showing any particular interest in females ten long years ago, he recalled, surprised that he could still feel bitter about the experience. He had been a callow youth of four and twenty at the time, too absorbed with his burgeoning career in the Army to pay much attention to the ladies. And then during his return to London on leave to visit his ailing mother, Richard had met the deliciously innocent Lady Helen Dalton. At least he had imagined her sweet innocence to be genuine, Richard recalled cynically. And, fool that he was, he had believed her, believed that he had caught a glimpse of paradise.

Richard frowned at the memories that rose unbidden in his mind. He had not thought of Helen in months, but every time he did, the full force of her betrayal returned to haunt him. A glimpse of paradise, indeed, he mused scornfully. How could he, even in that intoxicating flush of first love, have been such a lackwit as to believe that Lady Helen could return his regard? And even if she had, he reminded himself with painful honesty, her sentiments had not been strong enough to withstand her first glimpse of his fair-haired brother.

Impatient with the direction of his morbid thoughts, and unwilling to venture further into those painful memories which still haunted him, Sir Richard paused at the desk of the officer on duty. It was Lieutenant Jefferies, he noticed, returning the younger officer's salute, a shy immature young man, much as Richard had been ten years ago.

"Where is she?" he barked, instinctively taking refuge from his intrusive memories in the sternness he affected with subordinates and fellow officers alike.

Jefferies jumped and looked alarmed. "Who, sir?" he asked.

"The lady who is asking to see me," Sir Richard said coldly.

The younger man gaped in surprise, echoing the amazement the duke's announcement had recently elicited in his staff officers.

"In the sitting room, Colonel," Jefferies stammered uneasily. "Shall I announced you, sir?"

"I shall announce myself, thank you," Sir Richard snapped, rather more sharply than he intended. Annoyed that he had allowed his past to intrude upon the present, he strode over to the sitting-room door and stepped inside without knocking.

The woman standing at the window looking out onto the parade grounds at the back of the building did not immediately acknowledge his presence, but one glimpse at that mass of pale gold ringlets peeking out from the stylish green shako perched rakishly on her small head told Richard all he needed to know.

He groaned under his breath and drew himself up to his full height, unconsciously preparing himself for this unpleasant encounter with a female he had imagined—perhaps even hoped—he would never see again.

And then she turned so suddenly that Richard blinked, startled, and not a little captivated in spite of himself, by the brilliant smile she directed at him. The smile faded slowly, trembling for an instant at the corners of her generous mouth before it disappeared entirely, replaced by a frown of disappointment.

"You?" the lady uttered in the scathing voice he also remembered well. "What are *you* doing here?"

What did she imagine he was doing here? he thought impatiently. He was a soldier in the soldier's world he had made his own. *She* was the one who should not be here. And Richard could have kicked himself for not demanding the reason for the presence of the beautiful Lady Regina Heathercott in Brussels on the eve of battle.

"I understand you are looking for me," he snapped, deliberately omitting her title. It was as clear as a pikestaff what had happened, Richard thought, watching the conflicting emotions of outrage and frustration on her perfect countenance. Outrage undoubtedly triumphed because her voice turned glacial as she informed him, as though he were some tiresome underling of limited understanding, that she was looking for Charles.

He had known as much the minute he laid eyes upon Lady Regina's elegant figure and seen delight and disappointment chase each other across her lovely face. The sight of her thrust him deeper into the well of depression that had enveloped him moments before at the memory of Lady Helen's long-ago betrayal. A betrayal in which Charles had played a prominent part. At nineteen, Charles—blond and dashingly handsome even then—had thought it a fine jest to cut his more serious brother out with the earl's daughter.

And at nine-and-twenty Charles had done it again, effortlessly and with mocking insouciance, he had charmed Lady Regina into losing her silly head over him and cut off before it sprouted any fanciful notion Sir Richard might have harbored in his bruised heart regarding the duke's stunning daughter. Not that he cared a fig for the pampered, willful female, Richard had quickly convinced himself when it became apparent that Lady Regina's one and only attempt to tease him into a flirtation was provoked by boredom rather than any serious interest on her part.

But what if there had been an interest there? he speculated now, watching the excited flush recede from the lady's delicate cheeks, and her eyes turn into chilly green ice. Lady Regina's pale gold hair had reminded him so vividly of Helen at their first meeting that Richard had been hard-pressed to keep his expression bland. But that first impression had been deceptive he soon realized, for Helen's limpid blue eyes paled beside the expressive, dancing green of Lady Regina's. Except when they turned to green ice as they had now, Richard mused, wishing himself a thousand miles away.

Pulling his eyes away from Lady Regina's frosty gaze, Sir Richard mumbled some inanity through stiff lips, inclined his head, and turned toward the door.

"Wait!" came the sharp command from behind him.

Sir Richard turned reluctantly and glared at his unwelcome visitor from beneath hooded lids.

Lady Regina met his gaze unflinchingly, and Richard noticed for the first time that she looked tired and showed signs of nervousness.

"Do you know where I might find your brother, Sir Richard?" she asked mildly.

The sound of his name on her lips gratified him for reasons he did not care to examine, but his answer was no less brusque than before.

"No, I do not."

The green eyes flashed briefly, but when she spoke her voice was calm. "Are you being deliberately perverse?" she asked. "Or do you really not know where he is?"

"I really do not know," he said shortly, wondering how he might avoid having to help her find Charles, and knowing in his bones that he could not do so.

"I see," she said softly and sighed. "I am tired, dirty, and hungry," she added in a strangely passive voice, as though she had suddenly wearied of playing the duke's daughter. "Wellington seemed to think you might help me find suitable lodgings . . ."

She let the words taper off into silence. Then she smiled, and although it was a mere shadow of the smile she had obviously been saving for Charles, Sir Richard knew that this one was solely for him.

He relaxed. "It would be my pleasure, my lady," he said rather formally, using her title for the first time.

Her smile deepened.

"If you are ready, I shall be glad to escort you," he said, wondering what maggot had got into his head.

When she nodded her consent, Sir Richard opened the door into the hall. "Jefferies!" he called, feeling a strange sense of foreboding take hold of him. "Order us a carriage if you please."

And then her small hand was on his arm, and Sir Richard guided her out into the hall, past the discreetly curious Jefferies, down the stone steps, and into the waiting carriage.

As he saw the lady's luggage safely stowed, assisted her abigail into the carriage, and gave directions to the driver, it dawned on Richard that, unlike Charles, he had never been alone with Lady Regina Heathercott before. In the closed carriage her faintly erotic perfume tantalized him, and a number of inappropriate notions flitted through his mind.

The carriage rattled through the uneven streets and Richard

kept his eyes firmly fixed on the passing scenery. With any luck he would never find himself alone with her again, he thought.

Lady Regina was, after all, the woman who had come all the way from England to marry his brother.

CHAPTER THREE

Multiple Deceptions

Brussels, June 1815

Lady Regina leaned back against the dark green cushions and closed her eyes. No sooner had the colonel taken his place beside her in the coach than she felt his withdrawal and wondered at it. There had been a slight softening of his hostility in the sitting room, she was sure of it; but she could tell from the heavy silence that his face would be once again set in that harsh mold, and his mouth a thin line of disapproval. Did the man never smile? she wondered. All he had ever favored her with was that faint, reluctant stretching of the mouth that seemed to pass for a smile in Colonel Swinburn's pitiful range of social graces.

She opened her eyes and slanted a glance at him from beneath her lashes. He was gazing rigidly at the passing scenery and appeared oblivious of her presence. His profile was angular and decidedly rugged rather than elegantly aristocratic as Charles's was, she noted, wondering as she had that summer at Wexley Abbey how these two men, so different in every possible way, came to be brothers. It was not the kind of question she dared ask, of course, imagining the royal set-down she would receive from the colonel should she broach the subject. Undoubtedly there must be dozens of subjects she might bring up that would send the austere colonel up into the boughs, she thought, vaguely piqued at the notion of ruffling the gentleman's calm demeanor.

But this was not the time to provoke the tiresome man, she decided, glancing at her abigail, who sat across from her, wrapped in her drab cloak and nodding off under the hypnotic effect of the swaying coach. Poor Claudette looked exhausted, and was probably as hungry as she was herself, Regina thought. She must try to keep her temper in check and be on her best behavior if she wished to obtain any assistance at all for the dour colonel. How long this resolution would last, Regina did not care to speculate. The colonel gave every indication of being the kind of man who expected females to be meek and obedient, deferring in every instance to male guidance. Regina gritted her teeth at the very thought of acceding to such antiquated notions and closed her eyes again, wishing that it had been Charles beside her in the semidarkness instead of the unbending colonel.

In a relatively short time, Regina felt the carriage come to a standstill and opened her eyes in time to see Colonel Swinburn leap from the vehicle as though he could not wait to escape. Unexpectedly he turned to hand her down, and Regina was startled to find his hand comfortingly large and warm around her own. She assayed a small smile, which he chose to ignore, and followed him up the shallow steps to the front door, and listened to him rap loudly and with barely repressed impatience.

"Good evening to ye, Colonel."

Lady Regina glanced at the imposing giant who stood in the open doorway, and her first thought was that she had never seen a more incongruous-looking butler. He was an inch or two shorter than the colonel, but made up for this deficiency in his girth, which resembled more that of a pugilist than a butler. His face, scarred and deformed as only a follower of the Fancy's could be, spread out around the centerpiece, a mushroom of a nose, battered out of its natural form into a pear-shaped mound so red and shiny that Regina could easily visualize it glowing in the dark. Had it not been for his eyes, small and blue and twinkling irrepressibly, Regina might have been reluctant to place herself under the same roof as this extraordinary creature.

"Good evening, Burton," the colonel replied, ushering her into the hall. "We are to have guests, as you see. Lady Regina Heathercott and her maid will be staying with us for a day or two. See to her luggage, will you?"

Burton made no move except for one shaggy eyebrow, which rose expressively. His eyes lost some of their merry twinkle.

"I shall rack up with Major Laughton tonight," the colonel added in a colorless voice. "Has my brother returned?"

"No, sir," Burton replied in his sonorous voice. "Ain't seen Charley-boy since yesterday morning, Colonel."

"When do you expect the captain back, Burton?" Regina cut in, determined to assert herself in this odd household.

"Can't rightly say, milady," the butler replied. "But that ain't unusual for the captain, ye see—"

"That will do, Burton," Colonel Swinburn interrupted brusquely. "See that Lady Regina gets a hot bath and some food, will you?" He turned to Regina, who was savoring the novel experience of having a gentleman order her bath for her, not immediately sure whether to thank the colonel for his concern or take umbrage at his dictatorial ways.

"I shall call on you in the morning, my lady," he said, with a return to his formal manner, which he had relaxed noticeably with the butler. "I trust you will find the accommodations comfortable if not exactly what you are accustomed to."

"But are these not your own lodgings, Colonel?" Regina blurted out impulsively. The horrible notion that she was rousting Charles's brother out of his own house pricked her conscience. "I cannot deprive you of your own bed, sir. If anyone must go elsewhere, it should surely be me."

At the mention of the colonel's bed, Regina was startled to see a hint of amusement in the gentleman's dark eyes, and she dared not imagine what he must be thinking at her lack of decorum. Nevertheless, she could not stop herself from wondering at the direction of the colonel's thoughts, and to her disgust Regina felt her face grow warm. She was being nonsensical to a fault, she told herself sternly. Charles's brother was too cold and severe a man to allow himself such frankly forbidden thoughts, was he not? Now had it been Charles, she would have no doubt at all where his thoughts would be straying.

Nevertheless, there had definitely been a hint of something in the colonel's eyes that she had not seen there before. Regina lowered her own gaze, suddenly finding it impossible to stare the impertinent man down.

"Now that I will not allow," her host said in tones that brooked no argument. "I shall call on you tomorrow, if you will allow me—"

"It is your house," Regina broke in impatiently. "You may come and go as you please, sir. But what about your brother? Does he reside here, too?"

At the mention of his brother, the colonel's face hardened, and his dark eyes lost whatever hint of softness they might have had. "I shall make sure he stays away, my lady," he said stiffly. "And if I can find him, I shall bring him to you on the morrow."

And with that Regina had to be content, for the colonel wasted no further time in polite conversation. After conveying his instructions to the interested Burton, Colonel Swinburn gave her a curt good night and disappeared into the twilight.

When Colonel Swinburn left his unwelcome guest at the small house he shared with his brother on rue Lafitte, he did not immediately go back to headquarters, where the field marshal would no doubt be still shut up in the briefing room with his staff. Instead, he dismissed the carriage and strode off toward the nearest boulevard, where he entered a small milliner's shop tucked away in an alley off the main thoroughfare.

His entrance caused two young women, who had been arguing over the merits of a gaudy yellow straw bonnet festooned with a mass of daisies, to cease their chatter and focus their combined attention on the tall officer. Sir Richard ignored them, his mind busy with the task of divining which of his brother's lightskirts—which the captain seemed to gather around him wherever he went—might be able to tell him Charles's whereabouts. He had not seen his brother for two days, which was not unusual, since Captain Swinburn served in a regiment of light cavalry attached to the brigade commanded by Major Sir David Laughton, engaged for the past weeks in reconnaissance duties.

"*Bonsoir, monsieur le colonel,*" a saucy voice greeted him from behind the narrow counter.

"*Bonsoir,* Madeleine," Swinburn replied with a brief nod. "Can you by chance tell me where I might find my brother Charles?"

The pretty milliner's smile faded instantly, and her face took on a mulish expression. "Ah, so you have misplaced the charming *Capitaine Charles, oui?*" she mocked, her voice becoming shrill. "*Moi aussi.* And for your information, *mon colonel, je m'en fiche de votre frère.* He promised to take me riding in the park last Sunday, *et nom d'un chien!* I am still waiting for that *mensonger san coeur* to show his face."

As quickly as she had exploded into this display of rage, Madeleine seemed to forget the cause of her annoyance, and her eyes gleamed speculatively. With hips swinging provocatively, the little milliner sidled up to the colonel and leaned on the counter, giving him a clear view of her not unsubstantial charms.

"But you, *mon colonel,*" she murmured huskily. "You are, as we say here, *une autre paire de manches, n'est ce pas?* Would you care to console poor Madeleine this evening?" she whispered under her breath. "For you, I am free."

Instinctively Richard recoiled. The thought of picking up his brother's leavings filled him with disgust, which he schooled his features not to reveal to the little trollop who had, until recently, been Charles's favorite doxy. He was not surprised to learn that Madeleine had ceased to amuse his brother. Charles was notoriously fickle with women and fluttered from one to another with the inconstancy and insouciance of a gorgeous butterfly, sipping first at one, then at another, with a total lack of discrimination. No, Richard thought grimly, he would not be caught dead climb-

ing into a bed still warm from his randy brother's amorous skir-
mishes. The notion was almost enough to make him swear off females entirely.

With a slight smile, he shook his head. "Unfortunately, I am on
duty tonight, ma'amselle," he lied, keeping his eyes averted from
the pink mounds straining to escape from the tight cotton bodice.
"Some other time, perhaps," he added, driven by an ingrained politeness which prevented him from snubbing any member of the
lower orders, as Charles frequently did.

For the next hour, Sir Richard explored the most popular
haunts of junior officers to no avail. He was about to give up and
return to headquarters to seek out his friend and fellow officer,
Major Laughton, when he came across his brother at a rather
rowdy card-party hosted by Roger Morgan, Lieutenant-Major
Viscount Westbrook. Richard was not a particular friend of Westbrook's—the rivalry between them dated back several years—but
he knew his brother could always be counted upon to frequent
any card-party where the stakes were not too high.

"I need to see you rather urgently, Charles," Richard murmured, standing behind his brother's chair.

Captain Swinburn looked up in surprise, and then flashed his
charming smile. "I shall be with you directly, Dick," he drawled.
"Indeed, I am delighted to see you. Five more minutes and I
would have lost my last sou to these lucky gentlemen, anyway."

A few minutes later, as they stood on the damp steps of Lord
Westbrook's comfortable quarters, Captain Swinburn waved
vaguely in the direction of rue Lafitte. "Shall we walk home?" he
murmured. "I trust Burton will be able to find something edible in
the kitchen, for I am starved."

Sir Richard grunted noncommittally. "You may wish to play
least-in-sight for a few days, old man," he remarked. "We have an
unexpected guest, one whom you might not be too anxious to encounter."

Charles looked at him sharply. "You intrigue me, brother. Are
you going to tell me who this unwelcome guest might be?"

Richard made no move to reply, and saw a smile play at the
corners of his brother's sensual mouth. In one respect he envied
Charles his utter disregard for anything or anyone not directly re-
lated to his immediate comfort. At times like this, however, the
colonel felt a strong urge to wring his brother's neck for the heart-
break he would undoubtedly inflict upon yet another unsuspecting
female who waited so confidently for Captain Swinburn to live up
to his promises. Richard could have told Lady Regina earlier that

she had wasted her time traveling to Brussels with the expectation of forcing his brother into marriage. Promises came easily to Charles's lips—as Richard was in a position to know—and he was not above promising undying love and devotion to any foolish female who would not succumb to his charms any other way.

"Lady Regina Heathercott," he said coldly, his mind going back to that summer evening two years ago when he had stood in the dimness of the terrace and observed the two shadowy figures in the summer house at Wexley Abbey. He had seen them slip away from the ball and had followed them out onto the terrace, hounded by some incomprehensible urge to avoid a repetition of his brother's debacle with Lady Helen Dalton.

He had tried to tell himself that the situations were nowhere near alike. Helen had been an innocent chit barely out of the schoolroom, whereas Regina was two-and-twenty, a self-possessed, pampered Beauty accustomed to having her every whim gratified. And Helen had been betrothed to him, Richard recalled with a familiar stab of regret, their wedding date not two months distant, when Charles had taken her out into another summer evening, in another time, another place, and made her God only knew what empty promises. As Richard had watched Lady Regina fall into the same trap, the whole ugly scandal had come back to him. He had acted instinctively at Wexley Abbey, driven by the primal urge to protect this woman as, ten years ago, he had been unable to protect the one who was to have been his wife.

But had he succeeded? he wondered, staring at his brother's classically perfect features and glittering blue eyes, which seemed to have the power to mesmerize any female he chose to lay them upon. Young chit or bored matron, lowborn milliner or duke's daughter, all seemed incapable of detecting the real man beneath the glittering facade that Charles displayed to the world. Poor Helen had not seen it, and if her presence in Brussels, with no one but her maid to lend her countenance was any indication, Lady Regina had not seen it either. Well, Richard thought, clenching his teeth savagely at the picture of Wexley's daughter in his brother's deceitful arms, perhaps he could do a better job of protecting Lady Regina's reputation than he had done for his erstwhile betrothed.

"Steady, old man," he heard Charles murmur, as if from a great distance. "You look as though you would have my liver for breakfast, Dick." The captain paused to flick an imaginary speck of lint from his immaculate uniform sleeve. "And just who is this Lady Regina Heathercott, brother, if that is not too much to ask?"

Richard felt a sick feeling of despair mixed with disgust invade his senses and strove to keep his voice dispassionate as he replied.

"If you bothered to read your correspondence, you would not have to ask."

Charles merely smirked. "I have no use for sniveling missives from lovelorn females, Dick, as well you know. I find them too depressing by half. Now, are you going to tell me the name of this fair visitor?" He raised a languid eyebrow. "I presume she is fair?"

"Lady Regina of Wexley Abbey. Remember her now, brother? The Duke of Wexley's only daughter?" Richard heard the sarcasm and impotent rage simmering in his tone as he repeated the name. "Two summers ago, Charles? What perverse promises did you make to this one for her to travel all the way to Brussels to run you to earth?" His scorn was more in evidence now. "What vile seductive lies did you tell the duke's daughter to cause her to believe she is betrothed to you? Can you tell me that?"

Charles laughed then, the same clear, caressing laugh that Richard suspected had charmed dozens of unwary females into believing his brother's improbable promises. "I swear, Dick," he drawled nonchalantly, "you are beginning to sound like Mama. This Lady Regina," he added, his eyes brightening perceptibly, "is she a Beauty? I seem to recall a profusion of blond ringlets. Soft and decidedly alluring, old chap. Or has she turned into an ape-leader? Two years ago, was it? As far as I remember the wench was practically on the shelf even then. What is she now, four or five-and-twenty?"

"What the deuce does that signify?" Richard growled, fast losing control of his patience. "The fact remains that you must have promised to wed her. She is quite convinced of it."

"So she says," the captain sneered gently. "Why is it that these bloody females *will* read wedding bells into everything a fellow says?" he added, a peevish note creeping into his voice. "The sad truth is, brother, that women do not understand the art of pleasure. Take it from one who should know about these things. Not one of them has a sense of adventure, of gathering rosebuds before they fade. I forget who said it, but you know the sort of thing I mean, Dick."

Richard knew all too well what his licentious brother meant, and the knowledge that Charles held the lovely Lady Regina in no higher regard than any other of his casual conquests—held her on a level with the frankly promiscuous Madeleine, for example— made Richard's blood run cold.

"Unfortunately, I do," he growled. "But unless you are ready to put your head in the noose this time, I suggest you give Lady Regina a wide berth. She is quite determined to force the issue, I should warn you, and has the connections to do so. Known to Wellington himself. Could kick up the devil of a dust if she is crossed, you know."

Richard saw that he had captured his brother's full attention.

"How unsporting of her," Charles drawled laconically. "I can see that I owe you my eternal gratitude, Dick. Once again you have ridden to the rescue of your intemperate little brother and saved him from the jaws of matrimony. Seems to be your mission in life, old man." He let out a crack of cynical laughter at this witticism, which Richard failed to find amusing.

"If Lady Regina is installed at rue Lafitte, I shall have to find another place to go to earth," Charles added when his amusement subsided. "Be a good lad, and let me know when it is safe to show my face above ground again."

"You intend to stay away, then?" Richard demanded, wondering why his brother's words, painful though they might be to Lady Regina, had gladdened his heart.

"Bien sûr, mon vieux," Charles replied flippantly. "I am certainly not in the market for a wife, old chap, of that you may be absolutely sure."

With a careless wave of his gold-handled ebony cane, Captain Swinburn turned and sauntered away, singing in a lilting tenor, the lines the Scottish bard seemed to have written with him in mind:

The sweetest hours that e'er I spend
Are spent among the lasses, O.

In a strangely lightened mood, Colonel Swinburn strode away to find his own bed.

Two days after her arrival in Brussels, Lady Regina was no closer to fulfilling her most cherished desire than she had been in London. Colonel Swinburn had kept his promise and called upon her that first morning, dwarfing the small drawing room with his presence and sending Regina up into the boughs with his clipped assurances that he was doing his best to discover the whereabouts of his brother Charles.

"Your best is obviously not good enough, Colonel," Regina had snapped angrily when it became evident that her expectations were once again to be dashed. Only after the offensive words were spoken did she remember her resolution to curb her temper with this stiff-necked man who had gone out of his way to assist her.

But the colonel had not assisted her in finding Charles, and on the second morning, when he again stood in the cramped room glowering at her with those penetrating dark eyes of his, Regina had to exercise enormous restraint to avoid throwing a hideous porcelain figurine of a grinning goblin at him. Instead, she treated him to her coolest greeting and refrained from offering him refreshments.

This discourtesy appeared to be lost on the colonel, who told her bluntly that Captain Swinburn had been sent on a reconnaissance patrol and was not expected back for several days.

"And what am I expected to do in the meanwhile?" Regina stormed, striding up and down the minuscule space before the empty hearth in a swirl of green skirts, her resolution to remain calm forgotten. "Sit around this dreadful little house kicking my heels until Charles finishes this reconnaissance thing he is doing? I will not do it," she declared loudly, hearing the note of peevishness in her voice and feeling the growing urge to indulge in a full-blown temper tantrum.

Colonel Swinburn merely stared at her and said nothing.

Regina looked longingly at the ugly squat figurine, then resolutely turned to confront the colonel's gaze. "I can only assume that Charles has not yet been informed of my presence in Brussels," she continued heatedly. "And I *demand* to know why. I am convinced that he would return in an instant if you had bothered to advise him that I have come all this way to see him."

When the colonel still made no move to reply, Regina swung around and marched the four short steps to the furthest end of the worn rug before the hearth. There she swung around and glared at him, her temper several degrees closer to exploding.

"Well?" she hissed angrily. "Has Charles been notified or not?"

The colonel shrugged his broad shoulders, and Regina could have sworn that he was provoking her quite deliberately.

"By its very nature, a patrol does not remain in one place long enough to be easily reached. Only in the gravest of cases would any attempt to establish contact be made." The colonel's dry tone clearly suggested that her demands did not meet the required urgency, and Regina bristled at his condescension. She was not accustomed to her wishes being treated so cavalierly, and her fury increased.

"I consider my case more than urgent enough to warrant sending a message to the captain," she said, her voice beginning to quaver slightly with vexation. "And I shall *demand* that it be done this instant."

The colonel's black eyebrows went up, although his expression remained shuttered. "You *demand* it, do you, my lady?" The question, spoken softly and without heat, contained all the derision in the world, or so it seemed to Regina, whose reaction was instantaneous.

"Yes, indeed, sir," she snapped, drawing herself up to her full height and glaring at the offender in her most ducal manner. "I *demand* it, and if you refuse me, I shall apply to the Duke of Wellington himself."

For the first time during their interview, Colonel Swinburn smiled. At least Regina took the slight stretching of the thin lips for a smile, having no other way of describing this faint relaxing of the gentleman's facial muscles. There was no softness in the smile—if indeed it was a smile—and any humor it contained was derisive and faintly mocking. The impertinence of it set Regina's back up immediately.

"I do not recommend it," the colonel remarked dryly. "I seriously doubt that His Grace will welcome the interference of a female in his military campaign."

"I would not be interfering at all," she countered angrily. "I merely wish to let Charles know that I am here."

The colonel shrugged again. "Charles will know soon enough when he returns," he said slowly. "And then, if he really wishes to get himself leg-shackled, which personally I find it hard to credit, he will doubtless come knocking on your door, my lady."

Lady Regina stared at him in dismay. How had this odious man put his finger on the one insidious fear that had nagged at her for the past two days? she wondered. To cover her uneasiness, she took refuge in anger.

"You are insulting, sir," she said icily. "How dare you presume to cast doubt on the validity of my betrothal to your brother? Why, I wear his ring, Colonel," she added, extending her hand to display the small garnet she now wore on her finger, quite as though this pledge of undying love would silence the cynical baronet's doubts. And silence her own as well, she thought, glancing down at the wine-red stone as if it could confirm that her dreams had not been in vain.

Quite suddenly Regina felt her throat tighten and her eyes grow damp, a circumstance that rattled her considerably. Tears were foreign to her, and she could not remember the last time she had cried. Growing up with four elder brothers had toughened her to the point where she scorned all missish signs of weakness, either in body or spirit. Coddled by her father and brothers, who vied to gratify her every wish, her life had been relatively untouched by sorrow, Regina realized belatedly. Thus the anguish of her present unhappiness was doubly distressing and must be responsible for the unfamiliar urge she now felt to find release in tears.

Caught in the unfamiliar throes of the very weakness she so despised, Regina found herself wondering what the stiff-rumped colonel's reaction would be if she burst into an uncontrollable fit of weeping. She rather imagined he would either heap scorn upon her head, or beat a hasty retreat to higher ground.

The notion of discomposing the imperturbable gentleman who obviously prided himself on his self-control distracted Regina momentarily from her own woes, but she was prevented from becoming the watering pot she abhorred by the appearance of Burton, who burst into the drawing room without the obligatory knock.

"Beg yer pardon, Colonel," the giant butler blurted, his face showing signs of acute agitation. "But there is a *person* out here who insists upon havin' a word with her ladyship."

Regina turned to him in surprise. "A lady, Burton?"

Burton hesitated briefly. "I don't rightly know, my lady," he replied, casting an appealing glance at the colonel. "Said it was urgent, she did."

"And so it is, you great lout," a shrill feminine voice could be heard from the hall. And then Burton's massive bulk was thrust aside and a small woman, clad in a modest gown and spencer, squirmed her way into the room, bonnet askew and brown eyes blazing angrily.

Burton made as if to grab the intruder by the arm, but the lady dodged to one side and whirled to land a stinging wallop on the butler's ear with an old-fashioned, oversized reticule. Stunned, not so much by the blow as by the audacity of a five-foot female daring to attack him, Burton stood for a moment glaring ferociously at the young woman, who glared right back at him, arms akimbo.

"That is no way to treat a lady, Burton," the colonel remarked gently. "And perhaps you could bring up some refreshments, if you would."

Jolted out of her astonishment by the mild irony of the colonel's words, Regina turned to the butler. "Yes, Burton," she said firmly. "Please bring up the tea tray." Then she addressed herself to the small figure still regarding the butler suspiciously. "And what can I do for you, madame . . ."

"Mademoiselle," the diminutive female corrected her in a French that betrayed her humble origins. "Mademoiselle Marguerite Laporte, soon to be Madame Swinburn," she added with a satisfied smirk on her rather pretty, pugnacious face.

"I beg your pardon?" Regina said in a frigid voice, her head still swimming from the suddenness of this apparition.

"Please sit down, ma'amselle," the colonel cut in smoothly and with entirely too much gallantry, Regina thought. And before she could protest, the virago had flounced over to the wing-backed chair and plopped down in it with a deplorable lack of grace.

"Did you hear what she *said*, Colonel?" Regina turned to Sir Richard, an accusing, faintly alarmed note in her voice.

"Yes, I did indeed," the colonel replied brusquely, his countenance grave. "There must be some mistake, of course."

"Mistake?" repeated the visitor, her voice rising close to a shriek. "There is no mistake, Colonel Swinburn," she added, a note of amused malice clearly audible in her tone. "You are looking at your future sister-in-law, my dear sir, so you may as well get used to the fact."

"No!" Regina had no awareness of having spoken, but the negation echoed loudly in her ears. "I am afraid you are mistaken, Ma'amselle Laporte," she heard herself saying with a calm authority she did not feel. "You see, I myself am betrothed to Captain Swinburn and I am in Brussels to celebrate our marriage."

Mademoiselle Laporte laughed rather too stridently for politeness. "That is what I heard, but you deceive yourself, my dear lady," she insisted with such confidence that a cold feeling of fear began to settle in the bottom of Regina's stomach. "If anyone is to wed the charming *capitain*, rest assured it will be me."

"Nonsense!" Regina exclaimed, covering her sudden fear with a spurt of anger. She glanced appealingly at the colonel, who appeared to have withdrawn from the argument swirling about him. She turned again to the little Frenchwoman, who appeared to be much at her ease in Charles's drawing room. The notion that there must certainly be a connection, probably sordid in nature, between this young hussy and her dear Charles caused Regina's temper to run away with her.

"You will never convince me that Captain Swinburn, who has been betrothed to me for the past two years, would ever dream of offering you marriage, Ma'amselle Laporte," she said with chilly frankness. "And if you think you can extort money from us, my dear girl, you will soon find—"

This indelicate speech was suddenly cut short by Burton, who once again opened the door and gazed helplessly at the colonel, his misshapen features twisted into even stranger angles.

"Well, man," the colonel said impatiently, "out with it."

"Beg yer pardon again, sir, but there's another one of 'em out here, asking for the captain she is."

There was a moment of appalled silence, broken by an angry snort from Miss Laporte.

"Show the lady in, Burton," the colonel said in a resigned tone.

"This 'un ain't no lady, Colonel, and that's a fact," the butler grumbled and opened the door wider to allow the second visitor to enter.

"*Miss* Annette Gérard," the butler intoned, an imperceptible emphasis on the first word.

Regina saw immediately what had aroused Burton's disapproval. The newcomer, a pretty blond with startlingly beautiful pansy-blue eyes, was visibly *enceinte*.

There was an uncomfortable silence in the room, which Regina, social correctness bred into her very bones, was the first to break.

"Please sit down, Miss Gérard," she said, coolly polite. "We are just about to have tea. I hope you can join us?"

Under the circumstances, this inane cordiality sounded incongruous to a fault, Regina thought, fighting a wild desire to run screaming from the room. Yet nobody laughed.

"Thank you, my lady," the girl replied with equal politeness. "I have come to see Captain Swinburn. Perhaps you can tell me if this is possible?" Her voice was no more cultured than their first unwelcome guest, but her voice was low and pleasant.

Before Regina could divine her purpose, Annette Laporte jumped to her feet and glared menacingly at the new guest. "And what, may I ask, is your business with Captain Swinburn, *mademoiselle?*" she demanded, rudely drawing attention to Miss Gérard's lamentable condition.

Impervious to the snub, Miss Gérard looked at her in surprise. "It must be obvious what my business with the captain is," she replied with a shy smile, her hands coming to rest lightly on her expanding figure, and her cheeks turning a delightful pink. "I have come to insist that he keep his promise to me before our baby is born. We are betrothed, you should know, and would have been wed by now had not Charles encountered a run of bad luck at the faro tables."

Regina felt her knees buckle and was vastly relieved when Colonel Swinburn caught her elbow and led her to a drab-looking settee of no particular style, where she collapsed.

"I cannot believe *any* of this," she murmured under her breath. "Tell them both to go away and leave me alone." He patted her hand in a manner so at odds with his usual starched-up aloofness, that Regina glanced up at him, her heart sinking at the glint of pity she detected in his dark eyes. "Do *you* believe these women's preposterous stories?"

Regina never did hear the colonel's reply, for at that moment the door opened again to admit Burton, and something inside her snapped.

"No!" she cried, jumping to her feet, fury at the game the Fates appeared to be playing on her overcoming her momentary weakness. "I forbid you to let any more females into this house, Burton," she ordered in her most arctic tone.

Burton paused in the doorway, seemingly nonplussed. Then a mischievous twinkle appeared in his blue eyes—a most inappropriate liberty for a butler to take, Regina remembered thinking—and his lips twitched quite noticeably while he made her a very correct and entirely servile bow.

"It is only the tea tray, my lady," he said with impeccable formality.

Deflated by the ridiculous incongruity of the scene, and conscious of the hysteria rising in her throat, Regina sat down as abruptly as she had risen.

"Very well, Burton," she said, not daring to meet the colonel's eyes. "You may serve us, if you will."

CHAPTER FOUR

An Irate Father

Much to his dismay, Colonel Swinburn discovered that the presence of Lady Regina Heathercott in Brussels occasioned more disturbance in his life than he had bargained for. Not only had the advent of Charles's supposed betrothed—to say nothing of two additional females with claims on the captain's thankless attentions—disrupted his former peaceful existence at rue Lafitte, but his commander-in-chief, the Duke of Wellington himself, had inquired with considerable interest when the happy event of his marriage was to take place.

Cursing himself for not straightening out that unfortunate misunderstanding from the very start, Richard felt himself becoming dangerously enmeshed in an imbroglio that threatened to disturb the ebb and flow of his life in ways that did not bear thinking about.

Yesterday morning's call on Lady Regina had been a worse disaster than any campaign the colonel had yet had the misfortune to conduct. As first one, and then another young female, besides her ladyship, had invaded his bachelor establishment claiming betrothal to his rascally brother, Richard had never come so close to bolting for cover in his life. Had it not been for the sight of Lady Regina's anguished face, and the unspoken plea in her lovely green eyes, Richard swore to himself as he recalled the harrowing events of the previous day, he would have washed his hands of the whole affair.

But he had not done so, of course. Lady Regina had needed his protection; he had seen it clearly in her eyes even though he suspected she would never admit it. And something in the colonel had responded, a long repressed instinct that had lain dormant for ten years, ever since he had failed to protect his own beloved Helen from the folly of her youth and innocence. So he had stayed in that oppressive drawing room, drinking tea he did not want, and watching the conflicting emotions flicker across that beautiful face as the other two women argued—in language that grew progressively shrill and distressingly vulgar—the validity of their claims on Captain Swinburn's affections.

When finally he had risen to take his leave, and Lady Regina had accompanied him out into the tiny hall, he had felt driven to take her frozen hand in his and raise it to his lips—a courtesy he rarely employed with any female—and press a warm, comforting kiss on the cold fingers. She had raised her eyes to gaze at him, and for the first time Richard had admitted to himself that they were very lovely eyes indeed, but also more vulnerable than any woman's he had ever seen. Except perhaps for Helen's.

And it was because of those eyes, because of that unexpected vulnerability, and yes, because of his long ago failure with Lady Helen, that Richard found himself knocking on his own door the following afternoon as promised.

"Afternoon, Colonel." Burton greeted him with the informality that had existed between them since their early days together in the Army, when the colonel, a mere lieutenant at the time, had not hesitated to employ an ugly ex-pugilist as his batman.

"I would like to speak to Lady Regina. Alone, if you can manage it, Burton."

Burton's misshapen countenance cracked into a radiant smile. "Right you are, Colonel," he said. "It so 'appens that the two young . . . eh, ladies, are out on the strut, and 'er ladyship is quite alone, sir." The butler paused, then added in a hushed voice. "As cross as crabs, the poor wee lass, but when ye 'ear what 'appened after ye left yesterday, sir—"

Richard held up a hand to halt the flow of words. "I shall announce myself, thank you, Burton."

"Ah, Colonel!" Lady Regina exclaimed testily as soon as he entered the drawing room. She had been standing at the narrow window overlooking the walled garden the size of a pocket handkerchief at the back of the house, and Richard saw at once that Burton had been correct. The lady was definitely blue-deviled. As he strolled forward to greet her, he noticed that in spite of the fashionable gown of green striped lustring and the artful arrangement of golden curls around her small face, Lady Regina had every appearance of having sustained a severe shock.

"So," she snapped, glaring at him as though he had committed an unpardonable sin, "you have come. I rather expected you to play the Jack, Colonel. You surprise me." The sarcasm in her voice was unmistakable.

Richard felt his face go rigid. "I promised to call on you this afternoon, and I have done so," he said with deceptive softness. "But if you intend to pull caps with me, my lady, believe me, there are other more congenial pursuits I might seek."

Lady Regina stared at him as though he had slapped her. The

expression of shock, followed by outrage, that flashed across her countenance told him more clearly than words that her ladyship was unaccustomed to receiving set-downs. The discovery amused him. If she had expected him to grovel at her feet and meekly submit to any insult she cared to throw at his head, he thought with grim satisfaction, the lady was in for a nasty surprise. He had never allowed any woman to ride roughshod over him, not even his own Helen, and he had no intention of starting with the high-and-mighty Lady Regina Heathercott.

With a dismissive toss of her head, Lady Regina seemed to regain her composure. "What news do you bring of Charles?" she inquired coldly.

Richard shrugged. "I spoke with his commanding officer last night, and he assures me that my brother is not expected to return to headquarters for another four or five days." At least he did not have to lie to her again, the colonel thought. Major David Laughton had given him the information readily enough when Richard had explained to his friend that the rumors flying around headquarters had mistaken the facts. It was *Captain* Swinburn the lady had come to see leg-shackled, not the colonel.

"Thank heaven for small mercies," Richard had felt obliged to add when David Laughton had glanced at him sharply. Laughton was one of the few friends who knew of the old scandal with Lady Helen, and although Richard had told him few of the painful details of that lady's betrayal, Laughton must have guessed that this early disappointment had soured the colonel to wedlock and turned him into a confirmed bachelor.

"How very odd," Laughton had remarked, a thread of sarcasm in his voice. "If what you say is true, Dick, and I do not doubt it for a moment, of course," he added when Richard frowned at him. "Then I wonder why Captain Swinburn came to me only yesterday, begging to be sent out instead of Riddleton, who was scheduled to lead the patrol?"

Richard stared at his friend's quizzical smile for a moment before heaving a resigned sigh. "I hope I can depend on your discretion not to bruit this about, David. But I fear Lady Regina has come on a wild-goose chase. Charles is as little inclined to parson's mousetrap as I am myself, and it appears that his request for patrol duty is his way of avoiding the lady's clutches. I have suggested as much, with as much tact as possible, of course, but the lady is somewhat of a termagant, and a determined one to boot."

"A termagant?" the major repeated in surprise. "A very beautiful one if I remember correctly. And full of juice, too. Your brother must be a monumental sap-head to let this one get away, Dick."

"You have met her, then?"

It was Laughton's turn to shrug. "Briefly. She was with Wolverton at the time, but I know for a fact that Guy is as skittish about marriage as you are, Dick. It seems the lady has execrable taste or is foolish beyond belief to waste her time with libertines. Wolverton's reputation with the ladies is almost as bad as your brother's. Now why could the wench not have set her sights on me? I wonder. I cannot claim Charles's good looks or Guy's rank and wealth, but I am a decent enough chap, after all, am I not?"

"You?" Richard had exclaimed in astonishment. Popular though he was with hostesses on both sides of the channel, Sir David Laughton had shown no interest in any particular lady since the untimely death of his young wife several years ago. "Surely you jest, David?"

Laughton grinned. "I am not above temptation, my lad. And Lady Regina is bonny enough to turn any man's head, even an old fuddlecap like me. And say what you will, Dick, the wedded state holds certain attractions for a man of advancing years. Can you not imagine the fair Regina preparing a restorative posset with her own hands for an ailing husband?"

Richard could imagine no such thing, and as he regarded the lady across the cramped length of his drawing room, he realized that his friend had been roasting him. Indeed, the picture Lady Regina now presented was of a female who, when her bristles had been set on edge, would as lief comb a fellow's hair with a joint stool as cater to his infirmities.

"I see," she said icily. "I take it that you have not seen fit to send Charles a message, sir?"

The colonel raised his eyebrows. "I explained only yesterday the futility of such a step, my lady," he said with barely restrained impatience. "And by the way," he continued, before the lady could utter the protest that hovered on her lips, "the duke appears to be under the misapprehension that it is I you have come to wed, not my brother."

He was gratified at the look of blank astonishment this announcement produced, and oddly affected by the rush of color that flooded Lady Regina's cheeks. "Perhaps you can explain how this nonsensical confusion came about?" he added more gently.

Momentarily deprived of her icy control, Lady Regina opened

her mouth several times, but it was not until the third attempt that she blurted out a violent denial.

"No!" she cried. "That must be a Banbury story. I cannot believe that His Grace would be so stupid as to imagine I would come all the way from London to . . ." She hesitated and waved one slender hand in his direction.

"To wed me?" he suggested gently, his eyes missing nothing of her obvious consternation at the notion.

"Precisely," she snapped, recovering rapidly from her gaffe. "I told the duke most clearly that I was betrothed to an officer on his staff, but when I gave Charles's name, His Grace did seem rather taken aback." She paused, as if remembering that scene. "In fact, now that I recall, he laughed in a most vulgar manner."

"What name did you give?"

Her glance brought his mental faculties into question. "Swinburn, of course. Who else?"

"I see," he murmured, and indeed he did see how he had become unexpectedly betrothed in the mind of his commanding officer. He smiled thinly. "I am the only Swinburn on the general's staff."

She stared incredulously. "Charles told me that—"

"Regardless of what my brother told you, my dear lady"—he interrupted harshly, wishing that Charles were less given to embroidering the truth—"he is not on the duke's staff, and never has been." And never will be, he could have added, but the bleak look in the lady's expressive green eyes stopped him.

"I see," she whispered in a low voice that caught at Richard's heartstrings. It was patently obvious to him that Lady Regina could not bring herself to see Charles in his true colors. He fervently wished that he could say something comforting, but there could be no comfort in revealing that his brother—for all his charm and good looks—was a scoundrel of the first stare, to whom a broken promise meant as little as a broken heart, as long as it did not inconvenience him.

"Lady Regina," he said abruptly, no longer able to stand idly by and watch this splendid creature throw herself away on a worthless rogue, "please allow me to arrange passage back to London for you. It is not safe to remain much longer in Brussels in any case. I would escort you myself, but that is out of the question. I shall, however, send Burton to see you safely back to Dover."

Lady Regina looked at him then, her eyes wide with surprise

and something else he could not fathom. After a moment, she smiled, and Richard's heart ached at the sweetness of it.

"That is kind of you, Colonel." For once her voice was devoid of sarcasm. "You are telling me, I suppose, in a tactful manner, that it is pointless for me to wait any longer for Charles to return." She took a deep breath before adding what must have suddenly become clear to her. "He is not going to return, is he, Colonel?"

Richard cursed his brother for placing him in this untenable situation. Perhaps if he had not warned Charles of Lady Regina's arrival, the lying rogue might have walked into the trap and been forced to face up to his responsibilities. The Duke of Wexley's daughter was not without friends in high places, who could undoubtedly make Charles's life very unpleasant indeed if he openly jilted her. But Richard shuddered to think of the pain such a public scandal might cause to the lady.

"Not for several days at least, my lady," he said noncommittally, reluctant even now to admit the depths of Charles's depravity. "I strongly recommend that you return to London," he added, without much hope that Lady Regina would agree.

"I am sure you do, Colonel," she said in a stronger voice. "But I cannot do so as yet. Yes see," she continued, regarding him with a strained smile, "there has been a further complication in this rather sordid affair. One which I am determined to set right before I leave Brussels."

The colonel raised his eyebrows, wondering what new entanglement could possibly occur in an already absurd situation.

"You are aware, I suppose, that both Miss Laporte and Miss Gérard have taken up residence here?" At his silent acknowledgment, she continued. "They are under the impression that Charles's return will provide one of them with a husband. But after dinner last night, we had another addition to your brother's little harem that seems to be congregating on the premises, Colonel."

Richard caught the faint bitterness in Lady Regina's tone and marveled at her poise.

"And who is this third mysterious lady?" he inquired.

"The fourth, actually," she corrected him dryly. "You are forgetting me, are you not? I am also betrothed to your brother. But to answer your question, Colonel, the latest arrival is a Miss Jane Russell, an English governess, whose charges have been sent back to England this morning."

"The silly ninnyhammer should have gone with them," the colonel said harshly. So this was what Burton had tried to tell him, he thought, wondering how many more of Charles's conquests he would be expected to feed and house. "I will arrange passage for both of you, if you wish."

"I fear that is not practical," she said, returning to her formal curtness. "You see Miss Russell has confessed to me . . ."

"Yes?" Richard prodded, although he already knew what Lady Regina had been about to say.

"Miss Russell fears she is also increasing," she said, her green eyes fixed on him accusingly, as though he were responsible for the girl's condition. "I cannot abandon her," Lady Regina said, her voice quavering with emotion. "And I am counting on you to help me force your brother to wed her, Colonel."

Richard stared at her for a full minute, before trusting himself to speak, conscious that his world had suddenly turned into Bedlam.

"I was under the impression," he said slowly, choosing his words carefully, "that you yourself wished to wed my brother?"

Lady Regina laughed at that, a rather sad, brittle sound, but a laugh nevertheless. And Richard's heart was touched by this show of bravery under intense fire.

"Oh, no," she said softly, her eyes shimmering with unshed tears. "I have decided that we would not suit at all, Colonel. Not at all."

No sooner had this selfless decision to champion Miss Russell's cause been made, than Lady Regina began to doubt the wisdom of her continued presence in Brussels. Patience had never been one of her virtues, and the strain of having to endure the presence of three strange young females in the cramped little house, two of whom bickered incessantly, while the third had a seemingly bottomless well of tears, weakened her resolve to the point where she would gladly have strangled them all.

She said as much to Colonel Swinburn the very next afternoon when he paid his daily call, ostensibly to inquire after her comfort, but in reality, Regina suspected, to press his offer to have her escorted out of Brussels.

"If I do accept your kind offer," she remarked acidly as Burton set the obligatory tea tray on the low table before her, "it will be because I have committed murder on the persons of three witless females and must flee the magistrates. You would not believe the lengths to which these silly chits will go to convince me that they have prior claim on your despicable brother's affections. Why, at nuncheon today, which I was misguided enough to take in the dining room, Miss Laporte announced . . ." She paused to glance up into the butler's twinkling blue eyes. "And Burton will vouch for the truth of this Banbury tale, for he heard it all. Did you not, Burton?" she inquired sweetly, ignoring the colonel's disapproving glare.

The butler bowed and his ready grin broke through his artificial formality. "Indeed I did, milady. Me French ain't nowheres near perfect, but I got the gist of what the prattle-box was sayin' all right."

The colonel cleared his throat, and Burton gave Regina a saucy wink and resumed his rattling among the teacups.

"I should warn you, Colonel," Regina said, changing the subject abruptly, "that I have offered Burton double his wages to come back to England with me. It is entirely thanks to his unflappable good humor that I have retained my wits among these bedlamites."

"He will not go," came the dry response.

"How can you be so sure, Colonel?" Regina demanded, instantly on her mettle. "If need be, I shall offer to triple what you pay him, which is doubtless far less than he is worth." She threw a speaking glance at the object of this exchange.

"Let us leave my butler out of this, my lady," the colonel suggested blandly. "You have yet to tell me what the witless Miss Laporte announced over nuncheon."

Lady Regina felt herself blushing and wished she had not brought up the indelicate admission the Frenchwoman had made. As was her custom whenever she felt threatened, Regina attacked. "You are a monstrous slowtop if you cannot guess that, Colonel," she said, her tone heavy with condescension. "It appears that Miss Laporte will not be outdone by either Mademoiselle Gérard or Miss Russell. She has discovered—or so she would have us believe—that she, too, is in an interesting condition."

A pregnant pause followed this revelation, and Regina forgot her own discomfort as she watched the riot of emotions on the colonel's face.

"I believe I will need something a little stronger than tea, Burton," Sir Richard said finally, his voice ominously calm.

Interpreting this as a sign of defeat, Regina surprised herself by giggling. "I predict that within a few months you will have your hands full of mewling babies, Colonel." The picture this conjured up in her mind was so ludicrous that she laughed outright, and Burton did not help matters by almost dropping the glass of brandy he had poured for his master. "Perhaps I should not tempt

Burton away from you after all," she added facetiously. "How selfish that would be of me when you will obviously need his support during the trying times ahead."

In such moments as these, Regina thought after Sir Richard had taken his leave, she could almost feel affection for the dour colonel. Were it not for his dark, threatening demeanor, his ubiquitous frowns, his odious air of superiority, his insidious attempts to control her life, his thoroughly repellent habit of finding fault with everything she said, and his ridiculous penchant of treating her like an addlepated schoolroom chit, she might actually come to like the man.

His only redeeming quality, she admitted grudgingly the following afternoon as she sat awaiting the colonel's call, was his unwavering kindness to her and those three silly widgeons who had invaded his house and taken up residence there as though he were responsible for their predicament. And had she not done precisely the same thing to the unfortunate man? she thought, suddenly conscious of the debt she had incurred to a total stranger as a result of her impetuous flight from London.

The upshot of these uneasy thoughts was a decided softening of her attitude to the colonel when Burton showed him into the dowdy drawing room a few minutes later.

"Colonel Swinburn," she exclaimed, jumping up and advancing to greet her caller with her most glittering smile pinned to her lips. "How very good of you to come."

The colonel stopped dead in his tracks, a look of acute apprehension frozen on his face. His dark eyes scanned her countenance, and Regina was surprised at the intensity of his gaze, which caused her heart to skip a beat.

For the merest instant, Regina got the impression that she had penetrated the cool reserve he always maintained in her presence, but she brushed the feeling aside, and laid a small hand confidently on his sleeve. "Do not look so alarmed, sir," she murmured with more coyness than she had intended. "I have a confession to make." She drew him to the drab settee whose colors had long ago receded into a nondescript gray.

"I have been sitting here thinking," she began, and then made the mistake of staring directly into his eyes. What she saw there— or imagined she saw there, she later convinced herself—made her forget what she had been about to say. There was an intensity there, an intensity that faded before she could actually swear she had seen it. But the shadow of it flickered for a moment, and Regina felt the warmth of it reach out to envelop her. She held her breath as it dawned on her that this man was as vulnerable as she was beneath his shield of cynicism. The thought was totally new to her, and as she slowly released her breath, Regina wondered how many other annoying habits the colonel had adopted to protect the man who lay hidden beneath the bright red coat and glittering gold braid.

She tore her eyes away and glanced uneasily at the door. "I shall ring for tea," she managed to say in a normal voice. Suddenly Regina found herself wishing for Burton's comforting bulk and his huge hands rattling the teacups. The thought of the colonel's unusual butler calmed her, and she was able to resume her seat instead of rushing from the room in panic as she had, for the briefest instant, wished she could.

The silence was finally broken by the colonel. "And what were you thinking about as you sat here, my lady?" he said with an odd gentleness.

Regina scrambled around in her head to come up with an acceptable answer. She had been going to thank him for his kindness, she remembered, but that was impossible now. She dared not mention anything that might trigger that intense look in his eyes again. Feeling incredibly young and gauche, and in an attempt to hide her confusion, Regina took refuge in her ducal manner.

"I have decided that I wish to go out driving this afternoon," she announced, picking on the first thing that came into her head. "I find it extremely odd that you have never invited me to do so, Colonel. You do have a curricle, I assume?"

She looked at him then, feeling safe behind her facade of rank and fortune. But she had nothing to fear, for his eyes were hooded and his forehead creased in the familiar frown. So, the colonel was hiding, too, she thought irrationally, wondering if he would ever again reveal that other man she had glimpsed so briefly.

"As a matter of fact, I do not," he answered in a flat tone. "The battlefield is no place for a sporting vehicle."

"But Brussels is not a battlefield," Regina protested, annoyed that he had made her feel frivolous.

"It will be before very long," he answered shortly, his tone dismissing the subject. "I had hoped to find you in the mood to leave Brussels, my lady," he continued. "Before too long, it might be impossible to get away safely."

"I confess I am sorely tempted," she replied. "Miss Russell refuses to contemplate leaving. I have argued until I am heartily sick of listening to her futile hopes of forcing your brother to the altar." She paused and regarded him levelly. "Why did you not tell me the truth from the beginning, Colonel?" she demanded. "Did you think me a watering pot like poor Miss Russell, or a harridan like Mademoiselle Laporte, or perhaps a brassy hussy like Annette Gérard?"

He regarded her for a moment before answering. "Nothing of the sort, my dear. But it did occur to me that you were not yet prepared to hear the truth. I had no wish to have my eyes scratched out. Unless I am sadly mistaken, you can be very fierce when you are crossed."

Distracted and oddly flustered by the endearment, Regina wished that Burton would bring their tea before the conversation became even more stilted than it was. But when the butler did open the door moments later, it was not the tea tray he brought.

"Trouble advancing from the rear, Colonel," Burton said cryptically, in a crisp voice that Regina had not heard him use before.

The colonel sprang instantly to his feet, but before Regina realized what was going on, she heard a familiar voice in the hall and the sound of several pairs of boots.

And then Burton was unceremoniously thrust aside and the Duke of Wexley strode into the room, flanked by two of his sons, bringing with him a palpable aura of disaster.

"Papa," she said warmly, exactly as she would had her father walked into one of her mother's select gatherings at Wexley Abbey. "What a wonderful surprise. We are about to order the tea tray. Perhaps you would care to join us?"

She smiled coaxingly up into her father's grim face, but the Duke of Wexley made no move to return the greeting.

Lady Regina sighed and settled back to endure the tirade she knew, from long experience, was about to be loosed upon her head.

"I have seen you do any number of foolish things, Regina"— her father began in his most formal and intimidating voice—"but this latest start of yours is beyond the pale, child."

Regina shifted uneasily in her seat under the fierceness of her father's withering gaze. Not only was the duke in one of his rare furies, she noted with a tremor of apprehension, which would take every ounce of cajoling she could muster to coax him out of, but his grim expression and failure to greet his beloved daughter with open arms suggested that he had worked himself into a state of parental outrage such as Regina had never before had directed at her. Her father usually reserved such bouts of blind anger for

Robert, his eldest son and heir, whose rakehell ways the duke had attempted unsuccessfully to control for as long as Regina could remember.

"Your mother has been beside herself with worry"—the duke began in a tone that made Regina flinch—"as you would have known had you stopped for a moment to consider the consequences of this rash and childish act. For that alone you deserve to be flogged. And by Jupiter, if you were a son of mine, I would take a horsewhip to you myself. Perhaps I should have done so long ago to curb that obstinate streak in you." He paused to glare around the room, as if daring anyone to argue the point. "What could you have been thinking, child, to endanger yourself in this manner? The Continent is on the brink of war, and what do you do? Run off to the most dangerous place you could possibly find. If you had been so set against Wolverton, Regina," he continued, his voice less strident, "you might have told me, instead of taking things into your own hands and running off like some tradesman's daughter with no sense of what is due her station. I would not have forced you to accept his offer, child. Surely you must have known that."

"Wolverton was not about to make me an offer, Papa," Regina remarked coldly.

"Because you warned him off no doubt," her father shot back, his heavy brows lowered menacingly. "And who do you think will have you after this latest scandal becomes known? You will be well and truly on the shelf as I have warned you before, Regina."

"You know very well that I am already betrothed, Papa—"

"I know nothing of the sort, child," the duke stormed at her, his patience obviously wearing thin. "And if you think that I will allow you to wed some half-pay officer without a sou to his name, you mistake the matter, Regina." He paused to catch his breath and seemed to become aware of the colonel for the first time since he had burst into the room.

"And who is this?" he demanded haughtily, raising his quizzing glass to stare down the stranger. He let it drop almost immediately to inquire, "Your face is familiar, young man. Have we not met?"

"Yes, Papa, he is—" Regina began, only to be cut short by the duke.

"Let the man answer for himself, Regina," he snapped.

"Colonel Sir Richard Swinburn at your service, Your Grace," the colonel said with a brief nod.

"Swinburn?" the duke mused, his eyes running over the

colonel's tall figure. "Are you the bloody scoundrel who has tricked my daughter into this unseemly behavior?" he said with deceptive restraint.

Seeing the storm clouds forming in the colonel's dark eyes, Regina interrupted quickly. "Oh, no, Papa, Sir Richard—"

"Quiet!" the duke bellowed so unexpectedly that Regina jumped. "Now"—he continued less harshly—"is this or is this not your residence, sir?"

"Temporarily," the colonel admitted curtly.

"And my daughter has been under your protection here for the past week, I take it?" His voice was silky now but humming with such threatening nuances that Regina shuddered.

"You are mistaken, Papa," she cried, shocked at the direction her father's logic was taking.

"I have told you to be quiet, Regina." Her father whirled on her, his face pale and drawn. "I trust I shall not have to repeat myself. And now you, sir," he continued, turning back to the colonel. "I must ask you to oblige me by answering my question."

The room was suddenly so quiet that Regina could hear herself breathe. Her father, still flanked by her brothers Geoffrey and Nevil, faced the colonel challengingly, booted feet apart, aggression emanating from every line of his body. Regina had never seen her father like this before. He appeared so much the stranger that she felt a sudden fear grip her. Her brothers, too, stared at the colonel, their familiar faces as grim and forbidding as the duke's.

Nobody spoke.

Regina glanced at the colonel, her heart in her mouth. His rugged face was pale, his lips set in a stubborn line, his eyes almost black with an emotion Regina did not recognize. He made no move to answer her father's insulting question and her heart went out to him.

When she could bear the suspense no longer, Regina rose to her feet, breaking the crackling tension in the room. "Sir Richard is an innocent bystander in this Canterbury farce," she forced herself to say. "It is his brother Charles you should be badgering, Papa. If anyone is guilty of anything, it is surely Charles."

The duke turned slowly to regard her, his face now mottled with a fury that was almost palpable in the cramped quarters. "Innocent is he?" he snarled in a low, threatening voice, so unlike her father's that Regina's blood turned to ice. "I cannot recall soliciting your opinion on the matter, Regina," the duke continued. "And if this Charles is the man you have come to Brussels to wed, where is he? I intend to thrash him to within an inch of his life."

Regina swallowed. "Captain Swinburn is away from Brussels at the moment," she said, amazed that her voice did not waver. "And if you must thrash someone, Papa, thrash me, for this whole unfortunate imbroglio is my fault entirely."

"Well, I will deal with you later, child," the duke said sternly. "But when I get my hands on him, this captain of yours will regret he ever had the audacity to look upon you." He glared at the colonel as if daring him to come to the defense of his absent sibling. "And as for you, sir, I hold you responsible for the irreparable damage the insolent puppy has brought down on my daughter's head."

He paused, then glanced sharply at Regina as though some unpleasant thought had just occurred to him. "You are not wed already, are you, child?" he demanded abruptly.

Dazed at the virulence of her father's attack on the colonel, Regina shook her head, wishing that Sir Richard had not been sitting with her when the duke had descended upon the house on rue Lafitte.

The duke turned back to glare at the colonel, his face set in harsh, angry lines that made Regina's heart sink into the soles of her fashionable blue kid slippers.

"In that case, I believe that Colonel Swinburn and I shall have a little talk," he said slowly and deliberately, with a finality that brooked no argument. "Geoffrey, take your sister away. And you, too, Nevil. Leave us, if you please."

As her brother grasped her elbow and pulled her toward the door, Regina made one last attempt to halt the avalanche of disaster her father seemed determined to unleash upon them all. She pulled free of Geoffrey's grip and threw herself upon the duke's chest, her fingers plucking nervously at the lapels of his coat of expensive Bath tweed.

"Please, Papa, I beg of you . . ." Her voice tapered off when her father refused to lower his gaze.

"Papa," she began again, reaching up to touch his rough cheek in silent supplication, yet knowing from the cold fingers clutching at her heart that she could not reach him. For perhaps the first time in her life, her father had shut himself off from her. Regina felt tears of frustration and despair prick her eyes.

Without removing his gaze from the colonel's, the Duke of Wexley firmly removed his daughter's fingers from his lapels and set her away from him.

"Take her away, Geoffrey," he said heavily.

Her brother reached for her hand, and this time Regina did not resist. At the door, she cast an anguished glance over her shoulder, but the colonel also refused to meet her eyes.

From the wooden expression on his pale face, Regina knew instinctively that Colonel Swinburn expected no quarter from the duke. He had the resigned, unyielding look of a man facing a firing squad.

Regina could not blame him; she felt very much the same herself.

CHAPTER FIVE

A Question of Honor

In the oppressive silence of the shabby drawing room, Sir Richard felt like a condemned man awaiting his fate. He had a pretty fair idea of what was in the Duke of Wexley's mind, but the enormity of what lay ahead of him seemed to have addled his own.

The duke was the first to break the tension. "I can only guess at the misguided reasons for my daughter's attempt to throw dust in my eyes with this farradiddle about your missing brother," he said, his voice betraying no emotion. "But I have spoken to Wellington, who tells me that it is *you* who are to wed my daughter." He paused, as if to give the colonel a chance to deny this damning information. When Richard said nothing, Wexley sighed audibly.

"I would like to know why—if indeed you are a man of honor, as Wellington assures me is the case—you have not already done so, sir, instead of exposing her to the scandal which is even now brewing and will doubtless fall on her head when it becomes generally known that she has spent a week under your roof with none but servants to lend her countenance?"

The duke did not raise his voice, but then he did not have to, Richard thought bitterly. The weight of his ducal presence alone would be more than sufficient to bend most men to his will. Besides that, Wexley was an impressive figure, standing almost as tall as the colonel himself, who was taller than most. And if ever the duke had cause to bring the full force of his influence to bear, it must surely be now, Richard knew. For his precious daughter—and Richard remembered from two summers ago just how precious Lady Regina was to her father—had been compromised in the eyes of the world, and the family pride had been tainted. Both offenses would require immediate reparation, that much Richard could understand and accept. What he had not yet accepted was that such reparation must inevitably fall to him.

The colonel cleared his throat. "The general is laboring under the misapprehension that Lady Regina is betrothed to me," he stated baldly, wondering just how much of the imbroglio set in motion by that lady he should reveal to the indignant father.

"Whereas in fact, your daughter believes herself promised to my brother Charles."

"*Believes* herself to be?" the duke inquired sharply.

The devil fly away with Charles and his randy hide, Richard swore beneath his breath. "Precisely, sir. Her ladyship has been wearing my brother's ring for nigh on two years, and finally seems to have grown impatient with the delay."

"Are you actually confirming that the impertinent whelp had the audacity to give my daughter a ring?" The duke's astonishment was so genuine that Richard would have been tempted to laugh had the matter not been so frighteningly serious.

"So it would appear, sir," he replied.

A puzzled frown appeared on Wexley's noble brow. "Then how did it happen that Wellington is convinced that my daughter is in Brussels on your behalf?"

"Her ladyship inadvertently misled the duke when she informed him that she was betrothed to a Swinburn. Naturally, His Grace assumed that Swinburn to be me, although I did not realize the full extent of the misunderstanding until he demanded to be invited to the ceremony."

His brows lowered into an angry frown, Wexley appeared to ponder the logic of the colonel's story. Now that he was forced to review the confusing series of improbable events, Richard thought wryly, he had to admit that he had been remiss in failing to clarify the lady's situation immediately. But then how could he have done so without branding the lady as a jilted woman?

"And where, may I ask, is this disreputable brother of yours?" the duke demanded abruptly, his frown still very much in evidence.

Richard took a deep breath. He could see what the duke's questions were leading up to, and he did not relish the outcome.

"Captain Swinburn is out on a reconnaissance patrol, sir. He has been away for several days now."

"Then he must be sent for immediately," the duke stated flatly. "And after I have supplanted some of his teeth and broken his nose for him, he shall wed my daughter."

"I should be only too happy to wring his neck myself," the colonel admitted, "but as for the other, I should inform Your Grace, that my brother has no desire to wed your daughter."

Wexley stared at him in surprise for several moments. When he spoke his voice was flat and hard with anger. "He will do so, nevertheless, Colonel. And without any further delay, if you please.

Wellington warns me that it is no longer safe to remain in Brussels."

Richard sighed. He could find it in his heart to pity Wexley, but to some extent the duke had brought this scandal upon himself when he failed to curb his headstrong daughter.

"I fear that will not be possible, sir," he said slowly, conscious of the noose tightening around his own neck. "If my brother does not wish to be found, there is no way he can be forced to return."

Richard could feel the Duke of Wexley's fury building to an impossible pitch, his aristocratic features twisting under the force of it. "Are you telling me, Colonel, that your misbegotten brother has jilted my daughter?" The words fell slowly and distinctly into the charged silence, and to the colonel's overwrought senses they sounded like cannon shots.

With another silent curse at the perfidy of his absent brother, Richard straightened his shoulders. "That appears to be correct, Your Grace."

An even longer silence followed this admission, during which Richard could not prevent his agitated thoughts from squarely confronting the decisive blow, which even now he could sense rising to the surface of the ducal mind.

"Nevertheless," the duke murmured, his voice silky but implacable, "my daughter will be wed by this time tomorrow."

And that was that, Richard thought dispassionately. His fate had indeed been sealed, and he was powerless to escape the net he felt, almost as a physical presence, closing about him. Not that he had given much thought to escape, he realized, as his brain absorbed the implications of Wexley's decision. The incontrovertible truth was that he agreed with the duke; Lady Regina's reputation must be protected at any cost, even if he must sacrifice his freedom to do so. His own honor demanded it. And what did it matter if the lady was a pampered, self-willed termagant? What did it matter that he would tie himself forever to a female who did not even like him? One who certainly would never hold him in the slightest affection.

Richard repressed these uneasy thoughts and forced himself to speak. "Of course, Your Grace," he said through lips that felt numb, in a voice so unlike his own that a stranger might have been speaking.

The duke relaxed minimally. "I shall send my daughter to you, Colonel," he said briskly, one hand already on the doorknob. "The sooner this business is concluded, the better for all of us."

And with that he was gone, leaving Richard to stare at the

closed door, wondering just how he might convince Regina that there was no other way out of this impossible tangle.

"All I can say is that I hate you both," Lady Regina said cuttingly. "Never did I imagine I would live to see the day when my own brothers would turn against me. Especially you, Nevil," she added accusingly to her youngest brother, who sat fiddling nervously with the tankard of ale Burton had placed before the two gentlemen in the small breakfast parlor at the back of the house.

"Cut line, Sis," Geoffrey Heathercott snapped in a tone that reminded Regina uncomfortably of her father. "If you will behave like a feather-headed peagoose, you must expect to pay the price lass. Father is only doing what he must to head off the gabble-mongers before it becomes common knowledge that the Duke of Wexley's daughter has been living in Brussels under circumstances that are highly irregular, to say the least."

"I see nothing irregular at all about my presence here," Regina insisted stubbornly. But if truth be known, the past hour had been a sobering experience for her. Her father's unnaturally grave demeanor and his failure to bestow so much as a smile on his favorite daughter had warned her that this time her transgression had gone beyond the pale. And looking back at the events of the past week, Regina had to admit that perhaps she had acted unwisely. And certainly indecorously, she felt obliged to add, recalling the wild ride down to Dover in the company of Wolverton, one of London's most notorious womanizers. And the channel crossing, alone on a yacht full of rough sailors; and once in Brussels, how could she deny that she had accepted the protection and hospitality of Colonel Sir Richard Swinburn, a man she hardly knew?

"Then you are more lost to propriety than I had imagined," Geoffrey answered bluntly. "Wild and willful you have always been, Regina, but I was frankly appalled when Father came rushing over to the War Office to tell me that you had been seen boarding Wolverton's yacht in Dover. He wanted to believe that you had finally decided to accept Guy's suit—"

"Guy never had any intentions of making me an offer, Geoffrey, as you of all people must have known," Regina interrupted.

"Aye," Geoffrey drawled, regarding her with distaste. "I disabused him of that notion quickly enough, and also dissuaded him from demanding satisfaction from poor old Guy, who had wisely disappeared from Town until the dust settled."

Regina rose from her seat at the battered table and moved to the window. "I fail to see what all the fuss is about," she said crossly, although this was not entirely true either. "I came to Brussels to find my betrothed, and when I do—"

"If you mean that flashy captain of yours, Gina," Nevil cut in, "you can forget about him. That nasty piece of work is not about to come riding back to save you from dishonor, love. More than likely he is hiding his scurvy hide in some poor unsuspecting wench's bed—"

"Nevil!" his brother exclaimed sharply. "Moderate your language when you address our sister, or I shall have to wash your mouth out for you."

Regina did not so much as blink at this exchange. It was an argument she had been listening to since they were children, and as far as she could remember Geoffrey had yet to make good his threat.

"You have been talking to Burton, I take it?" she said.

"Burton? And who is he?" Geoffrey demanded.

"The sporting cove who passes for butler in this establishment," Nevil explained with a grin. "Says he trained with Barklay before he joined the Army. Give a pony to have a turn-up with that lad, I would."

"Save your blunt, Nevil," Regina advised her youngest brother, whose passion for violent sports had not diminished with age. "Burton would no doubt draw your cork for you in an instant if you were foolish enough to come to cuffs with him."

"Enough of this vulgar cant talk, Regina," Geoffrey warned. "If Father hears you there will be the devil to pay. On top of everything else," he added glumly, reminding Regina that her irate parent was still cloistered with Colonel Swinburn.

"Whatever can be keeping Papa?" she wondered aloud, drawing two uneasy glances from her brothers. Neither gave any sign of wishing to enlighten her, but she did not have long to wait, for at that moment the parlor door swung open and their father stood on the threshold, his expression unreadable.

Regina assayed a tentative smile, but the duke's countenance remained rigid. The fears that she had managed to suppress in the company of her brothers returned to twist her stomach. Something was in the wind, she thought uneasily, and if she knew anything about her father, it would not be pleasant.

"Colonel Swinburn awaits you in the drawing room, Regina," the duke said in those clipped tones he only used when his mind was firmly made up.

Regina stared at him. "Whatever for?" she demanded, although a hint of panic began uncurling inside her. She was dimly aware of her brothers' silent disapproval at this unwise remark.

"Do as you are told, girl," her father said with deceptive softness.

Regina forced herself to smile sweetly. "I have no desire to see Colonel Swinburn, Papa," she pointed out, trying to sound as though this were a normal conversation between father and daughter. It was no such thing, of course. Her wildly beating heart told her that this time her father would not be swayed from his course. He would, if necessary, force her to obey him.

The duke stared at her for a long moment. "It has been a long time since I took you over my knee, Regina," he said in the same low, conversational voice. "But let me assure you that if you defy me once more, I shall not hesitate to beat you."

Regina felt herself go pale. Her father had only raised his hand to her once, she recalled, the humiliation of it rushing back to flood her memory. She had been eight at the time, and in defiance of her father's express command, she had opened the gate of the South Pasture early one morning and let the sheep out into the hills. It had taken a good deal of time and effort to round the silly things up and drive them back to the estate, she recalled, and the damage done to neighboring farms had been considerable. She had never defied her father so openly again. Until now, Regina thought, returning her father's menacing stare without flinching.

"Geoffrey," the duke ordered quietly, "escort your sister to the drawing room, if you please."

With obvious reluctance, Geoffrey stepped toward her, but before he could touch her, Regina swung around angrily and, brushing past her father, strode angrily down the tiny hall. When she came to the closed drawing-room door, she paused, glancing speculatively at the front door.

"I would not recommend it, Regina," her brother said from beside her. "Father means to have his way this time. So you had best accept it gracefully." He reached around her and opened the door.

Pushing Geoffrey's hand aside, Regina flung the door open violently and swept into the small room, her silk skirts rustling. She heard the door close softly behind her, and the finality of it fell ominously on her ears.

"Well?" she snapped, glaring angrily at the man who stood leaning against the modest mantelpiece of nondescript, smoke-stained wood. "I trust you are not about to commit an act of indescribable folly that will haunt you for the rest of your days, Colonel."

To her vast surprise, the colonel's lips twitched into what may have been a smile. "And who are *you* to speak of folly, my lady?" His voice was heavy with sarcasm. "Try as I might, I doubt I could come close to the folly you have already committed by coming here. What but arrant foolishness caused you to imagine that a few idle kisses in the moonlight on a summer evening could mean anything to a man of my brother's stamp?"

Regina gasped in dismay. "You spied on us," she said, her voice quivering with indignation. "What a despicable creature you are!" Her indignation was such that she found it difficult to speak."

"Not spying, my lady," the colonel said coldly. "Merely watching out for your safety."

"Fiddle!" she exclaimed disparagingly. "Are you trying to suggest that Charles . . . that Charles . . ." Her voice faltered as certain events of that moonlit evening came back to her.

"Precisely," he said dryly. "No gentleman would have sneaked out alone with a young lady. And unfortunately I know my brother too well to trust him. To put it bluntly, I had no wish to see the Duke of Wexley's daughter in the same predicament as poor Miss Russell."

Regina felt the color rush up into her cheeks as the implications of the colonel's outrageous remark sank in. "You are odious beyond bearing," she said stiffly. "I shall not stay here to be insulted by some officious, pompous, impertinent jackstraw," she fumed, quite beside herself with fury. She glanced down and saw the squat porcelain figurine grinning back at her malevolently. She was prevented from snatching it up to hurl at the object of her ire by that gentleman's voice, which changed the direction of her thoughts.

"I do have some news that I trust will put you in a better temper, my lady," the colonel drawled.

She raised her eyes and stared at him, noting that his grim-faced expression seemed to belie his words.

"And what might that be?" she said coldly.

"Your father tells me that tomorrow you are to be wed, my dear."

As Regina listened to these words, a sense of relief washed over her and she smiled. They had found Charles was the first thought that came to mind. The second was less euphoric. She could not marry him, of course, not after what she had learned about his morals; but at least she would be able to tell him exactly what she thought of his libertine ways, and perhaps she could persuade him to correct the wrong he had done to Miss Russell.

"You have found Charles?" she said, not bothering to conceal her pleasure.

"No, I have not," the colonel replied with unexpected harshness. "Believe me, if I could, I would drag the blackguard back to Brussels myself to face up to his responsibilities."

"Then who . . . ?" Regina began but the odd expression she saw on the colonel's face stopped her question in midair.

The colonel grimaced and turned to kick at the unlit logs in the hearth. "Unfortunately, your father appears to think it is *my* duty to repair your damaged reputation, my lady."

The unexpected bitterness in the colonel's voice caused Regina to stare at him in growing dismay. She had fully expected that her father would insist upon her immediate marriage to Charles; indeed, she had counted upon such an eventuality before she set out from London. Perhaps even then, in a secret corner of her mind, she had doubted the promises Charles had made to her that summer in the moonlight. Perhaps she had suspected that the dashing captain might not be swayed by her pleas alone, and wished for the weight of the duke's presence in Brussels to press her case. What she had not anticipated, Regina thought wryly, was Charles's cruel deceit and his brother's unexpected kindness. And she had certainly not expected to find such abundant and undeniable proof of the captain's indiscriminate beddings.

The thought of the three females who had shared not only the colonel's lodgings with her over the past few days, and also the intimate affections—far more *intimate* indeed than her own—of her betrothed husband, sickened her. Had he told each of them he loved her? she wondered, her thoughts slipping back to that night in the summer house when Charles's hands and lips and laughing eyes had almost drawn her into wantonness. The memory of the liberties she had allowed the dashing captain to take with her made Regina's heart grow cold. What if she had . . . But the notion did not bear thinking of. She dragged her errant thoughts back to the present.

"What utter nonsense!" she exclaimed disdainfully. "As if I would consider, even for a moment, accepting such a ridiculous notion." She spoke bravely, but her heart wavered.

He turned to face her, and Regina realized she had angered him. When he spoke, however, his voice was tightly controlled. "I fancy you may not have any choice in the matter, my lady." His dark eyes were hooded, and Regina had the uncomfortable impression that she had lost an unwilling ally. Was it possible that Colonel Swinburn had sided with the duke against her?

Regina drew a deep breath. "Never say that you have agreed to such an absurd arrangement, Colonel?" she said with all the sarcasm she could muster.

"I dislike the notion as much as you do, my lady," he replied so harshly that Regina was startled. "Believe me, you are hardly the kind of wife I had envisioned in my future. But I agree with your father that you cannot leave Brussels unwed, so wed you will be. And since my brother is not here to do the honorable thing, I shall be obliged to do it in his stead."

"You are too, too kind, sir," Regina said bitingly. "Do not delude yourself into thinking that I will have you. If you were not such a slop-top, Colonel, you would have done as I suggested days ago and sent for Charles. Not that I would have him either, of course," she added disdainfully. "I am, after all, the daughter of a duke, and will not throw myself and my fortune away on a worthless scoundrel such as your libertine brother has turned out to be."

"You already have," he snapped impatiently. "Thrown yourself away, that is. You did so the moment you left London on this madcap venture. And since Charles has declined the honor, it falls to me to—"

"Do not flatter yourself, Colonel," Regina interrupted brusquely. "If your brother has chosen to play the Jack, it does not follow that you must cast yourself into the breach. And honor be damned!" she cried in frustration. "I will not wed a man who cannot afford to keep me in gloves and stockings."

No sooner had the reckless words left her mouth than Regina wished she could recall them. The mention of stockings was particularly rash, and she saw a glimmer of rare humor flicker in the colonel's eyes.

"I reckon that if I were to practice the strictest economy, I might manage to do so, my lady," he drawled, one corner of his mouth curling in self-deprecation. "But your father assures me that you would not be a drain on my pocket since you are well able to afford all the fripperies your heart desires."

Flabbergasted that her parent had spoken so freely to the colonel, and alarmed at the implications of such a financial disclosure, Regina felt her world totter beneath her feet and reacted in blind rage.

"So!" she exclaimed furiously. "Now we get to the heart of the matter, do we? It is money not honor that drives you to do my fa-

ther's bidding, is it not? Well, perhaps I should warn you, that if
you expect to benefit from my fortune, you will be sadly disappointed . . ."

The expression on the colonel's face caused her words to taper
off into silence and cooled her own anger. He had turned a pasty
white, and his eyes blazed with such murderous anger as Regina
had never imagined possible. His lips were drawn into a tight, forbidding line, and the ripple of muscle in his square jaw gave evidence of extreme stress.

For an interminable moment anger crackled in the silence
between them, and Regina understood that she had badly underes-
timated her adversary. The colonel was evidently not a man who
would tolerate insults from a female as her brothers always did.
And she had insulted him, she admitted to herself. She had deliberately set out to do so.

"Your father warned me that you were headstrong, arrogant,
and disobedient," he rasped, his breath uneven, fists clenching
and unclenching. "And that I might have to beat some sense into
you if I wished for a quiet life." He paused, and his expression
softened minimally. "The idea is repellent to me, but do not try
my patience too far."

After another uncomfortable silence, the colonel squared his
shoulders and moved to the door. His demeanor was coldly formal again, and Regina found herself perversely intrigued by the
momentary display of fire which she had glimpsed beneath the
cool surface of the gentleman's set expression.

"I shall inform your father that we are agreed upon the match,"
he remarked as calmly as though they had been discussing a drive
in the park.

"We are not agreed upon anything, sir," Regina protested
loudly.

The colonel regarded her dispassionately. "Then I shall inform
His Grace that you have *not* agreed to the match," he said unemotionally, opening the door.

"No!" Regina cried out, feeling the control of her life slipping
through her fingers. "No," she repeated, when the colonel paused
and looked at her over his shoulder. "Papa will beat me, too," she
said in a choked voice. "And besides," she added defiantly, trying
to rally against the despair that seemed to sweep over her, "you
have yet to make me an offer, Colonel."

"I have no intention of doing so," he replied curtly. "That
would indeed be ridiculous, given the circumstances."

His voice was brittle and filled with a world of cynicism, or so it appeared to Regina, who could think of no set-down crushing enough to communicate her displeasure at this insult. She glared at him, beside herself with fury and conscious of the humiliating desire to burst into tears.

Evidently taking her silence as acquiescence, Colonel Swinburn went out and closed the door with a finality that told Regina that she had lost that battle of wits.

Without conscious thought, she reached for the offensive porcelain figurine and hurled it at the door, taking intense pleasure as the ugly face of the grinning goblin shattered against the woodwork and fell in a dozen pieces to the floor, mutilated beyond recognition.

CHAPTER SIX

Unwilling Bride

At the sound of Claudette drawing the faded curtains the following morning, Regina opened her eyes to see the bright sunlight streaming across the bedcovers. For a brief moment, she luxuriated in the bright warmth, then flung the covers back, wondering if perhaps today she might not persuade Colonel Swinburn to escort her for a drive. The thought of Colonel Swinburn brought her abruptly back to reality.

"I have pressed the pale blue jaconet for you, milady," the abigail said, excitement evident in her voice. "And your bath is ready, but we must hurry if we are to have you ready for the colonel by ten of the clock."

Lady Regina's pleasure in the sunlit morning evaporated. This was to be her wedding day, she remembered, the previous afternoon's events rushing back in all their inescapable horror. In the bright light of the day, she found it difficult to believe what her father—the same adored and doting father she had trusted to fulfill all her heart's desires—had done to her. In a few hours, she would be married off to an insignificant baronet, a man she hardly knew, a man who did not want her, and all because of her father's stiff-necked sense of pride. What had happened to the father she thought had loved her? And her brothers? Why had they not spoken a single word in her defense?

For a long, miserable moment, Regina sat hunched over on the bed feeling utterly bereft; loneliness and pain washing over her. She wished she might die. That would show all those heartless men just how much they had hurt her, she thought resentfully. Of course, the inconvenience of dying was that she would not be there to witness their remorse. No, she mused, her eyes stinging with unshed tears, dying was not the answer to this heartless tyranny her father meant to force upon her. She would make one last desperate attempt to move him, and if that did not work, she thought wretchedly, she would make quite sure that he never forgot the great wrong he had done her.

She glanced dispiritedly at the cup of chocolate Claudette had set beside the bed. "I do not feel like chocolate this morning," she said defiantly. "And I will not wear the blue jaconet." The blue gown was one of her favorites, and Regina knew it set off her pale beauty to perfection. But she had no desire to look her best today. She felt miserable and was determined that everyone should know it. She slid out of bed and walked to the tiny armoire.

"I shall wear this one," she declared, pulling out a slate-gray carriage gown whose severe lines and modest lace frill at the collar had never pleased her. It suited her mood admirably, though, and when Claudette protested that her blue jaconet was far more becoming, Regina ignored her.

When Burton tapped at the door to inform her that her father awaited her pleasure in the drawing room, Regina girded herself with what little remained of her self-confidence and descended the narrow stairs, taking a perverse pleasure in the plainness of her appearance.

They were all there, she saw at a glance, four tall, silent men who stood about uneasily in the small room, and a fifth whose cheerful, ruddy face looked out of place among the somber countenances of the others.

"Ah, Regina," her father spoke up heartily, as though holding the nuptials of a duke's daughter in a dowdy drawing room with none but male relatives to attend her was an everyday affair. "This is the Reverend Thomas Crumbley, who has consented to perform the service for us this morning."

Lady Regina regarded the smiling curate with a sinking heart. She had little hope that the Reverend Crumbley would dare to take a daughter's side against her father, particularly if the father was the powerful Duke of Wexley. Nevertheless, she owed it to herself to try.

"I am sorry to have inconvenienced you, Reverend," she said pleasantly but firmly. "But I have changed my mind, and no longer wish to wed anyone."

In the silence that followed this pronouncement, Regina focused her attention on the reverend's round face, noting the puzzled frown that chased away his fatuous smile. She refused to look at her father or the colonel.

"Nonsense, child," the duke exploded in a loud voice, making the poor Mr. Crumbley jump nervously. "My daughter has an odd sense of humor, sir. Pay her no heed."

The curate appeared nonplussed, and looked from Regina to her father inquiringly. "I would not wish to go against the lady's—"

"Balderdash!" the duke exclaimed impatiently. "I am the lady's father, and I wish to give her to Colonel Swinburn here. You already have the special license to prove it, sir. There is no more to be said. Now come over here, Regina, and let me hear no more of this missishness from you." He glared at her and then abruptly seemed to notice her appearance. "And what is that dowdy thing you are wearing, child?" he fumed. "That gown is hardly what one would expect a bride to chose for her wedding day."

Regina could not repress a snort of disgust. "This is hardly the kind of wedding day I would have chosen, Papa," she said disdainfully. "And if you persist on going through with this ridiculous match, I shall never speak to you again. And I mean it," she insisted coldly. "You are no father of mine if you insist on a path that can bring nothing but unhappiness to all concerned."

After a short pause, during which Regina saw her father grow suddenly pale, the duke answered curtly, "You will do as I say, Regina."

She heard Nevil clear his throat behind her. "Father, perhaps we are being rather hasty—"

"Hold your tongue, boy," the duke snapped savagely, his patience obviously running out.

"I beg your pardon, Your Grace," the reverend began hesitantly, his ruddy face showing signs of stress.

"Let us get on with it," the duke ordered harshly. "I wish to leave Brussels within the hour."

And that, Regina thought bitterly as Mr. Crumbley quailed under the duke's command, was that. Short of swooning, which she had never been able to do at will, or throwing a monumental tantrum, which she seemed to lack the energy to pull off convincingly, Regina knew she had exhausted all alternatives to becoming Colonel Swinburn's lady.

Silently, head held high, lips compressed in anger, and eyes focused on the battered clock on the mantel, Regina stood passively beside the colonel, flanked menacingly by her father and brothers. She felt cornered, hemmed in by this unrelenting male presence that made her realize, for the first time in her protected, laughter-filled life, how very little her own desires really counted in a world ruled by men.

How well they had all deceived her, she thought with shattering insight. Her doting father, her beloved brothers, even Charles—the man who had stolen her heart; all had lulled her into believing that they really cared about her happiness. Regina had known, of course, even as a little girl, that her father's word was law, but her dearest papa had rarely exercised that awesome power upon his little Gina, his fairy-girl—as he had called her then. The memory of that pet name brought a lump to her throat. That life was behind her now, gone forever into the mists of memory, to be remembered as dreams are remembered, with no precise distinction between what was true and what had merely been imagined.

With an effort, Regina pulled her mind back to the present and with a start heard the echo of the curate's voice fading into silence. She had missed half the service, she realized, but the air of expectancy in the room warned her that she had also missed her cue. Beside her, the colonel did not move a muscle, but Regina became aware of a sudden tension in him. She withdrew her gaze from the clock and stared at the curate, noting that he was regarding her with acute anxiety, his cherubic mouth partly open as if to prompt her. He nodded his head encouragingly when their eyes met, and his lips mouthed the proper response in a grotesque pantomime.

"*Regina*"—she heard her father hiss in a loud whisper —"answer the question, if you please."

What question? she wondered distractedly, her mind aching to retreat once again into the comforting haze of the past. How could she answer a question she had not heard? "I do beg your pardon, Mr. Crumbley," she said impulsively. "It appears my thoughts were wandering. Would you repeat the question, please?"

A stunned silence followed this bizarre request, and Regina knew she had committed a frightful faux pas, but she did not care. Anything that would delay, even for an instant, the moment when she would be forced to give herself into the hands of a man who did not want her was to be cherished, unmannerly or not.

The Reverend Crumbley cleared his throat and began again. "Lady Regina Elizabeth Constance Heathercott, wilt thou have this Man to thy wedded husband . . . "

Regina closed her mind. Deliberately, she removed herself to that afternoon of her eighth birthday when she had insisted that her brother Nevil take her out on the lily pond in the rowboat. She had been determined to pet the baby ducks presented to her on that occasion by one of her father's tenants, and would not listen to her mother's warning that ducks did not take kindly to petting. Nevil had been game, as he always was for any adventure frowned upon by their mother, but his skill with the oars had been less than adequate. Particularly where speed and agility were required to catch up with the ducklings, Regina recalled with fondness. They had both ended up in the water, of course, and their father, minus coat and topboots, had rescued them amid much splashing, yelling, and laughter.

Yes, laughter. Regina recalled the laughter most vividly and sighed. That would be gone from her life, too, she thought. She doubted that Colonel Swinburn knew how to laugh. And yet she would have to accept him, she knew, hearing the curate's question coming to a close.

" . . . so long as ye both shall live?"

She opened her mouth to give the required response, but before she could do so, the door of the drawing room burst open and three females trooped in, evidently set to do battle. They came to an abrupt halt, scanning the room with avid eyes. Even the mousy Miss Russell was there, standing discreetly behind the burgeoning Miss Gérard in her flamboyant yellow gown, whose myriad ruffles and flounces called attention to her condition.

"What is the meaning of this intrusion?" the duke bellowed, glaring at the newcomers. Had she been less subsumed in her own misery, Regina might have found the appearance of Charles's three lightskirts amusing. As it was, all she felt was relief that the evil hour had been, once again, briefly postponed.

"Oh, I-I do beg your pardon, milord," Miss Laporte stammered, her sharp eyes darting around among the gentlemen present and finally settling on Colonel Swinburn.

"We heard there was a wedding taking place this morning," Miss Gérard added in her simpering French, "and wondered if my darling Charles had returned."

"*Your* darling Charles?" Miss Laporte repeated shrilly, whirling to confront her rival. "He ain't *your* Charles at all, *ma cherie*. He is *mine*. How many times have I to tell you?" She turned back to the duke and lowered her voice to a mincing simper. "We was afraid this *grand lady* here had stolen a march on us poor working girls, if you know what I mean, milord." The emphasis she placed on the *grand lady* was unmistakably lacking in proper respect, and Regina saw her father bristle.

"Actually, Captain Swinburn is betrothed to *me*," Miss Russell's cultivated voice murmured unexpectedly from the background, causing the two other girls to join forces against her.

"There are some of us who have a valid claim on the captain's affections," Miss Gérard declared haughtily, patting her increasing girth with evident satisfaction. "Just you wait until he sees the *petit paquet* I have here, and we shall see whom he chooses to wed, *ma cherie*."

"Who are these women?" the duke demanded in his most

quelling tone. He had listened to this exchange with an expression of outraged bewilderment on his face, but Regina felt quite unequal to explaining Charles's libertine tendencies to her father.

"They are my brother's harem," the colonel said shortly, in French.

All three pairs of female eyes instantly focused upon him, but it was Miss Laporte who spoke up in their defense.

"We are nothing of the sort," she argued hotly, her red curls bouncing angrily. "We are all respectable females, just like that grand lady there," she added spitefully, gesturing at Lady Regina, "who have been grossly betrayed by a heartless English rogue. And here is the proof," she cried, shrill with indignation. She held out her left hand defiantly, and Regina froze at the sight of the small garnet ring on Miss Laporte's finger.

"And here is my proof," added Miss Gérard, presenting her hand, where an identical garnet ring twinkled in the sunlight streaming in through the grimy window.

"And mine," volunteered Miss Russell, thrusting her own hand forward to display the garnet ring on her thin finger.

And mine, too, Regina thought disconsolately, furtively turning Charles's ring around on her finger beneath the folds of her gown. A ring she had thought stood for undying love and a promise of marriage. A promise she had gambled her reputation on. Gambled and lost, a small voice whispered in her heart.

Regina was suddenly overcome by a sick feeling of dizziness, but the pressure of the colonel's hand on her elbow steadied her. For a brief moment, she leaned into his large hand, gathering strength from it. Then she pulled herself erect and turned back to Mr. Crumbley.

She smiled gently at the perplexed curate. "It seems we must beg your indulgence yet again, Mr. Crumbley," she said calmly. "If you will repeat the question, sir, I am ready to answer it."

And answer it she did, her voice clear and devoid of any hint of the turmoil of emotions that roiled in her heart.

When the service was finally at an end, Regina turned her back on her new husband and walked regally from the room, brushing aside her father's tentative attempt to take her in his arms, and her brothers' awkward wishes for her happiness, ignoring the smirks of the two younger girls, and Miss Russell's faintly envious stare. In the hall outside, she accosted the butler.

"Burton, please have my trunk brought down and loaded onto the duke's carriage," she ordered in a cold, controlled voice. "Claudette should have finished packing by now."

Burton stared at her in surprise. "You are leaving us so soon, milady?"

"Of course," she replied, wondering how she could be expected to stay on in this house where all her dreams had been smashed, much as she had smashed the ugly figurine yesterday.

"What shall I tell the colonel?" Burton blurted out, forgetting his role in his astonishment.

Regina laughed shortly, the sound unpleasing to her own ears. "Tell your precious colonel whatever you wish, Burton," she replied airily. "It is no concern of mine."

And with that Regina turned about and walked up the stairs, her brave front belying the uncertainty in her heart.

The Duke of Wexley extended his hand and Sir Richard, surprised by this unexpected affability on the part of his new father-in-law, took it in a strong grip.

"Give the girl time to become accustomed to her new state"—the duke remarked with a heartiness that rang false in Richard's ears—"and I have no doubt she will make you an excellent wife, Colonel."

The colonel smiled fleetingly into the dark eyes that regarded him searchingly. This was probably as close as the Duke of Wexley would ever come to an apology, he realized, suddenly feeling a sense of kinship with the older man that had nothing to do with the relationship established between them that morning. The duke's life had been turned upside down, too, and perhaps in more drastic ways than his own had been by Lady Regina's indiscretion. From what little her brothers had let slip, Richard knew their father had envisioned a glittering match for his daughter with a man of rank and fortune comparable to his own. It must have been deeply disappointing to a man as proud of his lineage as the Duke of Wexley to be forced to settle for a baronet with an insignificant estate and modest means.

"Doubtless you are correct, sir," Richard replied, taking pity on the other man's need to defend his daughter's unpardonable rudeness to her new husband only moments before. The colonel himself was still reeling from the lady's decision to leave Brussels with all possible speed and her failure to seek his permission to do so. But what rankled most was her cavalier departure without a word of farewell.

She had been equally remote with her father, Richard noted, refusing to address the duke or acknowledge any remark he made to her. In essence, Lady Regina had made good her threat, uttered in what the colonel had taken to be a moment of pique, a last-ditch effort to thwart her father's wishes. What gave him pause for thought was that his wife seemed to have included him in the silent treatment she meted out to the duke. After remaining upstairs until the last possible moment, Lady Regina had swept regally down the stairs, brushing past her brothers and ignoring her father. She had made straight for the coach, and when the colonel had stepped forward to hand her in, hoping that she would unbend at the last moment, she had refused his assistance, climbing into the carriage unaided, in a flurry of sable and the lingering scent of gardenia.

And here was the duke, vainly attempting to explain away his daughter's odd behavior as post-marital jitters. But Richard was not such a flat as to imagine the duke misread Lady Regina's character so lamentably as to believe such a Banbury tale. The colonel did not for a moment believe it himself.

He smiled again wryly. "God speed you, sir," he said, suddenly wishing the parting was over and done with so he could be comfortable again.

"I shall take good care of her for you, Colonel," Wexley said, obviously wishing to say more but unable or unwilling to do so within his daughter's hearing. "Let us hear from you," he added and climbed into the carriage.

And then they were finally gone. His wife, Regina, whom he had not yet had the opportunity to kiss, Richard reflected. His father-in-law, the powerful Duke of Wexley, who seemed as much at a loss on how to manage his daughter as Richard himself. And her brothers, who had offered to escort the coach as far as Ostend before returning to active duty.

The colonel stared after the well-sprung coach as it rattled away down the narrow cobbled surface of the rue Lafitte and turned right into the boulevard, disappearing from view. He listened to the sound of the horses' hooves for several moments before its distinctive clatter mingled with other sounds and became lost.

He should be glad to see the last of her, Richard told himself wryly. But for some odd reason the scent of gardenia lingered in the air, and he found himself wondering if she rinsed her hair with that particular perfume, and what it might feel like to bury his face in that cloud of pale gold curls spread out on his pillow. The colonel closed his eyes briefly as a painful flash of memory brought back the vision of another pale-haired woman, about whom he had indulged in similar erotic fantasies. Those fantasies of a lovesick youth had never been realized, he recalled with a familiar twinge of bitterness. And all because of Charles, who could not keep his roving hands off any woman, even one promised to his own brother. And now Charles had brought him, by a strange quirk of fate, another woman who had rekindled those old, half-forgotten fantasies. But he was no longer the callow youth he had been ten years ago, Richard reminded himself, to be beguiled by such foolishness. And yet, the persistent aroma of gardenias could not be denied.

The colonel shrugged and turned back into the house.

Lady Regina sat in a corner of her father's traveling coach in a state of numb withdrawal. She still wore her wedding gown, and had thrown her sable cloak about her shoulders, in spite of Claudette's warning that the heavy fur would be far too warm for the bright June weather. For once, the abigail had been wrong, Regina thought, repressing a shudder. She was cold to the very marrow, and no matter how deeply she snuggled into the lavish folds of the fur, she could not seem to escape the chill that had invaded her heart.

She was returning to England a married woman, she reminded herself for the tenth time since leaving the rue Lafitte, clasping her gloved fingers together in an attempt to warm them. That had been the culmination of her fondest dreams when she set sail from Dover barely a week since. Had it only been a week? she wondered, her eyes staring blindly at the countryside flashing past the window. And now here she was, her dreams realized, only by some malicious quirk of fate they had not materialized as she had expected. Everything had turned topsy-turvy. The man she had loved so blindly—Regina did not allow herself to speak his name, even to herself—had jilted her. *Jilted her*, she repeated to herself, still reluctant to admit that such a fate could befall the Duke of Wexley's daughter. And the man she had disliked on sight, that odious, pompous, grimly stern oaf of a colonel, had rescued her from that ignominy by offering himself in his brother's stead.

No, she reminded herself with painful honesty, he had not offered himself at all. He had deliberately refused to make her an offer of marriage. Ridiculous, he had called it, and of course he had been right. The notion of a match between them had seemed laughable at the time. But ridiculous or not, it had become a reality, and she was a married woman, but married to the wrong man for the wrong reasons. Regina felt a sudden urge to burst into tears.

They had stopped briefly for refreshments, not at *La Poule Verte* this time, but at the largest posting inn in Ghent, which was doing such a thriving business with carriages of all shapes and sizes making their way toward the coast, that the duke's equipage had difficulty entering the crowded yard.

Regina refused to leave the coach, ignoring her father's insistence that she should join him for a light meal. Instead, she instructed Claudette to bring her some freshly baked chicken pies and a mug of strong tea, and sat in the carriage with the abigail until they resumed their journey.

By the time they reached Ostend, dusk had long since fallen, and she boarded her father's yacht by the light of the captain's lantern without taking leave of her brothers, who had ridden beside the carriage and would return immediately to their posts with Wellington in Brussels. Instead of retiring to her cabin, as her father suggested, Regina took up a stand beside the railing and watched the lights of Ostend disappear into the darkness behind the ship until the only sign of land that remained was the beam from the lighthouse, flashing intermittently in the night.

When even that faint reminder of her sojourn in Brussels had been lost from sight, Regina remained on deck, listening to the rush of the water against the sleek hull of the *Seabird*, and wondering when, if ever, she would see Colonel Swinburn again. She could hardly blame him if he never came back to England to claim her, she mused, unhappiness coloring her thoughts as black as the enveloping night. She was, after all, an unwanted wife. He had made no bones about admitting as much. Just as he had not, by so much as a flicker of those dark inscrutable eyes of his, given her the slightest hint that he might have wished her to stay. No, the colonel had let her go without a murmur of protest. Perhaps he had even been thankful to be rid of her, she thought, giving rein to her most desolate suspicion.

The prospect was sobering indeed, and Regina, who had never wasted much time feeling sorry for herself, suddenly felt cast adrift in a world as dark and unfamiliar as the night around her. On impulse she drew off her left glove and touched the gold band Colonel Swinburn had so recently placed on her finger. Did the ring really mean anything? she wondered. Or was it merely an empty symbol of an unwanted marriage? Her fingers traced the small shape of the garnet ring on the same finger. She knew all too well what that ring symbolized. It had meant absolutely nothing to the man who had given it to her.

With sudden fury, Regina tore it from her finger and threw it as far as she could out into the dark sea.

CHAPTER SEVEN

Disobedient Wife

London, June–October 1815

"Have you not considered, my dear Regina, that perhaps Lady Swinburn might be expecting you to join her in Kent?" Lady Egermont remarked over the breakfast table one morning several days after her niece's return to London. Her wide blue eyes regarded Regina anxiously. "I cannot believe that Colonel Swinburn did not make arrangements for you to join his mother, particularly since he knew that a battle was imminent when he sent you home, dear."

"He did *not* send me home, Aunt," Regina responded quickly, pausing in the process of slathering her toast with her favorite strawberry preserve. "I made that decision myself just as soon as that dreadful little curate had finished posing those absurd questions. Everyone knew perfectly well that I had no wish to marry Colonel Swinburn, but what could I do with Papa standing there like some medieval dragon breathing fire at the slightest hint of opposition."

Lady Egermont sighed and passed her cup to the butler to be refilled. "Your father loves you, Regina," she said gently, "of that you can be sure. And he only did what he had to do. Did you honestly believe you could keep that quite shocking escapade of yours under wraps, dear?"

"To be quite honest with you, Aunt, I did not think that it would kick up such a dust. Wolverton never said a word about a possible scandal when he escorted me to Dover."

Lady Egermont threw a speaking glance at her butler, who silently left the room. "Wolverton!" she exclaimed in tones that clearly indicated her disapproval. "Scandal is Wolverton's middle name, child. And how you came to trust yourself to such a rakehell is beyond my comprehension."

"I have known Guy since I was in the nursery," Regina said, as if that explained everything. "And besides, he is bosom bows with Robert and, like my dear brother, has no desire to be legshackled."

"That is precisely the point, my dear innocent," Lady Egermont said with growing exasperation. "For that very reason, it was doubly rash of you to go loping off with him. I am only surprised that your father did not insist that Wolverton wed you instead of poor Colonel Swinburn."

"So am I," Regina said, amusement at her aunt's notion breaking through the apathetic mood that had plagued her ever since she had left Brussels behind her. "At least Guy would be more diverting. Did I tell you that the colonel never, ever smiles? He was forever badgering me about something. Can you believe that he could not take me driving because he did not own a curricle? Now what sort of a gentleman does not own a curricle, can you tell me, Aunt? Guy has two of them, and a spanking team of grays that is bang up to the nines."

"I imagine that a sporting vehicle would not be much use to the colonel in a battlefield," Lady Egermont said dryly. "And it is unfair of you to compare the colonel to Wolverton, dear."

"And why not?" Regina said, aware that she was being deliberately contentious and unable to stop herself. "Guy was in the Army, too, you know, before his twin brother was killed and he came into the title. You are beginning to sound like the colonel, Aunt," she added crossly. "That is just the sort of thing he would say, about the curricle in the battlefield. In point of fact, he did say it, now that I think on it. A dashed dull dog, if you ask me. I would as lief have wed Guy, even though he is a rake."

"You would regret it within a week, love," the countess said prosaically. "Just as you would have regretted being wed to your charming Captain Swinburn, had your father been able to lay hands on him long enough to get him before the curate, of course."

"I would *never* have wed that scoundrel," Regina burst out, conscious of a dull ache in the region of her heart. "And I do not wish to hear his name mentioned again, if you please, Aunt. It is quite bad enough that I find myself chained to his brother for the rest of my life." She paused, conscious of the rising lump in her throat and the uncharacteristic desire to burst into tears again, an urge that had plagued her at the oddest moments ever since her return to England.

She took a vicious bite out of her toast and chewed it, grimly determined not to succumb to melancholy.

"It seems to me that you are in the colonel's debt in more ways than one, dear," her aunt remarked. "I should warn you, my dear Regina"—she continued in a worried voice—"that your father told me last night that Napoleon has joined his army in the north and that he appears prepared to engage the Prussians at Ligny. Dispatches to that effect arrived late yesterday afternoon at the War Office, he tells me, and the general feeling is that it cannot be much longer before Wellington must confront the French."

"I do not wish to talk about my father either," Regina retorted coldly. "He has broken my heart and destroyed any hope I had of finding happiness."

"Pooh! You broke your own heart, Regina, when you gave it to that handsome scoundrel," her aunt said with unusual severity. "And if you insist on punishing your poor father for protecting your reputation and saving you from a disastrous marriage, you have windmills in your head, dear child."

It was Regina's turn to speak sharply. "My reputation may have been salvaged, Aunt, but at what price? This marriage *is* a disaster, but nobody would listen to me. And was it not you, Aunt Phoebe, who reminded me not long ago that the Heathercotts never wed below the rank of earl? Swinburn is only a baronet, and an obscure one at that. A nobody!" she exclaimed, bitterness at the hand the Fates had dealt her making her voice harsh.

"But a far better man than his brother, Regina, as you would see if you but opened your eyes. An honorable man, and obviously responsible and kind, although he was sadly misguided when he agreed to wed you, dear, as I would have told him had I been in Brussels at the time."

Regina waved this comment aside, but she could not deny that some of what her aunt had said was true. A match with that traitorous captain would indeed have been a disaster, but it did not follow that being wed to his brother would bring her the happiness she had dreamed of two short weeks ago. No, she thought dejectedly, that dream was gone forever, and all she had to look forward to was a life of placid boredom as mistress of an obscure country manor in Kent with a man who was neither exciting nor amusing. And far from fashionable. A man who would doubtless take refuge in his Army career to avoid having to live with her, she realized, suddenly and quite inexplicably lonely for the colonel's solid presence. At least she could depend on him, she mused, remembering the occasions when the colonel had shown uncanny insight into her feelings. The memory of his strong hand steadying her when she had faltered at the sight of three other identical garnet rings on the fingers of Charles's *amourettes* still lingered in her mind. If nothing else, her new husband was kind she had to agree; but Regina had wanted so much more than kindness.

She glanced at her aunt and found that lady regarding her with a frown on her beautiful face. Thank goodness for Aunt Phoebe, Regina thought, not for the first time since her father had set her down on Lady Egermont's doorstep when she had adamantly refused to cross the portals of Wexley Court on St. James's Square. Her aunt had received her with open arms and instantly agreed that her niece was welcome to stay with her for as long as she chose.

Impulsively, she reached for her aunt's hand. "You are very sweet to let me stay with you, Aunt Phoebe," she said a little shakily. "When I come into the bulk of my fortune next year, I shall set up my own establishment, so I shall not long be a burden to you, dearest."

Lady Egermont stared in amazement. "What nonsense you do talk, Regina," she exclaimed laughingly. "I am delighted to have you, child. But let me suggest that before you rush into anything, it might be wise to pay a visit to Kent. Perhaps you will find that life at Willow Park suits you more than you think, dear. Summer in the country can be quite pleasant."

Regina laughed. "I rather think not, Aunt," she said archly. "If the colonel's lodgings in Brussels were any indication, I imagine his taste must run to stuffy drawing rooms filled with old-fashioned furniture and ghastly porcelain figurines of dubious origin. The only amusing person in the house was his butler, Burton, who is a quiz of the first stare. I would give a pony to see Mama's face were she to see Burton serving tea. His hands are like hams, dear, and he rattles the teacups most dreadfully. I was surprised he never broke any."

"Well, if you are set against visiting your mother-in-law, Regina," Lady Egermont said with an elegant shrug, "I wonder if I might prevail upon you to accompany me to Brighton next week. I have a house there, as you know, and was quite resolved to remove there for the summer before you descended upon me."

Regina's spirits rose instantly. "I think that is a splendid notion, Aunt," she cried enthusiastically. "I have always enjoyed Brighton. And if the Regent is in residence, there should be enough amusements to entertain us for some time. I shall take my mare Medea with me, of course, and have Dodson drive my curricle down. Do you take your own mare, Aunt? I do so enjoy a good gallop in the mornings."

Her aunt eyed her reproachfully. "You must learn to comport yourself more decorously, my dear Regina," she suggested. "Now that you are a married lady, you will be expected to behave appropriately, which does not include galloping wildly down the Strand, let me tell you."

"I shall be as decorous as you, my dear aunt," Regina shot back with a teasing smile, for her dashing aunt was not precisely known as a pattern card of respectability. "Will that suit you?"

"I am a widow, dear," her aunt responded gaily. "And that is a very different affair, let me tell you."

Regina was not at all sure she wanted to be constantly reminded of her married state, yet her aunt's careless words reminded her that she might soon be a widow herself, a notion she found singularly unsettling. In her youthful dreams—discarded with the meaningless garnet ring she had tossed into the sea—marriage had always implied the presence of a loving husband. What sense did it make to be married and have no husband? she asked herself later as she dressed for dinner. If she could have pretended the whole Brussels affair had been a particularly unpleasant dream, she would have done so. But for some reason, Regina could not rid herself of the notion that she owed the colonel an apology. She rarely apologized to anyone, but she knew she had behaved badly in Brussels, and her heart would not rest until she had admitted as much to her husband.

Unfortunately, he was not there to hear her, and as a result, Regina found herself thinking of the colonel far more often than she had intended to.

Much as Regina had wished to escape from London, now sadly thin of elegant company, she was reluctant to do so after an unexpected visit from her mother. The Duchess of Wexley burst in upon Lady Egermont's drawing room the afternoon before their planned departure with disturbing news that banished all thoughts of Brighton from Regina's mind.

"Your father would have come himself," the duchess remarked dryly, taking a seat on the green brocade settee beside her daughter, "but he feared you would not receive him, Regina."

Regina resented the reproof in her mother's voice. She also resented the fact that the duchess was entirely in agreement with her father's decision to force his daughter into what could only be considered, at least in Regina's eyes, a *mésalliance* of the worst kind.

"He was right to stay away," Regina said curtly. "I have nothing more to say to him."

The duchess reached for her daughter's hand, balled into a fist in her lap. "You are making him very miserable, my dear," she said gently. "I beg you will not be so stubborn, Regina; he is your father, and he loves you."

"Does he imagine that I am not miserable, too?" Regina demanded coldly, touched in spite of herself by her mother's words. "And if I am stubborn, he was doubly so when he forced me into marriage with a man I dislike and who dislikes me. What does he imagine my future will be like, Mama, can you tell me? I shall be forever perusing the casualty lists in the *Gazette* to discover whether or not I am a widow yet."

The duchess squeezed her daughter's cold fingers reassuringly. "If you dislike the colonel as much as you say, Regina, I cannot see why finding his name on those dreadful lists of officers fallen in battle should upset you, dear. Although I myself would certainly grieve for him. I found him a thoroughly decent young man that summer he visited the Abbey with Lord Uxbridge."

Regina shuddered at her mother's words. Yes, she thought, she disliked the dour colonel and wished him in Jericho, yet the idea of all that masculine strength and kindness laid waste on some obscure battlefield distressed her with an intensity that took her by surprise.

"I do not wish to be a widow," she observed in a dampening tone. "Now, are you going to tell us what news you have from Brussels, Mama, or are we to sit here biting our nails?"

The duchess set her cup on the low boulle table beside her and turned back to her hostess, a worried frown on her face. "Wexley heard some distressing news this morning at the War Office," she began. "It seems that Prince Blücher was defeated three days ago at Ligny, and that the emperor is deploying his forces along the Bruxelles-Charleroi road. The prime minister believes that even as we speak a decisive encounter may be taking place between the Duke of Wellington and Napoleon's forces."

Regina stared at her mother, thoroughly alarmed. She had known that sooner or later this battle would take place, but had been so caught up in her own pain at Charles's dastardly betrayal, that the horror of it had not touched her. Now the reality of war and the bloody consequences of this crucial encounter between Allied and French armies hit her with sudden force. She might well be a widow after all before the day was done, she realized, her heart cold at the thought. A widow before she had ever been a wife. Would she lose the husband she was determined to dislike? A man she would remember more for his small kindnesses than for any real harm he had done her. Would she never get the chance to thank him for taking on the responsibility of a wife he obviously had not wanted?

"When will we know if . . . ?" Words failed her. Regina had two brothers with Wellington's forces, as well as a husband, and the thought of losing any of them rendered her paralyzed with fear.

Her aunt seemed to sense her anxiety for she intervened, her calm manner going a long way to restoring some of Regina's equilibrium. "If this battle of Ligny took place three days ago," she said practically, "then it is highly likely that any encounter between the armies has already taken place. I do not doubt that Wellington will be successful. Only consider his successful Peninsular campaign, my dear Sybil," she said to her sister-in-law. "I understand that Colonel Swinburn was with the duke in Spain. And as for Geoffrey and Nevil, they are both seasoned officers, dearest, so it is pointless to expect anything but their safe return."

Regina threw her aunt a grateful glance. Lady Egermont's logic was not unassailable, but her intentions were of the best. If her brothers were seasoned officers, her husband was even more so, and Aunt Phoebe was right. There was no point in expecting the worse.

"Wexley is to attend one of Lord Liverpool's political dinners at Fife House in Whitehall this evening," the duchess continued, "and he is confident that by that time there will be further dispatches arriving from the Continent. By morning we should know the outcome of the battle at least."

"You will let us know immediately, will you not, Mama?" Regina said in a low voice.

"Of course, child," the duchess replied, giving her daughter a compassionate look. "But I wish you and Phoebe would come to Wexley Court to wait there to learn whatever tidings your father will bring, my dear. It would please him so."

But Regina was adamant in maintaining her distance, and so it was Lady Egermont who carried home the next distressing news after a short call on her sister-in-law the following afternoon.

"They are saying that Wellington's losses were enormous," her distraught aunt reported to Regina, who waited nervously in the drawing room, fiddling distractedly with her empty teacup. "The duke routed Napoleon, as I knew he would, but it appears that the cost was much higher than expected."

"And do you bring news of Geoffrey and Nevil?" Regina demanded. "And the colonel? What of him?" she added, unwilling to sound as anxious as she felt.

"Ah, there's the rub, dear," her aunt said with such an air of distress that Regina immediately thought the worst.

"Not all lost, surely?" she whispered, suddenly unable to breathe.

"Oh, no, dear," her aunt hastened to add. "Geoffrey was able to send word that both he and Nevil received slight wounds, but the worst part concerns the colonel, dearest. Lord Liverpool confirms that Lord Uxbridge lost over forty percent of his men. The earl himself was wounded, as were several of his commanding officers, although your papa says that as yet they do not have their names. Sir William Ponsonby was lost, and . . ."

But Regina was no longer listening to her aunt's grim recital of names. Her heart had frozen in her breast at the mention of Lord Uxbridge's great losses. Colonel Swinburn was one of Uxbridge's most trusted officers and would doubtless have been with the earl in the field. Was her husband among the wounded? she wondered. Or was he lying out there on the battlefield, as yet unidentified among the heaps of dead? Regina shuddered.

"Dispatches are arriving hourly, my dear Regina, so do not give up all hope until the casualty lists are complete," her aunt advised, pouring her niece another cup of tea and forcing her to drink it. "We must not despair, child," she added philosophically. "No doubt the colonel will send us news when he is able."

As it was, news of Colonel Swinburn's fate came from quite another quarter. Not two weeks after the guns of the Tower and Hyde Park had rattled the windows of London in celebration of the victory of Waterloo, Regina received a missive in an unfamiliar hand, which turned out to be from her mother-in-law, the Dowager Lady Swinburn, in Kent.

Regina tore open the letter impatiently. As she read the long-awaited news that both Colonel Swinburn and his brother had come through the battle unscathed, the relief she expected to feel slowly turned first to annoyance, and then to a simmering anger that caused her fingers to tremble as they crushed the offending missive.

"Whatever is the matter, love?" her aunt inquired anxiously. "Never say that the colonel—"

"The colonel is hale and hearty," Regina cut in ruthlessly. "At least, so it would appear from what Lady Swinburn reports. She tells me that Sir Richard sent word a week ago that both he and his worthless brother survived the ordeal. How she dares to mention that scoundrel to me is beyond my comprehension," she added angrily.

"I very much doubt the poor lady knows anything about the captain's scandalous goings-on," Lady Egermont remarked gently. "What else does her ladyship say, dear?"

Regina gave an inelegant snort. "She presumes to advise me that the colonel expects to return to Willow Park before Christmas and dares to suggest that I had better be there when he arrives."

Lady Egermont gasped in astonishment. "Never say those are her very words, dear?"

"No, of course not," Regina snapped, her anger at being snubbed by her husband causing her to forget that moments before she was agonizing over his safe return. "She says that Sir Richard might be seriously discomposed if he returned to find his bride not in residence. But the implication is clear would you not agree, Aunt? I must run home like some schoolgirl to oblige her precious colonel."

"You are married to the gentleman," her aunt pointed out, much to Regina's annoyance.

"Well, I will not be ordered about like some genteel governess who has caught a baronet in her snare," she said coldly. "And now that we know that Swinburn will not appear on the casualty list"—she abruptly changed the subject—"I propose that we leave the city, which is becoming unbearably hot, and remove to Brighton as we had planned. What do you say to that, Aunt?"

Lady Egermont had no objection whatsoever, and before the week was out, the ladies had ordered their trunks packed and set out in the elegant Egermont traveling chaise.

And the colonel might go hang himself, Regina thought as the unpleasant summer smells of London faded behind them. It would take her at least until Christmas to forgive him for not writing to her directly. That was a slight she had never expected of him, and she was not disposed to forget it in a hurry.

"Buck up, lad," Burton said cheerily as the two men dismounted in the bustling yard of the Blue Stag Inn, one of Dover's less pretentious posting houses. "To look at ye, a man might think ye be off to the wars instead of comin' home fer good, as like as not, what with Boney put away all right and tight."

Colonel Swinburn glanced at his merry-faced batman and then down at his own travel-stained clothes and muddy boots. They had but recently disembarked from the ferry after a rough crossing, and the colonel was tired and hungry; he also needed a shave and a bath, and his boots were definitely ruined. And as if that were not enough to dampen a man's spirits, the chill October rain showed no signs of abating. He found nothing cheerful about the prospect at all.

No, he thought later that night as he lay awake listening to Burton snoring in the truckle bed the landlord had set up in the small room, there was nothing cheerful about this homecoming. On the contrary, Richard felt that same insidious tension he was accustomed to experience before a battle. That tightening of the stomach muscles, the racing of the pulses, the mental reconciliation to what might result from the encounter ahead of him. All of this was familiar to him, but why he felt these pre-battle anxieties when he was on his way home, he could only guess. Would his life with Lady Regina be the kind of pitched battle he had seen other marriages turn into? he wondered.

Perhaps he should turn right about and return to France, Richard thought despondently. The Second Treaty of Paris was scheduled for November, and although he had done more than was expected of him by volunteering to escort the defeated emperor aboard the small brig *L'Epervier*, which carried his suite and baggage to the port, and to deliver him into the custody of Captain Maitland of the H.M.S. *Bellerophon*, Colonel Swinburn had wanted to remain in Wellington's entourage during the discussions of the treaty.

The Earl of Uxbridge had vetoed that idea and ordered the colonel home on a long-delayed leave, chiding him for leaving his new bride unattended for so long. The colonel had not wanted to correct his superior officer's delusion that his marriage to Lady Regina was anything but the stroke of good fortune the earl and fellow officers seemed to think it. Indeed, Richard had been forced to endure a great deal of good-natured ribbing on his sudden and quite unexpected alliance with a duke's daughter of vast wealth and beauty.

And so here he was, the colonel mused as they set out the following morning in the continuing drizzle, back home and far from feeling that joy he supposed a normal husband must feel at the prospect of being reunited with his new bride. But he was not a normal husband, Richard reminded himself somberly, and Regina was as removed from being the loving wife a man such as himself might have envisioned as any woman could be. He sighed and dared not speculate what the rest of his life might be like with such a female.

It was not until later that afternoon, as they rode through the village of Langley and turned off the Maldstone Road into the oak-lined drive to Willow Park that the colonel had the sudden premonition that his wife would not be there to greet him. Why should she be? he asked himself. He had sent her no word of his arrival, and it occurred to him that he may have committed a serious tactical error in not doing so.

As a result of these uneasy meditations, Richard was halfway prepared for his mother's welcome, unaccompanied by his wife, as old Tobin, the Swinburn butler for upward of fifty years, ushered him into the drawing room.

Lady Swinburn jumped to her feet and flew across the room. "My dearest Richard," she exclaimed, her voice escalating into a twitter as it always did when she was overset with emotion. "I have been distraught, my dear boy," she added quite unnecessarily, reaching up to fling her arms about the colonel's broad shoulders, a feat she could only accomplish by standing on tiptoe. "Oh, how I have prayed for your safe return. I cannot tell you how I have dreamed of this day. Ever since I received notice of the battle, I have been beside myself with worry, dear. Come and warm yourself by the fire, you must be frozen to death. It has rained for almost a week," she rattled on, drawing him toward the brightly burning logs in the generous hearth. "Robinson was barely able to get the last of the crops in, it has been so damp. And would you believe that—"

The entrance of Tobin with the tea tray, followed by Mrs. Tobin, their housekeeper, who had come up from the kitchens to welcome the master home from war, put a stop to Lady Swinburn's outpouring of chatter.

"Sir Richard, it is a relief to see you back at Willow Park," the plump housekeeper said, bobbing him a curtsy, her face wreathed in smiles.

"And it is glad I am to be back, Mrs. Tobin," Richard responded, striding over to embrace her plump form enthusiastically. "I have sorely missed your gooseberry tarts."

Clearly bursting with pleasure, the old retainer took her leave, vowing that her dear Sir Richard would no longer want for his favorite tarts, since she had put up a generous supply of gooseberry preserves for that very purpose.

Quite suddenly Richard felt as though he were really back home again. His mother's ceaseless chatter, the genuine affection of the housekeeper, who had remembered to put up the gooseberries, and the uninhibited welcome accorded by old Tobin himself, all combined to give Richard that sense of well-being that comes to a man at peace in his own home.

Now if only his wife could fit into this picture, he mused, accepting a steaming cup from his mother and settling back into his favorite chair. But that would be asking for a miracle, of course. And Richard had long since ceased to believe in miracles. He sighed and glanced toward the door. Obviously his wife was not here, and he should have been relieved, but all he felt was an unexpected sense of dread. Regina was a battle that still had to be fought, if he knew anything about the duke's daughter.

Lady Swinburn must have noticed his glance, for she paused in her recital of the new babies born in the parish since the colonel's last leave, and said in a tense little whisper. "I suppose you are wondering why Lady Regina is not here to greet you, my dear. Well, I wrote to her in London as soon as I received your letter. I thought it only my duty to let your wife know what I had heard, although no doubt you wrote to her yourself, dear," she added hastily. "Her ladyship responded with a very proper little note, informing me that she had made plans to spend the summer in Brighton with her aunt, the Countess of Egermont."

Lady Swinburn had risen from the settee during this breathless explanation and rummaged around in the top drawer of a cabinet set in a corner of the room.

"Ah!" she exclaimed in delight, as if upon discovery of some hidden treasure. "Here it is, dear. Very condescending of her ladyship, I must admit, to take the time to inform me of her plans, dear, as I know you will agree."

There had been no hint of irony in his mother's words, and Richard knew from long experience that Lady Swinburn was incapable of guile and that an unkind thought had never entered her head.

Grimly he took the letter she held out to him and read it through quickly. It was as he thought, brief and bordering on rudeness. Lady Regina was pleased to inform her ladyship that since the colonel would not return to Kent before Christmas, she saw no need to do so herself.

She would spend the summer in Brighton and perhaps return to London for the Little Season if she tired of the seaside resort by September.

There was no mention whatsoever of traveling to Kent, and Richard knew, with sudden intuition, that Regina had meant the missive for his eyes as well. Was his wife serving notice that she was not about to jump to do his mother's bidding? he wondered.

Or his own? he thought, a wry smile twisting his lips at the notion.

The note, written in bold, slanting strokes, reminded him forcefully of the female he had—in a moment of mad quixotism he had yet to understand—taken to wife. The memory of her blond loveliness swamped his consciousness so vividly that she might have been standing there before him in all her stubborn, imperious, willful, yet tantalizing beauty. His wife, he mused, a woman he had yet to hold in his arms, to kiss, to make his own. He wished he had more experience with females of Lady Regina's stamp. He wished that they had met under different circumstances. He wished that he knew the key to her heart.

He wondered if he ever would.

CHAPTER EIGHT

Uncertain Future

Brighton, October 1815

"I do believe it is getting time to think of returning to the Metropolis, my dear," Lady Egermont remarked over the breakfast table in the sunny parlor one morning in early October. "We have already outstayed most of the *beau monde* who came down to Brighton for the summer. And the Regent returned to London weeks ago, Regina."

"Are you saying that we must ape the Prince's every move, Aunt?" Regina responded rather dryly, picking dispiritedly at her food. "I rather enjoy the Promenades when they are less crowded, and one can drive about without being gawked at by a parcel of old Tabbies."

Lady Egermont laughed, "I daresay it is the *manner* in which you drive that scandalizes them, dearest," she said with the perennial good humor that never failed to please. "I have driven out with a good number of whipsters in my time, love, but I declare that none of them can match you in reckless disregard for life and limb."

"I have yet to overturn the curricle, Aunt," Regina pointed out in offended tones. She rather prided herself on her skill with the ribbons, and had been permitted the rare privilege of driving the teams of such high sticklers as the Honorable Willoughby Hampton and the Duke of Wolverton. "Willy Hampton told me that I am a first-rate fiddler," she added defensively, "and Wolverton assured me that if the Four-in-Hand Club admitted females, I would undoubtedly be elected a member. Guy says I would look bang up to the nines in that toggery they wear." She took a tentative bite of toast, glancing with amusement at her aunt's expression of distaste.

"I have no earthly idea what a *fiddler* is, dear," the countess said crossly, "and I do wish you would refrain from using such stable cant at the breakfast table. It is unseemly." She motioned to Higginbotham to refill her cup. "I warned your father years ago how it would be, when he taught you to drive his own team," she added after the butler had filled her cup with steaming brew. "But he would not listen, naturally. Nothing was too good for his little fairy-girl—as he used to call you, remember? He doted on you, poor Roger did, and how do you repay him, dear? You will not receive him when he comes down to Brighton expressly to patch up your ridiculous quarrel."

Regina shrugged her shoulders. "I, too, warned him how it would be," she said, the mulish expression this particular argument always provoked marring her face. "And again he would not listen. And I still do believe that he might have arranged for me to return to England with no one the wiser. There was no need to rush into this absurd marriage."

Her aunt grimaced. "You have windmills in your head, dearest. From what your papa told me, there was not a single officer in Wellington's Army who did not know that the Duke of Wexley's only daughter had arrived in Brussels to force Swinburn to the altar. To say nothing of the colonel's own men and half the population of Brussels."

Regina was appalled. "I did no such thing," she protested loudly.

"Are you trying to tell me that you did not intend to badger the captain into honoring his offer of marriage?" her aunt demanded rather caustically.

"No, I did not," Regina was quick to reply. "Besides, Charles never did actually offer for me, you see. He intended to, I am sure of it, but he said it was too soon to speak to Papa—"

It was Lady Egermont's turn to look astonished. "I can well believe it," she cut in scathingly. "The rogue had no intention of doing anything of the sort, Regina. You are an innocent ninny to have believed the scoundrel."

"Oh, but he did," Regina protested angrily. "He gave me a ring, you see."

The look her aunt gave her was withering. "The gift of a ring means nothing to a man, dearest," she said pityingly. "They give them to their mistresses all the time, but they rarely wed them. *Very* rarely," she repeated with heavy sarcasm.

"That I discovered for myself," Regina responded bluntly. "There are at least three other females in Brussels with identical garnet rings."

"The rogue undoubtedly purchased them by the dozen, dear," her aunt said in a softer voice. "To a woman, a ring has a great deal of sentimental significance, and some men—being the scoundrels they are—use this to breach a female's defenses, dear. And, fools that we are, we are too often taken in by such perversity." She paused to regard her niece speculatively. "I trust that you were not so deceived, Regina," she added hesitantly.

Regina bristled. "Whatever do you take me for, Aunt?" she cried, mortally offended by the question. "However, I did allow the colonel to believe that Charles had seduced me," she added hesitantly, a faint blush tingeing her cheeks.

"You never did such a thing!" Lady Egermont exclaimed in consternation. "I have known you to indulge in harebrained starts, Regina," she added censoriously, "but that is beyond the pale. How could you deceive the poor man in such a fashion?"

"I only wished to scare him off, Aunt," Regina admitted, heartily wishing that she had chosen some other means of doing so. "But he only became more insistent on doing my father's bidding. I could not believe the man's stubbornness."

"It is to his credit that he insisted upon righting the supposed wrong his brother did you, dear child." Lady Egermont paused for a moment, and Regina knew that further probing would follow.

"I assume you have since confessed the whole to him, dear?" she queried, one slender eyebrow raised.

Regina wished she could answer in the affirmative, but she had been so intent on escaping from her new husband that she had failed to enlighten him on the subject.

"No, I have not yet done so," she said in an offhand manner, wishing her aunt was not so perceptive. "But I will," she promised, seeing the condemnation in Lady Egermont's eyes. "The very next time we meet, I shall confess the whole. I promise you, Aunt. Now," she continued, abruptly changing the subject, "you were discussing our return to London. Are we to miss the last assembly at the Castle Inn then? I have already promised two waltzes to Lord Westbrook dear, and I would hate to disappoint him," she added ingeniously.

"Ah!" her aunt said in a different tone of voice. "I have been meaning to speak to you about our so handsome Major Westbrook, dear. His attentions are becoming far too marked of late, Regina, and you must not wander off with him as you did at Lady Bedford's ball last week. It caused quite an unpleasant amount of gossip among the matrons. And another scandal is something you do not need at the moment, my dear."

Her aunt's rebuke immediately put Regina on the defensive. "Major Westbrook is a friend and fellow officer of the colonel's," she retorted. "In fact he confided that Sir Richard asked him to look me up if he was in London. He came down to Brighton expressly to pay his respects when he discovered I had removed from the Metropolis. I thought that was very considerate of him, do you not, Aunt?"

"Oh, yes indeed," Lady Egermont drawled sarcastically. "I wager our Major Westbrook has a string of broken hearts in his wake to rival Captain Swinburn's. Two of a kind, they are, and make no mistake about it, love, he intends to break yours, too."

"Then he will be disappointed," Regina said carelessly. "I have no heart to break again, Aunt, so you may rest easy on that score."

She had spoken lightly but her aunt's warning returned to impair her enjoyment of Lord Westbrook's fulsome compliments two evenings later when the ladies were set down in front of the Castle Inn where the last assembly of the summer Season was to be held.

The first gentleman the ladies encountered upon entering the assembly room was the Earl of Westbrook himself, who appeared to have been lying in wait for them.

"My dear Lady Egermont," he drawled, bowing with innate grace over that lady's gloved hand. "I was beginning to think you had forgotten your promise to save a dance for me tonight. And Lady Swinburn," he cooed, raking Regina's elegant form with practiced eyes. "How magnificent you look tonight, to be sure. I swear that my poor heart is quite revived in the glory of your presence."

Regina murmured a polite response to these flowery and—at least to her ears—insincere phrases and was about to pass on into the ballroom with her aunt, when the earl detained her. "I have a friend here, fresh back from the Continent, my lady, who is anxious to make your acquaintance."

Some inner voice told Regina that Major Westbrook was anything but pleased to be forced into this introduction, and when she heard the name of the newcomer, she knew why.

"Major David Laughton at your service, my lady," the tall dark man who stepped forward to raise her fingers to within a hairbreadth of his lips observed in a deep voice that reminded her instantly of the colonel's.

There was something about the slow smile that curled his lips and the engaging twinkle in his black eyes that made Regina feel at ease with this total stranger. Well, perhaps not a complete stranger, she thought, returning his smile with one of her own. The colonel had mentioned Major Laughton several times, and she was sure that Sir David was truly one of her husband's friends. Richard had never mentioned Westbrook at all.

Her smile broadened. "I trust you intend to honor us with your company, Major," she remarked, genuine pleasure in her voice. "I hope you bring me tidings of Colonel Swinburn, who is not the kind of correspondent one might wish for."

"I had intended to request the pleasure of a dance, my lady," the major responded with smooth courtesy, as Regina had hoped he would.

She extended her hand. "You are in luck Major Laughton," she said with a gay little laugh. "My first set is completely free."

Before the major could take it, however, Lord Westbrook spoke up in mock distress "I had hoped you would have saved the opening set for your most devoted admirer, my dear lady," he said in caressing tones that implied a certain understanding between them.

Regina bristled, her aunt's admonition regarding the earl ringing in her ears. "If you must presume to hope where there is no guarantee of achieving success, my lord"—her tone of voice had a distinct edge to it—"then you must be prepared to take the consequences, must you not?" She accompanied this set-down with a faint smile to take some of the sting out of the words, but the earl's eyes went hard, even as he smiled and offered his arm to Lady Egermont.

Major Laughton led her onto the dance floor, smiling down at her in frank admiration. "I am relieved not to be in your black book, my lady," he observed with an infectious grin. "I have heard some pretty effective set-downs in my time, but I actually have it in my heart to feel sorry for Westbrook. Whatever did he do to deserve that crushing remark?"

"His lordship can be too encroaching at times," Regina replied, wondering whether this was the real reason she had felt the need to cut off any hint of intimacy between Westbrook and herself in front of Major Laughton. "Tell me, Major," she continued, not wishing to examine the question too closely, "is Westbrook a good friend of Richard's?"

Laughton's smiled diminished. "Has he told you that he is?"

Regina chided him. "Will you not answer mine first? Please?"

"Do you always answer one question with another, Major?" she added, instinct telling her that she could trust this man to give her the truth.

"I would hardly call Westbrook one of Richard's bosom-bows," he answered, his tone of voice telling Regina all she wanted to know.

"And I take it that you are, Major Laughton?" she inquired, feeling a smile twitching at her lips.

"Yes," he said readily. "At least I like to think so. Our lands march together in Kent, so we are neighbors. We practically grew up together. Richard is a couple of years my junior, but he was always a serious lad, so we got on well together."

"That I can believe. But surely you do not consider yourself another *serious lad*, Major?" Regina asked in surprise. The major's dark eyes held a constant gleam of secret humor that belied his words, and his face was lined with laughter.

"Oh, but I am, my lady," he replied in a serious voice, but his eyes gave him away, and Regina burst out laughing.

"I think you are bamming me, sir," she protested before they joined a set that was forming for the opening cotillion and further conversation was curtailed.

As the major led her off the floor at the end of the set, Regina demanded to know what news he had of the colonel.

"Richard has not written to you recently, I take it?"

"No," Regina answered shortly, shrinking from confessing that her husband had not sent word to her at all. "The last we heard, he expected to be home for Christmas."

Major Laughton glanced at her curiously. "His plans have changed since then, my lady," he said. "Or Uxbridge changed them for him, I should say. The last I heard, Richard was to sail from Calais the week after I did myself."

Regina stared up at him, her mind racing. "Then he could be at Willow Park even as we speak?" she asked hesitantly.

"Quite likely," the major responded laconically.

"How tiresome of him," she said crossly. The notion that her husband was already in England and might well be expecting to see her at Willow Park made Regina suddenly nervous. "I trust he is not always this inconsiderate," she complained. "I should let my aunt know, of course. We were planning to remove to London next week."

"Inconsiderate?" Major Laughton repeated in surprise. "That is the last word I would use to describe your husband, my lady. He has never been so to me."

Regina sensed the unspoken rebuke, and retorted without thought. "But then you are not wedded to him, Major," she observed rather sharply. Instantly remorseful, she met the major's dark gaze frankly. "Forgive me," she murmured, "I did not mean to snap at you, Major. But I find your news unsettling. He did not want to, you know," she added enigmatically, suddenly quite sure that the colonel had confided in his friend.

"So he has indicated," the major replied at once, confirming her suspicions. "Neither did you, I understand?"

For a terrible moment, Regina thought she was going to burst into tears, but after a short pause, she was able to reply. "No," she murmured, her thoughts on the man whom she would have to face sooner or later. "No, I did not. But it is done, thanks to my meddling father." She looked up into the major's eyes, finding them full of silent sympathy. She smiled faintly. "I intend to make the best of it," she said more firmly, surprised at this sudden decision that had sprung unbidden to her lips. She meant it, too, she realized, sensing that this man who was Richard's friend approved of her. "Yes," she repeated in a firmer voice. "I shall do my best not to be the termagant he must think me."

"I am relieved to hear it, my lady," the major said solemnly. "He deserves the best. I wager you will not be disappointed in him either when you know him better."

A sudden troubling thought occurred to her. "If the colonel is already at Willow Park, he must be wondering where I am," she murmured, almost to herself. She shot a veiled glance at the major. "Do you suppose he will come looking for me here?"

Major Laughton grinned widely, his white teeth flashing. "If I were your husband, my dear, I certainly would," he said, frank admiration in his eyes as he observed her. "I would not leave you a moment longer than absolutely necessary in the company of a man like Westbrook," he added, glancing around the room as if searching for the object of his criticism.

Then his smile abruptly broadened. "But your question is plainly moot, my lady," he drawled, amusement in his voice. "For here he is, quite obviously looking for you."

Regina's gaze followed the direction Laughton indicated, and she went suddenly very still. Yes, there he was, she thought. Her husband. She savored the taste of the word. Looking quite unexpectedly tall and splendid in his bright red-and-gold Hussar's uniform, Colonel Swinburn stood at the entrance to the assembly room, scanning the milling crowd. Was he really looking for her? she wondered, surprised at the racing of her heart.

Before she had time to consider her own question, their eyes met, and Regina knew the answer.

Colonel Sir Richard Swinburn stood at the entrance to the Castle Inn assembly rooms and scanned the swirling crowd on the dance floor. He had left Willow Park on impulse that morning and traveled to Brighton on the off chance that his wife had not yet removed to London for the Little Season. It was only after he and Burton had taken rooms at the Green Stag Inn, a modest posting house on the outskirts of the town, that he gave any thought at all to how he was to handle Lady Regina's refusal to assume her proper place as the wife of a very minor baronet in Kent.

Had he really expected she would? he asked himself a dozen times as he made the journey along the coast, listening with half an ear to Burton's jocular confessions about some skittish lass he had once fancied as a youth in the nearby village of Bexhill.

"As sweet an armful as a man could wish, was me wee Alice," the batman mused nostalgically. "But she wanted me tied tight to 'er apron strings she did, more's the pity. And at twenty-two I was not ready to give up me roaming ways, lad, and that's the truth. Now if I 'ad to do it over again, there's no telling but . . ."

The colonel ceased to follow Burton's rambling reminiscences and wondered how he had ever been fool enough to imagine that this impulsive marriage he had entered into with the duke's daughter might bring him any satisfaction. He still had difficulty convincing himself that it had happened at all. Had he not himself accompanied Wexley when the duke set out to obtain a special license from the Anglican prelate attached to Wellington's entourage, Richard might have considered the episode part of an absurd dream. But he had seen the license, purchased the plain gold band from the obscure jewelers, and brought the marriage lines safely back to England in his pocket. The document was even now lying in his strongbox at home.

And now, what did he imagine he would say to her when they came face to face again? His more cautious self had several times suggested that the wise—however cowardly—strategy would be to give the lady a wide berth. Yet a stronger, more primitive urge led him to seek out what was his own, although the thought of reminding Lady Regina of this indisputable legal fact to her face made him falter as he dressed with particular care, later that evening, for the formal call he intended to pay on his wife.

"Their ladyships will be most put out to have missed you, Sir Richard," Lady Egermont's ancient butler informed him some time later with what appeared to be genuine distress. "They left not an hour since for the assembly rooms, sir, and are not expected home before midnight. Most partial to dancing are their ladyships," the butler continued with the natural informality of the trusted retainer. "Would you wish me to send word to the Castle Inn, sir?"

But the colonel decided, again on the spur of the moment, that he would seek the ladies out himself. The notion of watching his wife dance, perhaps even of dancing with her himself, suddenly appealed to him, and so it was that shortly thereafter, Richard found himself standing at the entrance of the assembly room among several other unattached gentlemen.

He scanned the dance floor for several minutes, acknowledging two or three officers of his acquaintance. The sight of one in particular drew a deep frown and caused his lips to thin suspiciously. What in Hades was that jackstraw Westbrook doing in Brighton? he wondered, observing the graceful figure of the handsome blond earl with distaste. Always the peacock, the major was not in uniform, the colonel noticed, but wore an exquisitely cut coat of pale blue satin which outlined his lean figure admirably. A darker blue waistcoat, lavishly embroidered with silver thread, and white satin knee breeches completed the dandy's attire, and Richard had no doubt that Westbrook had patronized the most expensive tailor in London to achieve that air of casual elegance.

After the unpleasant shock of encountering his old rival in Brighton had worn off, Richard noticed that Westbrook had not yet seen him. The earl's gaze was fixed on a couple engaged in dancing the cotillion in a set at the far end of the room. As the gentleman, dressed in the familiar red Hussar's uniform, moved in the pattern of the dance, Richard had a clear view of his partner. The sight of her took his breath away. He had known of course that his wife was a beautiful woman, but the colonel had never seen her in such splendid looks as she was that evening. Her gown of heavy green silk clung provocatively to her slender yet shapely form, hinting in the movement of the dance at the long length of slim leg beneath the rustling gown.

As he watched, spellbound at the fairylike loveliness of the woman he could now call wife, Richard found his thoughts moving of their own accord in a direction he had hitherto not allowed himself to dwell upon. His eyes traced the delicate shape of her breasts rising above the low neckline of the green gown, and he felt his pulse quicken. This gorgeous creature was his, that primitive voice within him murmured suggestively, and the colonel felt a surge of possessiveness he had never experienced before. Not even with Lady Helen, he recalled, surprised at the thought.

The cotillion came to a close, and Richard saw his wife smile up at her partner with such sweetness that a knot of sudden rage twisted his insides. And then the gentleman turned to escort Lady Regina off the floor, and Richard saw with an odd sense of relief that the man was David Laughton. The major returned his wife's smile, and Richard relaxed further. If Regina was with Laughton, she would be safe, he thought. It was that libertine Westbrook who had set warning signals off in his head.

He glanced toward the earl, and his fears were confirmed. Westbrook was observing the couple on the floor with that predatory stare characteristic of a big, sleek cat. As Richard watched, the earl started across the floor, obviously intent on intercepting Lady Regina. Richard instantly pushed through the milling crowd, his eyes fixed on the couple. And then David looked up, and their eyes met. The colonel could not be sure, but he thought he detected a glint of relief in his friend's glance.

And then, before Richard was quite ready for it, Lady Regina glanced his way, and their eyes locked. The green irises widened in shock, followed instantly by a look of pleasure so unexpected that it took his breath away. And then he was standing before them, shaking David's hand warmly, and gazing down like some besotted moonling into his wife's green eyes.

"I do admire your friends, Colonel," Regina remarked to the tall, dark gentleman who rose as she entered her aunt's sunny breakfast parlor the following morning. Her husband had politely but firmly refused Lady Egermont's insistence that he take up residence under her roof, pointing out that he hoped to escort his wife back to Kent without further delay. He could hardly refuse her ladyship's invitation to take his breakfast with them, however, although Regina suspected the colonel would have preferred to break his fast at an earlier hour than that set by Lady Egermont.

"Westbrook is no friend of mine," the colonel replied without roundaboutation.

Reading a world of unspoken reproach into these few words, Regina bristled instinctively. If the colonel imagined for a moment he could criticize her choice of friends, he was in for rather a set-down, she thought resentfully. She had come downstairs this morning determined to be conciliatory, but her husband's first words seemed calculated to send her into the boughs.

"I was referring to Major Laughton," she said with a small smile, deciding at the last minute not to pick a quarrel with her new husband just yet. "He tells me we are to be neighbors," she continued brightly, motioning to Higginbotham to serve her tea.

She wished that she had waited for her aunt before coming down to face the colonel.

"Yes, David and I go back a long time," the colonel said, accepting the plate of thick ham slices and coddled eggs the butler handed him. "He was instrumental in my purchasing my commission ten years ago. We were together when Sir Arthur Wellesley—as Wellington was then—defeated the Danish forces under General Castenskiold near Riogo in 1807, and later we served under the duke on the Peninsula."

Not wishing to bring up the subject of their departure for Kent, Regina chose a topic which had intrigued her since Major Laughton had mentioned it the previous evening.

"Why is Major Westbrook no friend of yours?" she demanded, helping herself to a slice of toast. "He appears to be quite charming."

The colonel snorted disgustedly. "His lordship is certainly full of charm," he said noncommittally. When Regina was quite convinced he would say no more, he added dryly, "Westbrook reminds me of my brother, but his motives are even less admirable than Charles's. Unfortunately, Westbrook has a minor estate near Willow Park, so he is an occasional visitor. I would advise you not to encourage him, however."

"And why should I wish to encourage his lordship?" Regina shot back, instantly incensed at this first hint of husbandly authority.

"Females of your station have been known to become bored with country life," the colonel remarked dryly. "Personally, I prefer it to the meaningless social posturing one encounters in Town."

Regina felt her temper start to fray. If this was any indication of what their future life together would be—the colonel rusticating in Kent, while she pined for the excitement of London—things had reached a sorry pass indeed. As usual when she flew into a pelter, Regina spoke the first words that came into her head.

"If I become bored, sir," she said with icy hauteur, "surely it must be your duty to amuse me, Colonel. I shall certainly expect it of you," she added with cool defiance.

"Do you, now?" her husband said softly, and for the first time, Regina detected the lilt of Kentish brogue in his voice. "Then perhaps I should warn you, my dear, that you are bound to be disappointed. I have more important things to occupy my time on the estate than to dance attendance on a frivolous female."

Regina very nearly choked on her tea. She put her cup down

with a distinct clatter and glared at the colonel. To her chagrin he seemed blissfully unaware of the solecism he had just committed. She rose majestically to her feet, a theatrical gesture which was entirely wasted, since the colonel did not even glance her way.

"I am not a frivolous female," she said in her most cutting ducal tone. "And if you insist upon being uncouth and boorish, sir, then I shall accept my aunt's kind invitation to spend the Little Season in Town with her. *You* may travel back to Kent alone."

He looked at her then, and Regina saw from the expressionless stare of his dark eyes, which had turned the color of wet slate, that her husband was angry. "I rather think not," he said in the same soft country drawl. "I have ordered a carriage for twelve of the clock."

"Then you may unorder it again, sir," Regina fumed, beside herself with indignation at this Turkish treatment. "I shall not go."

"I think you will, lass," he said in a tone that should have warned Regina that his mind was made up, but by this time she no longer cared what she said.

"You are mistaken," she said icily. "And who are you to dictate to me where and when I go?" she snapped, wishing that she had never come downstairs at all this morning.

The colonel observed her dispassionately, but Regina saw the muscles in his jaw bunch stubbornly. "I am your husband, lass," he drawled, with truly remarkable restraint Regina thought. "A deplorable circumstance, to be sure, but one we must live with." He returned to his plate of ham as if the matter were closed.

"Deplorable indeed," Regina cried indignantly. "No one deplores it more than I, and I shall insist that Papa obtain an annulment immediately," she added, quite on the spur of the moment.

"You seem to forget that you are not speaking to your father, my dear," the colonel pointed out with enervating logic.

Regina had it on the tip of her tongue to tell him that he was a dolt as well as a boor, but at that moment the parlor door opened and Major Laughton strolled in, a welcome smile on his weathered face.

"Sorry to be so late, old man—" he began, then seemed to notice the tension in the room, for he came to an abrupt halt and regarded both occupants curiously. "Ah, I see I am interrupting a conjugal tiff," he remarked lightly. "Shall I return later?"

Since the major's arrival was closely followed by that of Lady Egermont, the unpleasant moment passed, and Regina set herself to charm Sir David into telling her something of her Kentish neighbors, ignoring her husband entirely.

When the colonel's hired chaise pulled up at Lady Egermont's front door shortly after twelve that afternoon, however, Lady Regina's trunks were waiting in the hall. She had bullied Claudette into a whirlwind of packing, and as a result of the abigail's efforts, Regina was able to receive the colonel with calm indifference when he arrived. She was delighted to see that Major Laughton intended to accompany them into Kent and insisted on having her mare, Medea, saddled so that she might ride at least part of the way with the gentlemen.

Regina's one disappointment was her aunt's refusal to accept the colonel's unexpected invitation to accompany her niece to Willow Park for a short stay before her projected journey to the Metropolis.

"I shall come to you for a long visit next summer, child," Lady Egermont promised as they said their farewells not much more than an hour after the time appointed by the colonel for their departure. "And by then I hope you will have some interesting news to share with me, love," she murmured as she caught Regina in a perfumed embrace. An amused trill of laughter escaped her as Regina's face flamed in embarrassment, and she patted her niece on the cheek. "These things have a way of working themselves out, dearest, so I count on it. Would you not agree, Burton?" To Regina's acute mortification, her ladyship had the audacity to address this last improper remark to the colonel's man, who was standing at the mare's head, ready to toss his new mistress into the saddle.

"I daresay you may be right, milady," the ex-pugilist responded with a wide grin, dashing any hopes Regina may have harbored that the saucy rogue had not heard her aunt's indelicate suggestion. She glowered at him, but his twinkling blue eyes refused to be cowed by her ducal displeasure. "And I be willin' enough to lay a coachwheel on it, if ye have a mind for it, milady," he quipped with serene impertinence.

"You will do nothing of the sort," Regina snapped, angry at her aunt for encouraging the shameless rascal.

"Burton making a nuisance of himself again, I see." The colonel's voice drawled from so close behind her that Regina jumped.

"He is a saucy rogue," she said sharply, glaring at the culprit as if daring him to open his mouth to deny the charge.

"What has he done now?" the colonel wanted to know.

"He has so far forgot himself as to offer to wager with Lady Egermont," Regina blurted out, only to wish she had held her tongue the moment the words were spoken, for Burton's grin only became more pronounced.

"And what was this wager, my lady?" the colonel asked her aunt, as Regina feared he would.

Lady Egermont had the grace to blush. "Nothing of any consequence, Colonel," she murmured, turning once more to embrace her niece to cover her confusion. "I shall see you both at Wexley Abbey for Christmas, I trust," she said, as the colonel lifted his wife onto her mare.

Distracted from her previous embarrassment by the touch of the colonel's large hands around her waist, Regina did not answer immediately. When he stepped back, she threw a speaking glance at her aunt.

"I would not count on *that*, Aunt," she said, her attention focused on bringing the frisky mare under control.

No, she thought to herself as the cavalcade set forth, and her mind turned toward the future that awaited her at Willow Park. Far better not to count on anything. She had counted on her father implicitly, and he had forsaken her. She had trusted Charles with a blind faith worthy of a witless ninny, and he, too, had betrayed her. How could she ever dare to place any reliance whatsoever on the colonel, a man whose bland manner concealed a will of steel?

The Fates, Regina concluded pessimistically as she rode out of Brighton toward an uncertain future, had dealt her a hand she had little chance of winning.

CHAPTER NINE

Reconciliation

Although the village of Langley, where the colonel's manor was situated, lay but fifty miles from Brighton as the crow flies, and might have been reached on a fast horse in less than three hours, Regina soon discovered that the colonel had no intention of venturing on country lanes with the loaded traveling chaise. Accustomed to the paces of her father's sixteen-mile-an-hour tits, and her brothers' neck-or-nothing style of driving, Regina was soon bored by the sluggish pace of the hired job horses and demanded that the driver be ordered to spring his horses.

"I very much doubt that the old codger knows the meaning of the word, my dear Lady Swinburn," Sir David responded with no little amusement. "And I suspect that even if he did, his old bones would not withstand the jouncing."

"Then let Burton drive the chaise. Or Dodson," she said impatiently, gesturing toward her trusted groom who had his work cut out for him keeping his mistress's highly-bred Welsh team down to the sedate pace of the ancient chaise.

"And who would drive your curricle, my lady?" the major asked innocently, when the colonel failed to make any reply to his wife's suggestion. "Never say that you will do so, I beg of you," he added hastily, a ready smile on his lips. "It would be most unseemly."

"Fiddle!" Regina exclaimed, waving her quirt in the air, a movement that caused her mare to prance about nervously. "I am used to driving about the countryside all the time at Wexley. I am no mere whipster, you know."

"That I can well believe," the major murmured, and Regina glanced at him sharply, wondering if she had imagined the irony in his tone. His smile was guileless, although his black eyes held the glint of secret laughter that always lingered there, as if Sir David found the foibles of the world vastly amusing.

Regina wished her husband would look at her with laughing eyes, but that would be like wishing her youthful romantic dreams would come true, she thought morosely. And such innocent dreams, Regina had discovered within the past few months, were indeed the idle fantasies Mr. Shakespeare had called them. She would do well to put them behind her for good, just as she had put that charming rogue Charles quite out of her mind. At least she had sworn to do so, but at times like the present, how comforting a little charm and light banter would be, she mused nostalgically.

Brusquely she brushed the insidious thought aside and turned to the colonel, who had yet to direct a single word to her since leaving Brighton.

"I am quite looking forward to making the acquaintance of your mother, Colonel," she said in a deliberately pleasant tone. "From her letter she sounds very amiable indeed, but she revealed nothing about her sentiments regarding your sudden nuptials. Is she displeased with it?"

"Displeased?" The colonel turned to glance at her in surprise. "No, quite the contrary in fact. My mother seems to think I have been extremely fortunate in my choice of bride."

This time Regina was quite sure she heard the cynical echo in the words, and the realization that her husband harbored such bitterness in his heart caused her own to sink.

She relapsed into a brooding silence, which not even Major Laughton's good-natured sallies managed to dissipate entirely. Not long after that abortive attempt to establish a polite exchange with the colonel, Lady Regina declared her intention of joining her abigail in the carriage. But it was the major rather than her husband who jumped to assist her in making the change. And no sooner was she installed inside the musty carriage than Regina wished she had not been so hasty in giving up the fresh air.

She envied Claudette the maid's ability to snooze away the dreary miles as the carriage lumbered along, jolting in and out of every rut and bump in the road. Regina's ruminations were as uneasy as the carriage's tortuous progress. Her marriage to the colonel seemed to be doomed to failure before it had begun. Why was it she was unable to converse amiably with the man? she fumed inwardly. This morning she had deliberately set out to be pleasant, and she had almost succeeded, at least until the colonel had made that quite odious remark about frivolous females. Frivolous females, indeed, she recalled, her anger stirring again at the memory of such callousness. When had she ever been frivolous? she wondered. True, she enjoyed fashionable gowns and other feminine fribbles which a gentleman might conceivably see as frivolous. But of course they were no such thing, she thought dismissively.

Regina was quite certain that the colonel's mother would be

anything but frivolous. In fact, the picture of her mother-in-law that rose to mind—derived mainly from the dowager's one and only letter and the little she had been able to draw from Sir David about his neighbor—was heartily depressing. Undoubtedly the elder Lady Swinburn never questioned a single one of her son's decisions. It was obvious to Regina that the colonel was far too accustomed to having his own way in everything. That would change once she was mistress of Willow Park, she told herself smugly. Gentlemen were never right in everything, and the sooner the colonel learned that basic truth, the more comfortably they would rub along together.

Having had plenty of time to develop this rebellious train of thought, Regina was in a battling mood when the creaking chaise drew up, well after dusk had fallen, in front of the neat Tudor manor house of yellow brick, glowing in the light of the two torchères set on either side of the carved oaken door. Her first encounter with the woman she had come to consider as her foe deflated her resentment within minutes of stepping into the spacious hall of Willow Park, however, and Regina soon found herself wondering how such a mild, unassuming female as Lady Swinburn could have produced such a bear of a son.

"My dearest child," the dowager murmured soothingly as she embraced her new daughter-in-law in a warm, motherly hug Regina rarely received from her own mother. "You must come and sit by the fire, dear. Your poor hands are quite chilled." As she spoke the dowager drew Regina into a cozy drawing room where a bright fire burned vigorously in the hearth.

"Tobin"— she turned to the ancient butler who had followed them into the comfortable room to throw another log on the already blazing fire—"arrange the footstool for her ladyship. And ask Cook if she can put dinner forward by half an hour. I am sure her ladyship is quite famished." She smiled down at Regina, who found herself warmly ensconced in a deep armchair close to the fire. "There, child," the dowager murmured in her soft voice, "we shall have you warm again in no time. I warrant my thoughtless son did not think to order warm bricks for your feet, dear, or an extra rug or two. He tends to believe we are all hardened campaigners, you know, and does not hold with coddling. As for myself, I have always believed that a little coddling never hurt anyone. Would you not agree, dear?"

Having experienced the unfamiliar lack of masculine attention ever since her return from Brussels, Regina heartily agreed with her mother-in-law and said so, receiving a charming smile for her pains.

Only after seeing her daughter-in-law comfortably settled by the fire, did the dowager greet Sir David Laughton with a warm embrace, quite as though he were another son. "It is good to see you home again, David," she said with evident affection. "You must know, dear"—she continued in the friendliest manner—"that David has run tame in this house ever since he was a wee mite. I disremember a time when he was not underfoot, and when I think of the innumerable bruises, broken limbs, and sundry other illnesses my three boys have plagued me with, I cannot but thank the heavens that they are grown up at last."

"Speaking of which"—Lady Swinburn continued before Regina could divine her intention—"you have met my youngest son, I trust? A regular charmer is Charles, and very popular with the ladies. In truth, I fully expected him to wed and settle down long before Richard here, who is not much given to the petticoat line, are you, dear?"

There was an uncomfortable pause, during which Regina shot a startled glance at the colonel, who came to her aid by responding shortly. "They have met, Mama." He cleared his throat and moved to the sideboard where he proceeded to pour two glasses of sherry. He carried one to his mother and offered the other to Regina, who took it gratefully.

It was obvious to Regina, from the dowager's innocent remarks, that the colonel had not informed his mother of the precise nature of the circumstances surrounding his nuptials with the Duke of Wexley's daughter. She was not sure whether or not she approved of keeping her mother-in-law in ignorance of the truth, but by the time dinner was over and the kindly dowager had insisted upon escorting Regina up to her chamber, which had been refurbished on the instructions of her new husband, Regina was surprised to learn from the lady's artless prattle, she felt that it would be heartless indeed to shatter the dowager's evident satisfaction in the magnificent match her eldest son had contrived to make.

Perhaps, she told herself as Claudette prepared her for bed that night, and helped her into the white silk nightrail her Aunt Phoebe had insisted upon purchasing for a bridal gift, if she managed to get into the dowager's good graces, the colonel might look on her less sternly. It might help her case, she also thought wryly, if the colonel were to catch a glimpse of her in the clinging white confection she now wore and with her pale gold curls cascading down her back. Regina had little hope of his doing so, however, since the colonel had not even glanced at her when she had taken her leave of Major Laughton and accompanied the dowager upstairs. Not that she was the least bit interested in his odious attentions, she told herself firmly, as she climbed into the empty bed, which—in spite of the warming pan wielded by a red-faced upstairs maid—chilled her to the bone.

Several mornings later, after a leisurely breakfast in a cozy parlor with the dowager, the harmony Regina had longed for in her new life came to an abrupt and shattering halt. The dowager offered to show her daughter-in-law around the manor, and had opted to start belowstairs with the kitchens and stillroom. Regina, who had never in her life felt the need to discover the exact contents of a pantry before, was intrigued at the multitude of items which, the dowager assured her, were essential to the smooth running of a moderate establishment like Willow Park.

The cordiality that was in a fair way to developing between Regina and the dowager was interrupted around mid-morning by the colonel, who came searching for them in the lower regions, a frown on his face.

"I have received a troubling summons from Wexley, Mama," he said abruptly, addressing himself to his mother rather than his wife, Regina noted with no little resentment.

"Troubling?" Regina responded before the dowager had time to gather her wits. "Have they received word from Alexander? Has something dreadful happened to him?" The exploits of her third brother, who had for several years been engaged in secret assignments on the Continent for the War Office, had often caused Regina to imagine him either rotting in some obscure French dungeon or a willing captive in the arms of a sinfully lovely enemy double agent, whose mission it was to divert him from his duty. She much preferred the later version, but every time the family failed to hear from Alex after several months, Regina always feared the worst.

Sir Richard glanced down at the missive he held in his hand. "No," he said. "The duchess says nothing of Alexander. It is the duke's health that prompts her to write."

"Papa is ill?" Regina asked in surprise, forgetting for a moment that she had vowed to distance herself from her tyrannical parent forever. "Papa is never ill," she added scornfully. "This sounds like some Banbury tale designed to trick me into spending Christmas at the Abbey. You may be sure of it."

"You had better read the letter yourself," the colonel observed dryly. "According to the duchess, Wexley is very ill indeed."

"I do not believe a word of it," Regina scoffed, but as she read through her mother's spidery message, her heart constricted within her. "And even if it were true, I would not go back," she declared, willing herself to recall the humiliation her father had caused with his willful tyranny. "I shall not do it," she repeated stubbornly, determined not to relent even if the thought of her father begging to see her broke her heart.

"But my dear child," the dowager began in horrified accents, "surely you cannot mean that."

"This is all a hum, my lady," Regina said, thrusting the offensive missive into the dowager's hands. "You may rely upon it. Read the letter for yourself, and you will see that it is only my father's way of trying to impose his will on me yet again." She glared at the colonel and saw his face was set in stern lines, a warning that she would have a fight on her hands.

"Impose his will?" the dowager murmured, puzzlement apparent on her kindly face. "But the duke is your father, child. Surely it is a daughter's duty to follow his advice?"

"Rubbish!" Regina said rudely. "Papa knew how it would be if he forced me to . . ." She hesitated, abruptly recalling that the dowager knew nothing of the circumstances of her son's marriage. "He knew how much I disliked the notion, but he insisted. Even though I begged him not to. I *begged* him, but he would not listen."

Regina could not keep her unhappiness from her voice, and the dowager must have heard if for she put a plump, comforting arm about her shoulders.

"My dear child," she murmured soothingly. "You are not making any sense at all. What is this notion you disliked so much?"

Regina met her husband's warning gaze and struggled to control her hysteria. Much as she would have liked to shout out the truth—that she had not wanted, had *never* wanted, to wed the dowager's eldest son—Regina found that she could not bring herself to wound the lady with this blistering revelation. Nor could she deliberately wound her husband, Regina realized after one glance at the colonel's unnaturally pale face and the bleak look in his eyes.

She drew a deep breath to steady herself. "It does not signify now," she said in a subdued voice. "It is done, and there is no undoing it. But you do see that I cannot allow my father to continue this tyranny over me." She threw a defiant glance at the colonel.

"That role belongs to your son now, my lady, and I trust that he will not be so pigheaded in exercising it."

The grim smile that curled her husband's lips told Regina all too clearly that her plea had fallen on deaf ears. "I am sorry to have to disappoint you, my dear, but I must ask you to prepare to leave for Hampshire this afternoon. I have already given instructions to your abigail."

Astounded and infuriated that the colonel could so blatantly disregard her express wishes, Regina bristled. "I shall not go," she snapped, tossing her head with regal defiance.

Regina heard the dowager gasp, and derived no little satisfaction in this open challenge of the colonel's command. He could hardly drag her into the carriage, could he? she asked herself smugly. Surely even the colonel would balk at such barbarous tactics to enforce his wife's obedience?

"I think you will," he said softly, his face betraying neither anger nor impatience at her rebellion. "I have ordered the carriage for two o'clock."

Conscious that she had made this exact same protest before with no success whatsoever, Regina raised her chin a notch and swept out of the kitchen, vowing that no matter how odiously the colonel behaved, there was no way he could force her into a reconciliation with her father.

Their journey into Hampshire was undertaken with a minimum of fuss and with considerably more comfort than that provided by the hired coach that had carried them from Brighton to Willow Park. The colonel took his own chaise and cattle and the pace was everything Regina could desire. The only drawback she could find was that the chaise carried her to Wexley Abbey, where she had no wish to be.

She had refused to give the colonel the satisfaction of renewing their argument, and had also refused his assistance in mounting the steps into the chaise standing at the front door, when she came downstairs at the exact hour he had indicated. She had taken a warm farewell of the dowager, loudly and sincerely regretting the need to go gallivanting off on a wild-goose chase—as she insisted upon calling her mother's summons to Wexley—before they could become better acquainted. It was already obvious to Regina that she would have no difficulty at all in warming to a lady who, even upon such short notice, had received her like a daughter. Any hope she might have cherished of achieving an equally comfortable relationship with the colonel was blighted by his odious insistence upon escorting her to call upon her ailing father.

As the early November dusk fell, the chaise pulled into the Turk's Head Inn at Petworth and Regina discovered that two of the inn's best rooms and a private parlor had been bespoken for them. The colonel's batman, blue eyes twinkling with his habitual good humor, was waiting to take the horses and to twit Claudette on her new bonnet, a pleasantry the abigail pretended not to hear.

The excellent service provided by the innkeeper, Mr. Greenwell, and the superior table kept by his wife, went a long way to reconciling Regina to the pointless journey. But the following morning, even a hearty breakfast and the unexpected warm bricks the colonel had ordered placed in the carriage, could not dispel Regina's apprehension as they passed through Eastleigh and turned under the monumental stone archway into the ancestral seat of the Dukes of Wexley. Was her father truly ill, or had he sunk to this deception to entice her back into the Wexley fold? she wondered, forgetting herself so far as to allow the colonel to hand her down from the chaise.

The answer was not long in coming. No sooner had the doors been flung open by the butler than Regina sensed in the unnaturally hushed atmosphere of the huge front hall the truth of her mother's words.

"How bad is he, Hobbs?" she demanded, her voice echoing eerily in the silence of the big house.

"Not well, milady," the old butler responded, more solemnly than usual. "His Grace has been feeling poorly since Michaelmas, milady, but in the past ten days he seems to have taken a turn for the worse."

Regina had not been prepared for the chaotic emotions which overcame her at the butler's words, and she sought refuge in her old bedchamber, even though Mrs. Hobbs had prepared one of the many guest suites for the colonel and his wife. It was here that the duchess found her twenty minutes later.

"My dear Regina," her mother said, giving her a warm though distracted hug, "I am so relieved you have put aside this silly feud you have with your father. But why are you here, dear?" she asked, looking around at the sea-green, silk-covered walls as if she had never seen them before. "I told Mrs. Hobbs to put you and the colonel in the Chinese suite in the west wing. I thought it would be most appropriate."

Regina glanced at her mother's beautiful face and noted that the duchess looked rather haggard. "Oh, I am sure it is, Mama," she murmured. "But I prefer to be here in my old room. And do not imagine for a moment that I have forgiven Papa for wrecking my life."

"Wrecking your life, dear?" the duchess repeated in surprise.

"Did Papa not tell you what happened in Brussels, Mama?"

"Of course, darling. Your father told me that he was able to prevent the truth about your exceedingly indecorous behavior with Wolverton becoming fodder for a public scandal, Regina. For that you should be eternally grateful to him, instead of upsetting him with all this foolishness. Of course, Colonel Swinburn is not quite what we had hoped for you, dear," the duchess said with unconscious condescension, "but under the circumstances, we must all be thankful that he let himself be persuaded to have you."

Regina stared at her mother in astonishment. "The colonel was *bullied* into accepting me," she said bluntly. "Papa must have threatened to ruin his career, or something equally overbearing. Otherwise there is no possible way the colonel would have done it."

"Of course, you silly child," the duchess said calmly. "Under normal circumstances we would never have countenanced such a *mésalliance*. Swinburn is hardly eligible for a duke's daughter, after all. But your father tells me it was either the colonel or his younger brother—a confirmed rakehell, I understand—so he had no choice. Besides"—the duchess continued, piercing Regina with her most accusatory stare—"your father assures me you spent a whole week in this man's lodgings, with only your abigail for company. If that story got bruited about there would be no living it down, dear."

For reasons she could not fathom, Regina's temper began to simmer as her mother painted the colonel in such derogatory terms. True, he was odiously autocratic, humorless, and pompous, and certainly stubborn and stiff-necked, but he had also been kind and considerate. And he had not forced himself upon her as Charles would certainly have done at the first opportunity. Without knowing quite why, she rushed to his defense.

"And so you think I am a slut, too, do you, Mama?" she hurled out angrily. "Do you imagine I jumped into the colonel's bed like some shameless hussy?"

The duchess let out a horrified gasp. "Regina! Ladies do not speak of such things," she said in distressed tones. "Never say you spoke to your father thus?"

"Papa obviously thought so," Regina continued, ignoring her mother's protest, "or he would never have insisted that I wed the colonel. A man who actively disliked me. Did Papa tell you that, too? Well, it is true. He disliked me so intensely he never so much as touched me. He would not have touched me had I attempted to throw myself at him," she continued, her voice growing shriller as she realized just how true this unflattering picture was. "And if you must know, he has still not touched me. He does not *like* me, Mama," she cried, a sob rising in her throat. "And it is Papa who has brought me to this pass. So do not ask me to forgive him, Mama, for I will not do so."

The duchess did not immediately respond to this emotional outburst, apparently deprived of speech by the torrent of her daughter's despair.

Unwilling to let her mother see the tears that threatened to spill down her cheeks, Regina moved to the window and gazed down on the park that stretched as far as the Home Wood in the distance. It was all so familiar and infinitely dear, and yet somehow lost to her since her marriage. Her father had cut her off from this, too, she thought disconsolately. She heard her mother behind her and felt the duchess touch her tentatively on the shoulder. Unlike her father, her mother had never been comfortable at expressing her love for her daughter. Regina had guessed long ago that the duchess preferred her boys, who made less emotional demands on her as they grew up. Her father was more outgoing in his feelings and could even, upon occasion, talk about them, a feat the duchess seemed incapable of.

"I had no idea things were so . . . so uncomfortable between you and the colonel, dear," she said now, and Regina knew how much it cost her mother to say even this much. "I wish there was something I could do."

She sounded so hopelessly contrite that Regina took pity on her. "There is nothing to be done now, Mama," she said bracingly. "Just do not force me to see Papa; that is all I ask."

After the duchess had gone, Regina rang for Claudette to help her change into one of her favorite afternoon gowns of dark blue velvet, edged in satin at the neck and hem, and closed with pearl buttons at the wrists. In spite of the warmth of the velvet, she felt chilled, and accepted a warm woolen shawl from Claudette before taking a seat by the fire in her small private sitting room and ringing for tea.

The scratching at the door did not bring the tea tray as she had expected. It was the colonel who strode into the room, dwarfing it with his broad frame. He was followed by Nevil, who crossed to the chaise longue and bent to give his sister an affectionate kiss on the cheek.

"I am glad you have come, Gina," he said, his handsome face grave. "Papa is not well, you know, and has been asking for you constantly. He knows you are here, and has sent us to bring you to him."

"Indeed?" Regina responded quietly. "What a short memory Papa seems to have, Nevil." She had been gazing into the fire but now she turned to stare at her brother. "You were there, Nevil, when I told him—"

"Yes," Nevil broke in impatiently, "I know what you told him, Gina, but that was what? Six months ago?"

"I do not care how long ago it was, Nevil," she replied sharply. "Things have not changed since then, and it is all Papa's fault. you will not deny that, I trust."

"And you will not try to deny that you were a silly twit to run off with Wolverton. *Wolverton* of all men," he repeated in an exasperated voice. "And then to blab to Wellington that you had come to Brussels to wed Swinburn. That beats the Dutch, miss, and no mistake." His tone was heavy with sarcasm, which prodded Regina to reply without thinking.

"That is exactly what I went there to do," she snapped. "I thought myself betrothed to Charles, who was not there."

"And a damned good thing he was not, my girl," Nevil growled. "No offense meant, Richard," he added hastily to the colonel. "But you cannot deny that brother of yours is a dashed loose screw. We should not want *him* in the family, I can tell you that."

Regina shot a glance at her husband from beneath her lashes, but the colonel was gazing into the fire, his face set in granite. What did he think of them? she wondered, watching the firelight play over the dark mop of hair that had fallen across his forehead. The duchess, who may well have admitted to his face that he was, but for a random stroke dealt by the capricious Fates, ineligible to wed her daughter; Nevil, who had just told him that his brother was a scoundrel. And the good Lord only knew what Robert may have said to him, her eldest brother not being known for being mealymouthed when it came time to speak his mind. Geoffrey was the only one who might be counted on to be polite, she thought, feeling vaguely sorry for the colonel. It was a good thing that Alex was not at home, too, for he was too much like Robert in his plain speaking.

During all this time, the colonel had not spoken a word, but now he glanced at Nevil, and her brother cleared his throat.

"Come on, Gina," he said. "Papa is demanding to see you."

Regina bristled. Nevil had always had the knack of saying the wrong thing, she thought. And relaying their father's demands was in every way the worst thing he could have said.

"I have just rung for tea," she said, changing the subject abruptly. "Would you gentlemen care to join me?"

Before either gentleman could assay a response, the door opened unceremoniously, and the Marquess of Gresham entered the room. His fashionable green coat and champagne unmentionables, cut to compliment the breadth of his shoulders and a pair of legs that were rumored to have caused grown females to sigh in rapture, proclaimed her brother a Buck of the first stare of elegance. But it was his silver-striped waistcoat, topped with the snowy folds of a cravat tied in the inimitable Trône d'Amour, and his bright golden hair brushed in a perfect Brutus that set him apart from the merely fashionable into a class by himself. He was, quite simply, Regina thought, not for the first time as she stared with affection at her eldest brother, quite the most devastatingly handsome man of her acquaintance.

"Robert!" she exclaimed, rising to receive his kiss on her upraised face, "I am glad you are —"

"Where else would I be at a time like this?" the marquess interrupted in a deep voice her Aunt Phoebe had assured her could make any number of unwary females commit extremely foolish acts. "I am glad you are here, too, Regina. Father wants to see you."

How like Robert to get straight to the point, Regina thought crossly, glancing uneasily at the three men standing in her small sitting room, their combined masculine authority aligned against her, pressuring her into acquiescence. She felt it and instinctively rebelled against it.

"I am about to have my tea," she said with deliberate coolness.

"That can wait," Robert said brusquely. "Come along, Regina. I shall escort you."

Regina waved away the proffered arm. "The colonel will escort me, Robert. Do not fuss at me, I beg of you."

The marquess glanced inquiringly at the colonel. "Very well, then." He stepped back and motioned toward Sir Richard, who moved forward until he stood at her elbow.

"It is time to set aside your reservations, Regina," she heard her husband murmur before settling his hand around her elbow. "Come, my dear, let me escort you."

Regina felt trapped. Trapped and helpless before the combined forces of the men around her. The pressure of the colonel's hand on her elbow increased until she could feel each individual finger bruising her skin.

Silently she walked between them down the wide hall to the ducal suite, whose elaborately carved doors were ajar. Her father's old valet must have been watching for them, for he opened the door, acknowledging Regina with a doleful glance and a nod.

And then she was standing at the foot of her father's bed.

The duke had not been bluffing about his health. He was deathly pale, and his strong, handsome face looked wizened in the relentless glare of the candles. He seemed to breathe laboriously, and with a shock Regina noted that the bedcovers hardly moved with the rise and fall of his chest.

He might well have been dead. The room seemed to sway around her, and Regina felt the colonel's breath against her hair.

"Steady there," he murmured, his hand returning to her elbow in a comforting grip.

Regina turned to gaze up at him, her mind in a frenzy of fear. He smiled faintly, reassuringly into her eyes. "It is not as bad as it looks, my love," he whispered in the uneasy silence of the room.

Oh, but it was, she thought, her eyes reaching out for her father again, probing the beloved face in a vain attempt to dispel the signs of weakness and decay. She moaned softly, unable to tear her eyes away.

The sound must have reached the invalid, for the duke opened his eyes, and Regina saw a faint smile stretch his lips, a pale shadow of the father she knew and loved.

"Gina, my pet," the duke said, pausing before adding, "how is my fairy-girl?" His hand moved gingerly in her direction on the counterpane, but Regina found it impossible to budge an inch.

The duchess, sitting beside her husband, glanced nervously at her daughter. "Do not excite yourself, Roger," she murmured, fussing with the bedclothes. "Regina, come and kiss your father, dear. He has so looked forward to seeing you."

Regina shuddered and felt the colonel's hand squeeze her arm.

"Yes, Gina," the duke said slowly. "Come and tell me . . . tell me how you go on, love." The words, spoken in the voice of an old man—a man who could not possibly be her own dear Papa, Regina thought desperately—washed over her. The duke struggled weakly to sit up, and Robert held his father while the duchess plumped up the pillows.

"Well, Gina," the duke spoke with an attempt at his old jocularity. "Do not be shy, lass. Have you no glad tidings for us, love?" His voice sounded stronger now, but Regina understood instinctively what her father wanted to know, and she could not bear the thought. She shrank back into the curve of her husband's arm.

The duke closed his eyes briefly, and Regina thought for a moment she was to be spared. But when he opened them again, the duke smiled, a shadow of his old teasing smile. "Tell me, Gina," he said, his eyes crinkling at the corners in the way she had always loved as a child. "Am I to have a grandchild, love? My first. From my fairy-girl?"

Her father's voice continued, but Regina heard no more. She had gone rigid with shock and mortification. How could he? she thought. How could he have forgotten that he had given her to a man who did not want her? How could he humiliate her in front of the whole family like this? In front of the colonel? She became aware of her mother's eyes, wide with shock and a glimmer of pity. Pity? Regina pulled away from the colonel. She did not want anyone's pity. She dared not look at her husband, fearful of what she might see in his eyes.

In the heavy silence, Regina realized they were all awaiting her reply. But what could she say? she thought. The notion—briefly considered and quickly discarded—of telling her thoughtless parent that he might wait until doomsday for a grandchild from her seemed utterly inappropriate. What was she expected to do? she asked herself, taking refuge in a rising tide of anger and hopelessness. Did her father expect her to beg the colonel to bed her? Her anger increased at the unfairness of it all.

Suddenly Regina could bear the tension no longer. Tearing her gaze away from the duchess's stricken stare, she turned abruptly and ran out of her father's bedchamber.

She ran down two flights of stairs, past the butler, who stared at her with his mouth agape, and out into the chill dusk of the evening.

It was only when she reached the summer house, the place where this farce of a marriage really began over two years ago, that Regina realized that there was no place for her to hide. No place at all.

CHAPTER TEN

Past Sins

The colonel was acutely conscious of five pairs of eyes—six if he included the duke's valet—staring at him in mute astonishment as the rustle of Regina's skirts could be heard growing fainter down the hall.

"What ails the child?" the duke muttered fretfully, after the silence had grown unbearably long.

No one attempted a reply, but the duchess, who had turned at her husband's question, shot a speaking glance at the colonel, and Richard saw a flash of accusation in her eyes before she veiled them. The devil take it, he thought uncomfortably, the duchess knew! Regina must have confided to her mother that their marriage was not as it should be. Why she had done so, he could not guess. Very little of what females did and their reasons for doing so was comprehensible to him. And his wife was a complete enigma. He had never understood why a female with Regina's beauty, wealth, and rank had chosen to throw herself away on a penniless petty officer with a roving eye. Charles had looks, of course, there was no denying that, and a charm that turned females into simpering idiots quite incapable of seeing beneath that glittering exterior to the shallow, selfish boy his brother had never ceased to be.

Richard had never understood Lady Helen either. She had been similarly bewitched by the captain's handsome face and glib tongue, Richard recalled. So much so that the lady he had thought to spend his life with had permitted Charles to take quite scandalous liberties with her person. The picture of the two of them together on the old green leather settee in his father's study that summer evening, when he was presumed to be elsewhere, had haunted Richard for months, nay years afterward. His dreams had been plagued with stark images of Helen's pale legs, skirts bunched above her knees, his brother's hand on her thigh, even after he had ridden hell for leather up to London with David Laughton to purchase his commission and escape into the Army.

Of late these disturbing dreams had returned, but the legs he saw were Regina's now, Helen and her iniquities having finally faded into the haze of the past. The man was still the same, however. His brother's laughing face now grinned up at him in these unwelcome dreams, daring him to blame a fellow for being irresistible to the ladies. That had always been Charles's standard excuse. Was it his fault if the silly wenches could not keep their hands off him? he used to say, his handsome face wreathed in that boyish grin he used when he had been discovered in some compromising entanglement.

Impatiently the colonel wrenched his mind away from these unpleasant thoughts. Excusing himself almost brusquely, he turned away from the staring eyes and strode down the hall. Regina was nowhere in sight, but from the hall two flights down he heard the front door slam and knew instinctively where she had fled.

Collecting a warm cloak from Hobbs, who was still staring at the door with an affronted expression on his wrinkled face, Richard walked quickly along the terrace, cutting off to the left on the brick pathway he remembered led to the summer house. The air was crisp without being cold, and the wind that had buffeted the Abbey earlier had died down. In the stillness of the November dusk, the colonel heard a stifled sob as he stepped up into the shrouded summer house and glanced around. The sound, heart-wrenchingly feminine and—to his heightened senses—helpless, touched a chord deep in the colonel's consciousness, and he cursed under his breath. This woman was his wife, he reminded himself, and regardless of what she had done or not done with his brother, she was his to protect and comfort for the rest of his life. It was his duty. He had vowed to do so before that insipid little curate in Brussels last June, and he had meant it then. He meant it now.

He stood motionless for several moments, probing the shadowy interior of the summer house until he saw her. She was standing at the far side, her back toward him, gazing down the second set of steps at the ornamental pond at the bottom of the slope. As he watched, Richard saw her shoulders shake with a repressed sob. He strode across to her and wrapped the warm cloak around her, feeling her quiver beneath his hands as he gently turned her around into the circle of his arm.

"You will take your death of cold out here, Regina," he said gruffly, quite expecting her to wrench herself away from him. When she did not, he pulled her closer until she was leaning against his chest. This was the first time Richard had held his wife in his arms, and the feel of her shivering against him caused such an abrupt swell of emotion to rise within him that he dared not trust himself to speak for several moments.

Gradually her shivering subsided and Richard felt her relax until her forehead rested on his lapel. The sensation of touching his wife was new and infinitely satisfying. When a fresh sob broke from her, the anguish of it cut through to his soul, and his arm tightened around her. With his other hand, he gently touched her hair, marveling at the silky feel of it beneath his fingers.

"Hush, my love," he murmured, overcome by a tenderness he had not imagined himself capable of. The endearment, too, surprised him, coming naturally to his lips as though quite at home there.

"Oh, Richard," she murmured in a choked voice against his waistcoat. "Whatever am I going to do? I cannot bear it. Papa is dying and I cannot bring myself to forgive him. I simply cannot . . ."

Her voice trailed off into an unintelligible murmur as she pressed her face into his chest, her shoulders wracked with sobs. Richard lowered his own instinctively against her hair and the scent of gardenia rose to weave a spell around his senses.

"Yes, you can forgive him, Regina," he whispered gruffly, cradling his wife more firmly in his arms. "He loves you, my dear. Remember that. No matter what you may think, Regina, your father wants only your happiness."

Abruptly she raised her head and stared up at him in the semi penumbra of the summer house. Instead of pulling away, she huddled closer to him, creating a chaotic reaction in his senses. "How can you say so, Richard?" she demanded fretfully, tears running unchecked down her cheeks. "How could he ask me . . . ? If he cared at all, he would not embarrass me so. You heard what he said. Oh," she cried, "how *could* he?" She buried her face against his chest again, and Richard felt the dampness of her tears against his skin, sending tremors of sensations shooting through him.

He touched her wet cheeks with his fingertips, reveling in the velvety feel of her. "You need to forgive him," he said gently. "For yourself as much as for him. You will find no peace until you do, my dear. You are his fairy-girl, remember? He needs you back in his life. Do you not see how much he needs you?"

She was silent for a moment, as if digesting his words. When she spoke, her voice was calmer. "Do you truly believe that?" she asked in a little-girl voice.

"Yes, I do," he replied with firmness. "And I think you do, too, Regina."

After a moment, she gave a shuddering sigh. "Perhaps you are right," she admitted tentatively, resting her head completely against him now. "Perhaps I have been unreasonable, after all. But I would not know what to do," she added plaintively. "What would I say?"

He grinned silently into the deepening night. "You are a silly widgeon, my dear," he said, hearing the tender amusement in his voice. "You need only kiss your father, and he will know you forgive him. That is all it would take, Regina. A kiss to tell him you still love him."

She was silent for so long Richard raised his hand to cup her cheek, gently wiping away the wetness with his thumb. She felt so fragile, so vulnerable at that moment that his chest tightened painfully. He would protect her, he vowed to himself. He would keep her safe from pain and sorrow, from predators like his brother and the Earl of Westbrook, even from himself, he thought with a touch of cynicism.

"That is all it would take, Regina," he continued, gently raising her face and tracing her lips with his thumb. "One kiss wills say it all," he added, suddenly aware that he might well be speaking of himself as well as the duke. "Follow your heart, my dear. Will you do this for me, Regina?"

He felt her mouth smile beneath his touch and without waiting to consider the consequences, Richard followed his heart, too, lowering his mouth until it rested lightly on hers.

He felt her go rigid with shock, but she did not recoil from him. He kept himself very still, his lips barely resting on hers, just enough to feel the warmth rising from them. After a long moment, his wife sighed, the gesture parting her lips slightly under his. The reaction of his body was immediate, desire springing alive and uncoiling slowly inside him. He opened his mouth and moved it against hers gently, experimentally, waiting for her to jump away. She did not do so.

Carefully, Richard gathered his wife into a closer embrace, enjoying the weight of her breasts against his chest and the increasing warmth of her parted lips under his. Wondering just how far he might go before arousing her alarm, he touched her tentatively with his tongue. She shuddered and quite unexpectedly leaned into him, another soft sigh escaping her.

His pulses went wild, and it was all Richard could do to stop himself from plundering her mouth of all its sweetness. It was only after he had fiercely reminded himself that this was the woman who had loved his brother, wanted to wed his brother, traveled all the way to Brussels to be near his brother, that he was able to bring his desire under control. This was the woman who had not wanted him at all, he told himself relentlessly. The woman he had not wanted either.

But whether he had wanted her or not, a voice inside him whispered maliciously, he had her now. And she was in his arms. And he liked having her there. Regardless of what she had or had not done with his brother. He put that unpleasant thought aside and concentrated on the warmth of the woman in his arms.

"Will you come with me?" she whispered against his mouth, and for a glorious, tumultuous moment, Richard thought she was talking of the two of them. Of being together. "I cannot face him alone, Richard," she murmured. "Will you?" And his pulses returned to normal—or as normal as they would get while his wife still snuggled in his arms.

"Of course," he managed to say, when he had regained control of his senses and chided himself for being a randy fool. "Of course, I will, Regina."

Regretfully but firmly, he disengaged from her, pulling his mouth away from the warmth of hers, letting his arms fall away from her slim body, forcing his mind away from the riotous thoughts that had deprived him—momentarily but shatteringly—of his habitual self-control.

"I am glad you have chosen to forgive, my dear," he said, thinking that he sounded ridiculously formal after the intimacy they had shared a moment ago.

"Come," he said, offering his arm. "I would not want you to catch cold." Which was also a ridiculous thing to say, given the heated atmosphere in the summer house.

"The sooner you forgive, the sooner you will be comfortable," he murmured as they made their way back to the house, his wife clinging to his arm.

"You are right," she said, with unusual meekness. "I should have forgiven Papa months ago. Truly I have been very silly to harbor a grudge."

It occurred to Richard that perhaps his wife might consider forgiving him for the same reason. But he dared not say so.

Regina felt nothing of the chill evening air as she walked back to the house with the colonel. She was aware only of a warm glow radiating from deep within her, and of the solidity of the arm to which she clung with unaccustomed meekness. Her husband's large hand covered hers with a protectiveness that made her feel deliciously feminine and fragile.

Her lips still tingled from the touch of his mouth, and Regina could not quite believe that this man, whom she had always considered hard and unfeeling, had really kissed her with an unexpected and shattering gentleness that had dissolved her fears and touched her heart. There had been no hint of the marauding male about the colonel's kiss, she reflected, and after the initial shock she had felt no inclination to retreat from it. The kiss had not even felt openly possessive as Charles's kisses had always been. Gentle, and warm, and infinitely comforting, and some other indistinct sensation that eluded her, but which had felt so right that she had abandoned herself to his embrace without further hesitation.

When they entered the brightly-lit hall, Regina allowed her husband to remove her cloak and hand it to Hobbs, who took it wordlessly. She made no protest whatsoever when the colonel tucked her hand into the crook of his arm and accompanied her up the long flights of stairs to pause before her bedchamber.

"I shall wait here for you to tidy yourself," he said in a formal voice, removing his arm. "Then I shall escort you to your father's room."

"No," Regina said quickly, before her courage failed her. She was not yet ready to relinquish the delicious intimacy they had shared in the summer house. Not with the weight of the colonel's kiss still heavy on her lips. "Come and sit by the fire," she murmured. "I shall not be long."

She felt him hesitate but the pressure of her fingers on his arm was enough to draw him into the dimly-lit chamber. The click of the door closing behind them caused Regina a moment of panic. She was alone with a man in her bedchamber, she thought. Not even her father had entered her chamber since she had been a schoolroom chit. Her brothers—particularly Nevil—occasionally sought her out in her private sitting room, but never in here, where the four-poster squatted suggestively on the far side of the fireplace.

To overcome her nervousness, Regina quickly took up a candle and touched the flame to the tall branched candelabra standing on either end of the mantelpiece. The room sprang to life and her panic subsided.

Only then did she dare to glance at the colonel, who had not moved from his rigid stance near the door. The sight of his tall, almost foreboding figure sent a second wave of panic shimmering through her, but she forced herself to smile and wave toward the delicate French settee before the hearth.

"Please sit down and let me pour you a glass of sherry. I believe I shall need one, too," she added with a self-conscious laugh, thinking of the ordeal awaiting her in her father's chamber.

The colonel seemed to relax and settled gingerly into the cushions of the settee. Regina realized with a start that her husband was as uneasy as she was at this novel situation. The knowledge heartened her, and she was able to serve the sherry, fetched from the adjacent sitting room, without mishap.

Sitting down before her dressing table, Regina studied her hair, noting that it was more untidy than she had imagined. On sudden impulse she removed the pins and let the heavy curls fall in waves of pale gold down her back. Slowly, languorously, she began to brush out the tangles until it crackled with life. Her hair was one of her best features, she knew, and she wondered if the colonel appreciated this fact. She was acutely aware of his masculine presence in the feminine sanctuary of the room, but dared not glance at his reflection in the beveled mirror before her. His continued silence gave her an odd sense of disappointment, so she abruptly gathered her hair into a simple knot and confined it again.

Perhaps, she thought wryly as they walked together down the long hall to the ducal apartments, her husband could not bring himself to admire a woman he suspected his own brother of seducing. Not for the first time, Regina regretted allowing the colonel to believe such a lie, and vowed to confess the truth at the earliest possible moment. Perhaps then, she mused as he threw open her father's door and led her inside, her husband would put aside his dislike and look at her once more with that warmth he had revealed in the summer house.

Her brother Robert was standing beside the duke's bed when she approached on the colonel's arm, and from the probing glance he gave her, Regina feared the marquess had guessed the cause of her previous distress. Robert had always been able to discover her innermost thoughts, she recalled, and was not surprised when her brother captured both her hands and looked down at her with his piercing sapphire eyes.

"Feeling better, Gina?" he asked, throwing a frowning glance at the colonel.

"Oh, yes, Robert," she replied, oddly pleased at his use of her nickname, a rare occurrence for her eldest brother. "I have come to make my peace with Papa," she added diffidently. "Richard has convinced me that I have been rather silly."

"We shall leave you, then," the marquess said firmly, in a voice that sounded so like the duke's that Regina glanced surreptitiously at her father. As the two men turned to go, Regina instinctively reached out to touch the colonel's sleeve.

"Please stay," she murmured, hoping he would understand the sudden need she felt for his solid presence. "You promised, remember?"

After Robert was gone, they stood together beside the bed where the duke dozed fitfully.

"Perhaps we should not wake him," she whispered, wondering if she might yet postpone the confrontation she had dreaded.

"No," the colonel replied immediately, and Regina heard amusement in his voice. "This is not the time to retreat, Regina. Remember, a kiss is all it takes to let your father know you still love him."

Regina glanced up at her husband and found him watching her, his dark eyes inscrutable. If only she knew what this man really thought of her, she mused. The incident in the summer house still puzzled her. The colonel had seemed quite different during that strange embrace. Less harsh and intimidating, more comforting and tender. Yes, she thought in wonder, her husband had revealed a tenderness she had never experienced with any other man, and had not dreamed of finding with the man she had married.

She considered what he had just said. *A kiss is all it takes.* Yes, perhaps, but some kisses turned out to be lies, she thought, remembering those Charles had given her two years ago, kisses that had turned her foolish head and captured her heart. Lies they had been, those kisses, sweet lies that she had believed implicitly, innocent that she had been then.

"Some kisses are lies," she murmured, unaware until the words were spoken that she had said them aloud. She saw the colonel's lips tighten and knew he had guessed where her thought had roamed.

"Not these, Regina," he said quietly. "Not these."

Regina instantly felt that he was saying far more to her than those simple words suggested. Did the colonel mean to include the kiss he himself had given her? she wondered, turning to gaze down at her father, and noting the soft rise and fall of his chest under the covers. His breath seemed less labored now, and she sighed, feeling a wave of love too long denied constrict her heart.

Without wasting another moment, she bent and placed a kiss on her father's beloved cheek, just as she used to do as a child.

The duke opened his eyes, and for a moment the two of them were alone in a private world together, a world in which love and understanding were miraculously restored.

"Gina, my love," the duke murmured, reaching up to touch her face gently with his knuckles. "I am glad to have my little fairy-girl back, sweetheart. I have missed you."

Regina felt the prickle of tears in her throat. "I have missed you, too, Papa," she said simply, kissing him again. "Richard convinced me that I have behaved very badly with you, Papa, and I beg you will forgive—"

The duke raised a hand and shook his head weakly. "It was not an ideal situation for any of us, love, but I had to do what I did. You understand that now, do you not?"

"Yes, Papa," she responded meekly, too glad to have her father back again to take issue with his masculine logic. "I see now that I am really to blame for what happened to me. I should not have thought . . . It was stupid of me to believe . . . " She swallowed, unable to say the name of the man who had betrayed her.

Her father reached for her hand and squeezed it. "No use fretting over what cannot be changed, love," he said comfortingly. "Besides, it seems to me that the colonel is the one who got the worst part of this bargain." He paused to smile up at his son-in-law, and Regina saw that he looked exhausted.

"Do not tire yourself, Papa," she scolded gently, hoping he would not drag in any more of her past sins.

"None of this bumblebroth was his fault, Gina," the duke continued, as Regina had feared he would. "None of it at all. And it seems to me you treated him rather shabbily in Brussels, my pet. I trust you have made your peace with your husband now that he has come back to you."

Regina flinched at her father's words, wondering briefly whether what had happened recently in the summer house might be called making peace with her husband. Perhaps so, she mused, but her father was wrong to imagine that Sir Richard had come back to her. The colonel had come back to Willow Park, to his mother; he had come back to take up his life again briefly before going off to the Army again, as she did not doubt he would. Regina felt herself to be only incidental in the colonel's life, and saw his recent softening as a deliberate attempt to make the best of having to acknowledge Lady Regina Heathercott as his wife. The thought disheartened her.

"Well, my dear?" the duke insisted, as was his wont. "Have you two made peace?"

"Yes, Papa," Regina replied quickly, unwilling to hear the colonel say anything different.

"Splendid!" the duke mumbled in a fading voice, closing his eyes and releasing his daughter's hand. "Then I may hope for a grandson, may I not?"

Regina clasped her hands together and kept her eyes firmly fixed on her father's ravaged face. The duke's words hung in the silence of the room and seemed to echo dolefully in her mind like a faraway church bell. What could she say, she wondered, that would not sound impossibly brazen? Her relationship with the colonel was hardly that simple. The kiss he had given her in the summer house was a start, but Regina imagined they had a long way to go before . . . She refused to complete the thought, feeling the color rising to her cheeks.

Without knowing quite what she would say, Regina struggled to move her stiff lips, but before she could utter a word, she felt the colonel touch her arm, and heard him speak in a perfectly normal voice.

"Yes, sir. I imagine you may."

A week later the atmosphere at Wexley Abbey had become noticeably less tense and funereal. Even the naturally pessimistic Hobbs had ceased to sigh gustily and shake his gray head every time Regina met the butler in the hall. Her father had improved so dramatically that the London physician, brought down to Hampshire at the duchess's request, had actually suggested that the duke might be carried downstairs to take his afternoon tea with the family in the not too distant future.

Regina, who spent most of her time sitting with her father, was delighted and relieved by Sir William Burton's optimism, and when the duke protested that he was quite well enough to dispense with the constant attendance of the eminent sawbones, she persuaded the duchess to allow Sir William to return to London. The whole house turned out to see the departure of the physician, which signaled, in the minds of family and staff alike, that the duke was on the road to full recovery.

By the first week in December, Regina's joy at being reunited with her father was augmented by the unexpected arrival late one afternoon of her brother Alexander, whom she had not seen since before her marriage. She was dressing for dinner when Hobbs brought her the news that her brother was closeted with the duke.

"Thought you might wish to know the instant Master Alex arrived, milady," the butler murmured diffidently, knowing full well that Regina's third brother was one of her favorites.

Glancing down at her clinging green silk gown with its fashionably low décolletage, Regina gestured impatiently for Claudette to clasp her diamond-and-emerald necklace around her throat and attach the matching earrings.

"Will you wear the ring that goes with this set, milady?" the abigail asked, causing Regina to glance down at her hands, devoid of adornment other than the plain gold band on her third finger. That ring was the only gift she had ever received from her husband, she thought, recalling the unhappy occasion during which he had bestowed it—with little enthusiasm, she suspected—upon her. Idly she wondered if the colonel would ever give her the expensive baubles she was accustomed to receiving from the other men in her family. Perhaps he could not afford to shower expensive trinkets on his new wife, she mused, standing impatiently while Claudette fastened a diamond- and emerald-studded comb in the cluster of pale curls that were dressed high on her head. And what if he did not wish to give her lovely things? an insidious voice whispered at the back of her mind.

Regina brushed the disagreeable thought aside and ran lightly down the hall to her father's chamber. The door was ajar, and she heard the buzz of masculine voices, interrupted by the unmistakable ring of the duke's laughter. Her heart swelling with joy at the sound, Regina pushed into the room, her eyes scanning the cluster of gentlemen around the bed in search of her brother.

"Alex!" she cried, moving forward impetuously, her arms wide. Her brother had been standing conversing with the colonel, Regina noted with surprise, but at the sound of her voice, he strode over and clasped her by the shoulders, planting an enthusiastic kiss on her upturned face. "Oh, Alex, how good it is to see you again, dearest," she murmured, searching his angular countenance for signs of change. "You are looking very well indeed," she said at last, satisfied that he did indeed appear in excellent form.

"Did you expect me to be in my dotage, love?" he quizzed her, the teasing light she loved so well twinkling in his hazel eyes. He placed an arm around her shoulders and urged her toward the colonel, whose gaze was shuttered as it had been all week, in spite of Regina's attempts to recapture some of the closeness they had shared in the summer house.

"I see you have already met Colonel Swinburn, Alex," Regina

said lightly, determined to ignore her husband's aloofness. "Has Papa told you that he is a member of the family?"

Her brother grinned. "I have known that for months, my pet," he said, sharing an enigmatic glance with the colonel. "You see, Gina, Richard and I have been friends for years, although, given the nature of my covert activities, I do not see him as often as I would like."

Regina felt stunned and not a little resentful as she glared from one gentleman to the other. Why had the colonel never told her that he knew Alexander? she wondered, anger at what she considered a deliberate deception beginning to simmer in her breast. And if this was true, she realized abruptly, then Alex must be fully aware of the circumstances of his sister's marriage. Regina would have given her favorite necklace to know exactly how her husband had described the event to her brother. She could well imagine the unfavorable light in which the colonel must have painted her. Her lips thinned dangerously, and she raised her chin defiantly.

"Indeed?" she said in quelling accents. "Then I must assume that you are familiar with all the sordid details of the affair, Alex." She dared not glance at the colonel as these ugly words came unbidden from her lips, but Regina saw immediately that her brother was taken aback by her reaction.

"Sordid?" he repeated, his expression suddenly sober. "The only sordid part of it, as far as I can see, is involving Wolverton in your freakish start, Regina. Wolverton no less," he added disgustedly. "Were you mad, love?"

"Guy Hawkhurst happens to be a friend of mine," Regina stated firmly. "And I knew I could trust him not to go running to Papa with the story. I should have been able to trust my brothers, of course," she added snippily, "but they are too scared of Papa to dare to cross him. I had no choice but to confide in Guy, who considered it a great lark, let me tell you." She glared at him defiantly.

"I can well believe that, you silly twit," Alex said shortly. "It is a miracle that Papa decided to give you to Richard instead of that jackstraw Wolverton. You should thank your lucky stars—"

"And you should not speak of things of which you know nothing, Alex," Regina interrupted tartly. "Papa *forced* us to marry, as the colonel must surely have told you. And if you intend to badger me, I shall wish you in Jericho."

Regina was to remember these hasty words that evening after dinner when the duchess asked her to entertain them on the pianoforte. She called to Nevil to turn the pages for her, but it was the colonel who came forward to stand beside her as she riffled through the sheets of music. She had every reason to feel put out with her husband, she thought, picking out a somber sonatina from Scarlatti that suited her present mood. During dinner, Alex had let it slip that Sir Richard was to leave in a day or two to return to Willow Park where estate affairs required his presence. Since this was the first Regina had heard of their departure, she had reason to feel peevish and was not about to hide the fact.

She opened the sonatina and laid her hands on the keys before turning to survey her husband. He showed no sign whatsoever of contrition at keeping her in the dark, a circumstance that only fueled her anger.

"I do think you might have informed me that we are to depart so soon," she said levelly, determined not to lose her temper again. "I resent having to hear of your plans through my brother's conversation at the dinner table."

The colonel met her gaze squarely, and Regina had the uneasy sensation that he was amused. "I thought you might like to stay on at the Abbey until I can join you at Christmas," he said easily. "Your father has told me he would hate to see you leave so soon."

Regina's first reaction was one of panic. "You wish me to stay here?" she demanded, fighting the shattering suspicion that her husband wished to be rid of her.

"That is not what I said, Regina," he said calmly. "I only want you to do as you wish, my dear. Your father asked me to allow you to stay."

"He said nothing to me," Regina said testily. She was not at all sure she approved of these men making decisions behind her back. Before the colonel could reply, Alex sauntered up to them, a cynical smile quite worthy of his brother Robert on his face.

"I suggest you postpone these little marital squabbles for the bedroom, Regina, and get on with the performance," he drawled. "Mama is getting impatient."

Marital squabbles indeed, Regina thought, gazing sightlessly at the music before her. Unless she was very mistaken, Alex was being deliberately provoking. If he was so friendly with Richard, surely he knew how matters stood between the colonel and his sister. Surely everyone at Wexley Abbey knew by now that her husband never came to her chamber to resolve little marital squabbles. Or to resolve anything else, she thought miserably, wishing she might get past the wall of indifference the colonel seemed to have erected between them.

She launched into the sonatina with less than her usual enthusiasm, scarcely able to read the notes on the page for the glaze of tears in her eyes. The sight of the colonel's hand as he turned the first page for her, brought her to the sudden realization that she did not want to stay on at Wexley Abbey if he was not there. She would go home with him to Willow Park, she decided, her eyes miraculously clearing. She wanted to go home. And home was where the colonel was, she understood with startling clarity.

Even if he preferred her to stay at Wexley Abbey, as she suspected he might.

The decision brought a faint smile to her lips, and Regina concentrated with renewed vigor on the sonatina.

CHAPTER ELEVEN

A Question of Trust

The journey back to Willow Park was conducted quickly and efficiently, with Burton handling the ribbons, and the colonel riding beside the chaise on his big roan gelding, Achilles. Regina wished she had thought to bring her mare, for the morning was crisp and sunny, and she wanted to talk with her husband, a feat she could not hope to accomplish from inside the carriage. As it was, she was condemned to listen to Claudette's gentle snores as the abigail fell into her customary doze after the first few miles.

Regina had been sorry to leave her father, but the duke appeared to be recovering his strength so quickly that she fully expected to find him back on his horse in the hunting field before another month was over.

"Take good care of my fairy-girl, sir," he warned the colonel as they stood beside his bed saying their farewells. "We shall expect to see you both back at Wexley for Christmas. And your lady mother, too, my dear boy, if she can be induced to travel in cold weather."

It had amused Regina to hear her father refer to the tall, broad-shouldered man she had married as his *dear boy*, but in a way it pleased her to know that her family had accepted him, in spite of the difference in his rank and fortune. She knew her father to be rather toplofty at times, but he had fallen into the habit of treating Sir Richard as another of his sons. And indeed the colonel seemed to have been accepted by her brothers, too, she thought, watching as they took turns thumping her husband jovially on the back as they stood grouped on the shallow front steps at an early hour that morning.

Even the duchess, who had not ventured out into the cold air but had made her farewells in the huge front hall, had shown extraordinary warmth toward her son-in-law. The same son-in-law her mother had so recently pronounced ineligible for a duke's daughter, Regina had mused cynically, watching the colonel's slow smile light up his face in response to some comment from the duchess. If only he would smile at her like that, Regina thought morosely, submitting to a bear hug from Nevil, who had come forward to assist her into the chaise.

"That husband of yours is a great gun," her youngest brother exclaimed enthusiastically. "And to think that Alex has known Richard for ages, Gina. Who would have credited it? You are a silly peagoose to turn up your nose at such a catch. He is a right'un, unless I miss my mark."

Regina gave her brother a withering glance and made no answer. She had had ample opportunity over the past few days to see that the colonel was—as Nevil had so inelegantly put it—a great gun. At least with the other gentlemen of the family. He had also charmed the duchess, a feat that many prospective suitors for her daughter's hand had attempted, but few achieved. Why the colonel had singled her out for Turkish treatment Regina could only guess. She felt unexpectedly hurt that, after that first kiss in the summer house, there had been no further intimacy with him at all. It was as though he regretted revealing that hidden tenderness in his nature that had surprised and delighted his wife.

As the light traveling chaise covered the rough roads at a speed that even Regina could find no fault with, she had ample opportunity to ponder the eccentricities of gentlemen in general, and of her husband in particular. She had arrived at no clear understanding of the colonel's coolness toward her by the time the chaise swept through the iron gates of Willow Park late that afternoon and pulled up with a flourish at the front door. All she had were suspicions, and as yet she was unwilling to admit that she deserved her husband's disdain.

The hall was comfortably warm when she stepped into it, and after Tobin had assisted her out of her fur-lined cloak and taken her gloves and fur bonnet, Regina felt as though she really had arrived home. She glanced in the mirror to tidy her hair, but her gaze was distracted by the reflection of the colonel divesting himself of his greatcoat, gloves, and scarf. As Tobin took the colonel's tall beaver, Regina saw her husband run his fingers through his hair, and was entranced at the disheveled effect he achieved, and by the lock of dark curls that fell forward over his forehead. He appeared as he had that enchanting evening in the summer house, she thought, feeling again the agitation her husband's first kiss had occasioned in her heart.

With a faint sigh, Regina put aside these memories and turned to the butler. "I think we could both use a cup of hot tea, Tobin," she said, glancing inquiringly at the colonel. "Unless you would prefer something stronger?" she added.

He shook his head. "Tea would be nice," he said in the polite, distant voice Regina hated.

"Her ladyship has this instant requested the tea tray," Tobin offered in his familiar way. "It will be up directly, milady."

As the butler shuffled away, Regina turned toward the drawing room, where the dowager would be sitting cozily before a roaring fire awaiting her tea. The prospect of joining her appealed to Regina, and her spirits rose.

But the dowager was not alone.

Regina had barely stepped over the threshold, when she recoiled at the sight of the gentleman sitting with her mother-in-law.

When he sprang to his feet and came striding across the room toward her, the well-remembered engaging grin on his face, both hands held out in an all-too-familiar gesture of welcome, Regina drew in a sharp breath and shrank back instinctively.

"My dearest Regina!" Charles Swinburn exclaimed in his insidiously caressing voice, his handsome face sporting the most innocent and charming of smiles. "I hear I am to congratulate you, my dear. Believe me I could not be happier for you."

The gross effrontery of this outrageous remark left Regina speechless. She felt the color drain from her cheeks as she stared aghast at the cause of all her misfortunes. Captain Swinburn had not changed a jot in the two years since she had last seen him. If anything, the rogue was even more dashingly attractive than he had been when he had kissed her in the summer house and made all those false promises to her. And now this handsome rogue—she could hardly deny that he still had the power to make her heart beat faster—had the colossal nerve to pretend that he was delighted to see her wed to his brother. The magnitude of this contemptible behavior was beyond anything Regina could have imagined.

She went rigid with anger.

The picture of three young females in Brussels, each convinced she was betrothed to this villain, each wearing his meaningless garnet ring, each one heavy with his child—or so they claimed—flashed suddenly through Regina's mind like a dash of cold water. This unhappy memory restored her bitterness at her own betrayal, and she straightened her shoulders, meeting the guileless blue gaze with frosty hauteur.

Her rejection must be unmistakable, she thought, even for a man as shameless as the captain. He came to a halt before her, his marvelous blue eyes shadowed with hurt. Even though she knew it to be carefully contrived, Regina had to struggle against the urge to relent.

She turned her regal stare upon her husband, who had remained silent during this shocking display of gall.

"I refuse to remain in the same room with that despicable creature," she said, ice dripping from every word. "I shall take my tea upstairs."

Neither of them said a word as she swept out of the room, leaving a heavy silence behind her.

By the time Regina reached her private sitting room, her fury was such that she slammed the door with unnecessary vigor behind her, causing the delicate figurines of shepherdesses to tremble on the mantel.

She marched over to the bellpull and rang it viciously.

If she were condemned to spend the rest of her days on earth confined to her private apartments, Regina told herself angrily, she would do so. Better that than having to listen to that lying, deceitful, heartless rogue prance about her house as though he were still her knight in shining armor instead of the evil sorcerer who had bewitched her heart only to break it into a thousand shards of ice.

The footman who brought up her tea tray placed it gingerly on the low table before the fire. He looked so apprehensive that Regina guessed the news of her tantrum had spread throughout the household. Well, she thought belligerently, let them talk. She would soon give them more fodder for gossip if the colonel made the slightest effort to force her to come downstairs until that wretch Charles had left the premises. The colonel had not yet seen her at her worst, she thought with grim satisfaction. And if he thought for a single moment that he could command obedience from her on this matter, he was all about in the head.

Regina girded herself for an ugly argument with her husband, relishing the opportunity it would afford her for venting her frustration on his head. So when she heard the scratching at her door a few minutes later, Regina smiled grimly in anticipation. But it was the dowager who slipped into the room, her kindly face shadowed with concern.

"My dearest Regina," her ladyship murmured, floating across to settle herself precariously on the edge of a ladder-backed chair, "I could not enjoy my tea knowing that you were up here by yourself. Will you not confide in me, my dear, and tell me what has so upset you?"

Regina was struck by the irony of the dowager's opening words, the identical ones the captain had used on her moments before. They only served to remind her that the insolent rogue was certainly still downstairs, probably enjoying his tea and cakes in front of the blazing fire at this very moment. The thought enraged her.

"Surely it cannot be my dear Charles?" the dowager continued hesitantly, when Regina made no move to reply. "I know he is often thoughtless and perhaps a little selfish, but he admires you so much, Regina. He has told me so several times since he arrived back from the Continent. What can he possibly have done to send you into the boughs like this?"

Astounded at such ignorance, Regina turned her angry gaze upon the dowager, causing that good lady to shift uncomfortably in her chair.

"I gather that the colonel has never told you the precise details of our nuptials, my lady?" she said coldly.

The dowager regarded her wide-eyed, and swallowed visibly. "Why no, my dear," she replied. "I was curious, of course, because I was not aware Richard was contemplating matrimony. But he never told me."

"That does not surprise me," Regina said dismissively.

She busied herself pouring herself a cup of tea. "Will you join me?" she said with a cordiality she did not feel.

"Perhaps you should tell me yourself, dear," the dowager said unexpectedly, ignoring the teacup Regina placed before her. "About how you and Richard met, I mean."

Regina glanced at her pityingly. "Believe me, my lady, you would not wish to know," she said abruptly.

"Oh, there you are wrong, my dear. I need to know why you are so unhappy. If it is anything my son has done you can be sure—"

"Your precious son has lied to me, made me false promises of marriage, and jilted me when I went to Brussels to seek him out," Regina cut in angrily, exasperated beyond bearing at the lady's misplaced belief in Charles's innocence.

The dowager stared at her open mouthed, her kindly blue eyes wide with shock. "B-but my dear Regina," she murmured disjointedly. "Surely you are mistaken, child. That does not sound like the kind of thing Richard would do."

It was Regina's turn to stare. "Richard?" she repeated stupidly. "I am not talking about Richard, my lady. The villain in this Canterbury farce is your younger son."

"Charles?" The brief flicker of understanding that flashed

across the dowager's face took Regina by surprise. It disappeared so quickly that she was not at all sure she had really seen it.

"I see," the dowager said after a moment of silence. She lowered her eyes to the dancing flames in the hearth and sighed. "So"—she continued in a distressed voice, as if talking to herself—"Charles has done it again."

Somewhat flabbergasted by the direction the interview had taken, Regina grasped the armrest of the settee and leaned forward. "I beg you will explain yourself, madam," she said coldly. "What has Charles done again?"

"He has obviously attempted to create discord between Richard and the bride of his choice, my dear." The dowager's pale blue eyes were clouded with pain. "He must compete with his brother in everything, and cannot bear to lose, you see. Particularly with the ladies."

"I was not Richard's chosen bride," Regina said baldly.

"You were not?"

"No, I was not. Richard was forced to marry me. He never wanted me at all, of course, but my father can be very overbearing when he chooses. Charles never did either, apparently," she added bitterly, "although he deceived me into believing quite the opposite."

"What a tangle, indeed," the dowager said after a pause. She regarded Regina with so much compassion shining in her eyes, that Regina felt a lump rising in her throat. "But you are wrong about Richard, my dear," she continued in her soft voice. "I cannot believe he did not wish to marry you, child. You are exactly the kind of female he favors, my dear."

Regina stared at her mother-in-law in amazement. A part of her wanted desperately to believe what she had just heard; the mere thought of it made her blood sing in her veins. Her more practical side dismissed the dowager's logic as hopelessly biased in favor of her son.

"I fear you are mistaken in this instance," she forced herself to say, as if it mattered not a fig to her what kind of female the colonel favored. "Sir Richard has given me not the slightest indication that he is content in his marriage to me." This was not strictly true, Regina thought, the memory of her husband's one and only kiss still fresh in her mind. But since he had made no move to repeat the embrace, the only explanation that sprang to her mind was that he had no desire to continue the intimacy.

"Oh, but he will, dear," the dowager said with a confidence Regina could not share. "I know my son, Regina. Richard would not have entered into a contract with you had he not intended to honor it in every respect."

"But my father forced—"

"So you say, dear. But not even a duke could have forced Richard into taking a step he was not comfortable with. You may depend upon it."

Regina did not believe a word of this sentimental farradiddle, and her expression must have said as much, for the dowager smiled. "Give him time, my dear. Richard is not the innocent young man he was ten years ago when he was betrothed to Lady Helen. But he will come about if you are patient, I know he will."

"Lady Helen?" Regina repeated sharply, her curiosity instantly aroused. "And who is Lady Helen, if I might ask?"

The dowager looked surprised. "Richard did not tell you? No, I suppose he would not. It was very painful for him when the lady changed her mind. And you are so like Helen in many ways. In others of course, you are quite different, my dear," she added hurriedly, as though the mysterious Helen had possessed less than desirable qualities.

"Tell me about Lady Helen," Regina said brusquely.

After a slight pause, the dowager sighed. "I do not know the whole, of course. Richard is so closemouthed about his personal feelings. But a month before the wedding, he came to tell me he was joining the Army. There was to be no wedding. He would say no more, but I know that Charles was somehow involved. I have always suspected that Charles had a hand in the breakup, but all Helen would say to me—after Richard had gone, of course—was that she had behaved very foolishly indeed."

Regina stared unseeingly into the fire. Could the colonel's charming brother have contributed to his betrothed's foolish behavior? she wondered, knowing in her heart the answer to that question before it was fully formulated. Of course he must have done so. And the ugly triangle of ten years ago seemed to be repeating itself, except that the colonel was now tied to the woman who professed to love his brother.

But she no longer felt any attraction at all for Charles, Regina realized with a start of surprise, recalling the smiling face and charming manner that had momentarily brought a tremor to her heart. But that tremor had lasted no more than a passing moment, replaced by a deep-seated disgust for the man who had made a game of her love. No, Regina thought, a sudden sense of relief lightening her heart. How it had happened she could not fathom, but her infatuation with the handsome rogue she had wanted to wed had dissipated as completely as the false promises he had made two years ago.

The sound of a sigh distracted her from this exploration of her feelings. "Do you wish it had been Charles rather than Richard?" the dowager murmured gently, reaching out to touch Regina's tightly clasped hands.

"No!" The answer sprang forth instantly, surprising Regina with its intensity.

The dowager looked vastly relieved. "I am glad to hear you say so, my dear," she said, picking up her teacup. "You are exactly the kind of wife my Richard needs, you know. I am sure you will find a way to make him forget that unhappy experience with Lady Helen."

And Richard was exactly the kind of husband *she* needed, Regina saw with startling clarity. Had she any sense at all, she would have seen it that summer he had come to Wexley Abbey with Charles. But she had been blinded by the dazzling younger brother. She had been as foolish as Lady Helen must have been; beguiled by the charm, she had ignored the better man and brought unhappiness down on her head.

Now that her eyes were opened, she vowed with renewed optimism, she would find a way to undo the harm she had done. And perhaps she would be lucky enough to undo the harm Lady Helen's foolishness had done to Colonel Swinburn's heart.

The following morning, Regina awoke feeling refreshed and optimistic, although she had spent a considerable part of the night thinking about her husband. Nevil had been right about the colonel, she finally concluded. Richard was as solid as a rock compared to the bubbling, ever inconstant flowing of his brother's shallow waters. A rock any female with her wits about her would want to cling to. A safe haven in the swirling ebb and flow of life's illusions and delusions. Charles had been just such a delusion, Regina realized, a glittering promise of endless love and laughter that burst into a rainbow of dancing spray, bewitching her heart, before dashing ever onward to new delights, an unruly, rudderless force that had almost swept her away with it.

But Richard was the rock that had saved her from imminent destruction. And he was *her* rock, she thought, smiling to herself in the darkness. It amazed her how foolish she had been to imagine she could have found happiness in the shallowness of Charles's regard. What if her father had approved of the match she had yearned for two years ago? she wondered. Regina suddenly saw that hypothetical future with clear eyes. She would have had to share the captain with countless other females from every station in life. That had been one of the distressing truths about the captain she had learned in Brussels. No less than three other females had worn his ring, had they not? And all had relinquished to him their virtue, if her eyes and ears had not deceived her. Was it Mademoiselle Marguerite Laporte, the redheaded French girl, or the pretty blond Annette Gérard, visibly *enceinte* with Charles's child, who had accused her of being one of them?

Regina shuddered and pulled the warm covers closer under her chin. Might she not have been beguiled into surrendering to him, too? she wondered, appalled at the thought. She had come dangerously close to disaster, she recalled, seeing herself with clearer eyes and hearing again with wiser ears the seductive pleas of the man she had thought to marry. Yes, she had come close to being one of those unfortunate females who had placed their ultimate trust and treasure in the unworthy hands of a lying scoundrel. It did not bear thinking of.

But the colonel had been there instead, and he had saved her from her own foolishness. And if his mother was to be believed— and who better than a mother to know her own son?—the colonel had agreed to wed her not because of the duke's insistence, but because he had chosen to do so. Regina still found this explanation hard to believe, but something in her willed it to be true.

And what if it were true? she mused. What if by some miracle the colonel had looked upon her with favor? What if he had really intended to keep those marriage vows, uttered so unemotionally in the presence of that cringing curate? Had he intended to honor her and keep her safe from the vicissitudes of life in the shelter of his arms? The notion brought a lump to Regina's throat. And how had she repaid him? The question rose accusingly in her mind and she shuddered again. She had not behaved like the compliant wife any right-thinking man would want, had she? She had abandoned him on their wedding day without a backward glance. Without a thought for his feelings.

For the first time since her marriage, Regina wondered how her husband had spent his wedding night. This novel thought naturally gave rise to another. What would have happened had she stayed to keep her own marriage vows? The notion intrigued her, and since she was alone, and the darkness of the chamber hid her blushes, she spent a significant amount of time speculating on the possibilities of such an event.

Before she dropped off into a deep, dreamless slumber, Regina had faced the surprising discovery that she would not be averse to assuming the duties she had once thought beneath her, the duties she should have assumed six months ago in Brussels.

"The master sent word that he wishes to see you, milady," Claudette said in a flustered voice as she placed the hot chocolate on the table by the bed and went to pull aside the thick curtains at the windows.

Regina opened her eyes to the weak December sunlight. She had slept extraordinarily well, comforted by the decision she had made during the night to become the kind of wife the colonel might admire. Her course in life had been set for her, she had decided, and although at the time it had been against her will, Regina had come to see that the man her father had given her to had definite possibilities. She had come to see that she much preferred the safe harbor the colonel had provided for her to the turbulent uncertainty she would certainly have encountered had she followed her own inclinations in choosing a husband.

Nevertheless, the abrupt summons from the colonel startled her. She had fully intended to confront her husband sooner or later. What she would say to him she had not as yet determined, content in the certainly that she would take the first step toward a better understanding between them. But his summons caught her off guard.

"At ten o'clock in the library, milady," the abigail concluded her message as she began laying out her mistress's fresh undergarments on the bed. "Will you wear the blue merino this morning, milady?"

"What time is it now?" Regina demanded, scrambling out of bed in a flurry of bedclothes and gossamer silk nightrail.

"It has just turned nine, milady. Shall I have the merino pressed for you?"

"I shall need the scarlet riding habit," Regina said, suddenly making up her mind to cajole her husband into taking a morning ride with her. She needed to see him alone if she were to begin her campaign to become the perfect wife for a simple baronet. The notion of Lady Regina Heathercott aspiring to such a position made her want to giggle. She vividly recalled her Aunt Phoebe's reminder that no Heathercott had ever wed less than an earl. Well, she thought, without the slightest remorse, she had broken that tradition with a vengeance. It was up to her now to make sure that she did not make a mull of this odd alliance.

With this comforting decision uppermost in her mind, Regina

tapped on the library door a little after ten o'clock, convinced that the Duke of Wexley's daughter could carry it off with style.

The first person she saw when she stepped across the threshold was Captain Swinburn, sprawled at his ease in an armchair beside the fire. He leaped to his feet at her entrance, but after the initial shock of seeing him there at all, Regina ignored him and turned to her husband.

"You wished to see me, sir?" she inquired, dismayed at the cool hauteur she heard in her voice. Regina had envisioned this meeting very differently, but then she had not bargained on having her husband's brother as a witness. Her fingers curled unconsciously around the handle of the riding quirt she held in one hand. Something was terribly wrong here, she thought, staring into the colonel's eyes, which had turned dark and bleak as a winter sky.

Valiantly, she tried to smile. "I had thought to persuade you to ride out with me this morning," she said, hoping that she did not look as apprehensive as she felt. "I have not yet had a chance to see the estate."

Her words died away into an uncomfortable silence, which was eventually broken by the colonel's cold voice.

"I am to meet my steward this morning," he said formally, "but I am sure my brother would be glad to ride with you."

Regina felt she had been slapped in the face. The colonel's eyes never left her, but Regina heard the captain clear his throat behind her, as if preparing to utter one of his meaningless pleasantries.

Regina could not imagine why Richard seemed determined to throw her into the company of a man he must know she despised, but she would have none of it. "I can imagine few things I would dislike more," she said clearly in her coldest, most dismissive voice.

After a lengthy pause, the captain cleared his throat again. "In that case, I see I am very much *de trop*," he said smoothly, and Regina was sure she detected amusement in his voice. The villain was laughing at her, she realized, wishing she had the courage to slash his deceptively handsome face with her quirt.

When she heard the library door close softly behind the captain, Regina relaxed a trifle. Perhaps now she could talk to her husband about their future together, about her desire to be a real wife to him. His first words dashed these hopes entirely.

"You surprise me, my lady," he said in his formal voice,

touched with a hint of cool mockery. "I had thought you would jump at the chance to be alone with the man you love."

Regina gaped at him. There was an undercurrent to the colonel's words that set off an alarm in her head, but she failed to grasp the significance of it. All she knew was that her husband was in no mood to listen to her plea for a better understanding between them. There was something much more important to settle first.

"Then you thought wrong, Colonel," she said slowly and distinctly. "I have nothing but disgust for your brother. How you can imagine that I would have any other feeling for that lying knave is incomprehensible to me. Have you so soon forgotten those poor, unfortunate females in Brussels? Can you honestly tell me that the captain has done the right thing by any of them?"

"Charles did not do the right thing by you either, my lady," he said softly, his face blank and eyes never leaving her face.

"That is hardly the same case at all," she said, conscious of the warm color that rose to her cheeks. "Those three young women were misled into quite scandalous misconduct by false promises."

"Am I to assume you were not, my lady?"

Regina felt the blush fade from her cheeks and the floor tilt alarmingly beneath her booted feet. What was he insinuating? she wondered, unwilling to take the colonel's ugly words at their face value.

"Of course not!" she exclaimed angrily, her voice trembling in spite of her efforts to maintain her calm. "And I find it most insulting that you appear to have assumed otherwise."

"My brother tells me it *was* otherwise," he said in a voice that had grown colder and ever more distant. "I can only assume that one of you is being less than honest with me."

"And naturally you prefer to believe your brother, sir, is that not so?" she said with equal coldness.

"He has given me reason to believe his story."

Regina felt her heart freeze within her. The warm sense of contentment she had experienced at the prospect of informing her husband that he need have no further fear that the Duke of Wexley's daughter was displeased to be his wife faded slowly away and left a dark, empty pit of incipient loneliness where the joy had so recently been. She licked her dry lips, willing herself to conjure up the words to ward off the despair that threatened to overwhelm her. But no words came.

The color of his eyes had become even darker, if that were possible, she thought, as though the winter sky had lowered its storm-filled clouds to flagellate the exposed earth with heavy lashes of icy rain. Regina shivered, feeling exposed and vulnerable to this man's silent wrath, a wrath all the more terrifying because it had yet to shatter over her head. Her rock had failed her, she realized, with a sinking sensation of having lost her footing on ground she had thought secure.

Regina drew a desperate breath of air into her lungs. She had, for a brief, terrible moment, felt she was drowning. The effort of breathing released her from the paralysis that had immobilized her, and she lifted her chin defiantly. Lady Regina Elizabeth Constance Heathercott was not to be beaten down by adversity, she told herself firmly, reaching down into her deepest, most secret reserve for the fortitude, the anger, the determination that would see her through this devastating scene.

"I can think of no legitimate reason whatsoever why anyone should believe such a blatant lie," she said in carefully controlled fury. "I can only assume that—contrary to what your mother almost made me believe—you are willing to go to any lengths to find an excuse to cast me off. I am disappointed that you felt you needed to stoop so low, sir. You had only to tell me . . ."—her voice almost broke at this point, but Regina swallowed the hurt that threatened to undo her and continued icily—"to tell me that you wished to be rid of me."

There, she thought, she had said it. The dreadful words had been torn from her throat and she had not died from the mortification of having to admit that he really did not want her after all. Regina silently cursed the complaisant dowager for misleading her into believing . . . But what did it matter now what she had wanted to believe?

Wanting more than anything to be gone from the presence of this man who had the power to cause such pain to her heart, Regina turned abruptly toward the door. One hand on the knob, she paused, pride in who and what she was—and what she was not—made her cast a disdainful glance over her shoulder.

"If you are so certain your brother is telling the truth," she said icily, "if you are so sure he knows me as no man has ever known me, then perhaps you should put him to the test." She permitted herself a frigid shadow of a smile at the scandalous suggestion she was about to make. She would never have dared mention such a thing had her very honor and sense of decency not been called into question. Her fighting spirit was thoroughly aroused, and Regina knew—as surely as she knew she was innocent of her husband's veiled accusations—that she owed it to her father to defend the Heathercott name from such slander.

"Perhaps you should ask him to tell you where my birthmark is," she continued defiantly, a mocking smile twisting her lips. "I have a very distinctive one as it happens. But then you would not know anything about that either, would you?" She deliberately curled her lip cynically at the corner, and noted, as if in a haze, that the colonel's face had gone pale.

Regina laughed, a brief, mocking laugh that hid the sound of her dreams crumbling around her.

"Neither does your brother," she said coldly, and swept out of the room, her head high, the full skirt of her gay red riding habit swirling about her like a froth of blood that matched the ruins of her heart.

CHAPTER TWELVE

A Revelation

"What do you mean, she is not in the house?"

"It-it appears that her ladyship did not ring for her chocolate this morning, sir," the ancient butler stammered in response to the colonel's startled question. "Her ladyship is partial to hot chocolate in the morning—"

"Yes, yes," Richard interrupted impatiently. "But what happened this morning?"

"This morning there was no ring from her ladyship's room, sir. So at ten o'clock, Cook Gibson sent up a cup with one of the maids . . ."

The colonel rubbed the palm of his hand across his face, keeping his impatience in check. He knew from years of experience that Tobin could ramble on forever if he lost the thread of his story. Even now the butler had paused, a puzzled expression on his homely face.

"And then?" Richard prodded insistently.

He had spent a wretched day yesterday after the emotional encounter with Lady Regina in the library. He had expected her—nay, he had *wanted* her—to deny the charge he had been fool enough to make, but he had never in his wildest dreams imagined he would see that haunted look flood those marvelous green eyes, as though her very soul had been trampled. He had been prepared for anger, for heated denial, for one of those crushing ducal snubs she delivered with such aplomb. But he had been unprepared for pain. He had been immediately contrite and devoutly wished he could recall his ugly insinuation. But once uttered, that veiled accusation seemed to take on a life of its own. It grew and expanded until the library had been heavy with it. He had felt stifled, smothered by his own pride, and quite unable to undo the damage he had plainly inflicted upon his wife.

"And then, sir, we discovered that her ladyship's room was empty and her abigail was not to be found anywhere."

"Have you searched the servants' quarters?"

"Yes, sir. Nothing unusual there, of course. Claudette is a neat lass and not given to leaving her room in shambles like some I could name."

Richard brushed this sententious remark aside. Old Tobin was eternally dissatisfied with the younger members of the staff, considering them lacking in the proper habits of good servants.

"And her ladyship's room?" Richard demanded, a tremor of apprehension beginning to vibrate in the pit of his stomach.

The old butler coughed discreetly, and Richard was astonished to see a glow of pink invade the old man's cheeks. "Everything was neat and tidy, sir, which is unusual at that hour. Even her ladyship's bed"—the butler lowered his eyes in obvious embarrassment—"was made up, although the upstairs maid swore she had not been in the room all morning."

"Are you suggesting that her ladyship might not have slept in her bed last night, Tobin?" Richard exclaimed sharply, realizing as he said it that the butler had believed just that, but had attached a far different significance to Regina's unruffled bed. Richard grinned mirthlessly. How ironic that the logical explanation embraced by his staff was the least likely to be true.

The butler's face turned a brighter pink, and Richard felt sorry for the old man. In spite of his superficial informality, Tobin had always maintained a strict regard for propriety, an invisible line across which he never stepped, even during the Christmas festivities when he was known to tipple a little too liberally.

The colonel's question had clearly crossed that line.

"That was one possibility that did occur to us, Colonel," Tobin replied stiffly, his pale eyes focused on a point above his master's right shoulder. It was evident to Richard that wild horses would not drag the other possibility from between those tightly clamped lips. And if Regina had not slept in her bed last night . . .

The colonel strode into the hall and took the stairs two at a time. He opened his wife's bedchamber door and stepped inside. The silence that greeted him chilled his heart. Had it not been for the faint scent of gardenia, he might have believed that Regina had never set foot in here, had never married him six months ago, and abandoned him on their wedding night.

But the perfume told a different story. It was the one she always wore, the flowery aura that trailed after her as she moved about the house, the scent that had delighted his senses in the summer house at Wexley Abbey. The memory of that evening flooded back in all its sensual enchantment, and Richard remembered vividly that the scent of gardenia was not all that had delighted his senses that night.

Had he lost her? Richard wondered. Yesterday morning in the library his wife had accused him of wishing to be rid of her, he re-

called. And for a while—particularly when he met his brother's
mocking gaze over her head as Charles had left them—he knew
himself guilty of just such a wish. He had wanted to distance himself—to run away as he had ten years ago—from a woman who
had preferred his brother.

But what if Lady Regina did not prefer Charles, as Helen obviously had? What if she were telling the truth? What if Charles
knew nothing about the birthmark Regina had mentioned? The
notion of exploring a birthmark on his wife's body channeled
Richard's thoughts into an area he had deliberately denied himself
access to. He had no stomach for an unwilling woman, and his
wife had given ample evidence that she wanted nothing to do with
him. His name had been forced upon her, but Richard saw no reason why he should force himself on her, too. There were enough
willing females in the world without having to resort to that, he
thought. As a soldier, Richard had met his fair share of them and
had been quite satisfied with these brief encounters that made no
demands on his emotions.

Richard glanced around the empty room, searching for some
physical sign of his wife's recent presence. The length of red ribbon lying on the dressing table reminded him instantly of the
scarlet riding habit she had worn yesterday. She had looked magnificent, he recalled, a slim, regal figure in red velvet, her pale,
shining hair topped by a jaunty black fur shako. He picked up the
scrap of ribbon and held it to his nose. It smelled strongly of gardenia, and Richard knew his wife had used it in her hair. Without
being entirely conscious of his action, he slipped the red ribbon
into his waistcoat pocket as he left the room.

"Tobin," he shouted as he descended the stair. "Have Burton
bring a fresh horse 'round for me immediately. I intend to ride
over to Laughton Hall." It was quite possible that Regina has paid
a call on Lady Laughton, he thought, although his instincts told
him he was deliberately ignoring the obvious.

The butler pulled a long face. "Mr. Burton did not come up for
his breakfast this morning, sir," he said tonelessly.

Burton gone, too? The notion that his trusty batman might be
involved with his wife's disappearance gave Richard pause for
thought. He knew that Burton doted on Lady Regina, and allowed
her to bully and cajole him as no other, including Richard himself, would dream of doing. Burton's absence, coupled with that
of the abigail, suggested a conspiracy that he vowed he would get
to the bottom of.

"Send down to the stables to find out if her ladyship ordered her mare this morning, will you, Tobin?" he ordered. It was entirely possible, Richard tried to convince himself while he waited impatiently for word from the stables, that Burton had accompanied his mistress on an early morning ride, perhaps over to Laughton Hall. And then again, perhaps not.

The colonel's fears were confirmed the moment he was ushered into Sir David Laughton's study twenty minutes later.

"Lady Regina?" his friend exclaimed in surprise, rising from behind the desk. "No, she is not here. Why are you raising such a dust, old man? You look as though someone landed you a facer."

"I seem to have lost her," Richard said bluntly, ignoring Sir David's witticism. To tell the truth, he had been forced to face the possibility he had tried to ignore all morning that his wife had fled Willow Park. Regina's mare had been reported still in her stall, but her ladyship's curricle was missing. Now why would a lady choose to drive out in an open carriage in the chill of December when there were two closed vehicles in the stables? Richard had asked himself a dozen times already. The answer that came most readily to mind was not the one he wanted to hear.

"Now I know you are daft, Dick," Laughton said bracingly, although the colonel noticed his friend's face was solemn. "How can a man lose his wife in an out-of-the-way place like Langley? Now if this were London, I can think of a dozen different tangles a female might get herself into, but Kent?" He studied Richard for a moment before adding, with an obvious attempt at nonchalance, "Where is that brother of yours?"

Richard's face twisted into a grim smile. "Charles rode over to Canterbury at first light this morning," he said, wondering for the first time if his brother's errand to look over a promising young hunter had been trumped up for his benefit.

Laughton gazed at him intently, his pale eyes hooded. "And, as always, you believed him?"

Yes, Richard thought disconsolately, he had believed Charles's glib explanation without hesitation. Just as he had believed his brother's earth-shattering confession—which Charles had let slip the evening of Richard's arrival back from Hampshire—that he had been rather more to Lady Regina than the colonel had perhaps been aware.

Richard had not wanted to hear what his brother had to say, indeed, he had accused Charles of being in his cups, which he undoubtedly was at the time. But as had always been the case when his brother felt the need for absolution, there was no stopping him once he launched into the confessional diatribe. It had all begun with a minor peccadillo committed when Charles was but nine, some trifling offense long forgotten, and had progressed until it climaxed, as it invariably did when his brother became maudlin with spirits, in an orgy of profuse, almost tearful apologies and moral flagellations, designed to elicit Richard's forgiveness for the part Charles had played in the downfall of Lady Helen.

All should have ended there, Richard thought, the bile rising again in his throat at the memory of his brother's unhealthy, almost unmanly he had always thought, insistence on spreading his dirty linen out for Richard to examine. The words of comfort and reassurance he had used so often they had become automatic and insincere trembled on his lips, when Charles had mentioned Regina.

Richard had reacted instantly, the knot of suspicion that had festered in his heart ever since that strange wedding morning in Brussels—he could still hear Charles's French doxy accusing the duke's daughter of being no better than she—becoming abruptly a lump that seemed to strangle him. His attempts to steer his brother's jumbled apologies into safer channels had failed, as they always had, for Charles seemed to derive a perverse pleasure from this uninhibited flow of sordid details he expected his elder brother to judge, and condone, and absolve, and ultimately forgive with nary a hint of blame for the penitent.

Richard had been unable to forgive his brother's revelations about Lady Regina. He had long ago forgiven Charles for coming between him and Lady Helen, but Regina was another matter entirely. Regina was his wife. She had become increasingly precious to him, and his heart rebelled against the insinuations that threatened to break it all over again. He refused to believe that this second female of importance in his life was no better than the first.

Before he realized what he was going to say, he blurted out the hurt that was gnawing at him. "Charles confessed that he knew Regina," he said with unnecessary harshness. "Really *knew* her, if you get my meaning."

Unexpectedly, Sir David let out a crack of sarcastic laughter. "And you believed that, too, you clodhead, did you not?" His friend observed him keenly, a look of disgust on his craggy face. "Just as you believed his so-called *confession* regarding Lady Helen. You are a genuine sapskull, Dick, and no mistake."

Richard found the direction of Laughton's conversation offensive. "You seem to forget that I was there," he said stiffly. "I *saw* them together on the library settee. My brother's later confession merely confirmed what I already knew." He picked up the brandy his host had served upon his arrival and drank it down in one gulp.

"The devil fly away with your damned brother and his confessions, Dick," Sir David exclaimed angrily. "All you know about the affair is what he chooses to tell you. Did you think to ask Helen how she happened to be on the settee with that wretch? Did you stop to consider that all was not as it seemed? Of course you did not. You are too stiff-necked for your own good, my lad, as I have said many a time. And now you are willing to believe some trumped-up Canterbury tale about Lady Regina just because you hear it from your brother's sacrosanct lips. You are a bloody fool, Dick, as I have also said before."

He paused to regard the colonel from beneath lowered brows, and Richard saw a sudden arrested look in his friend's eyes. "Never say"— Laughton began in a hushed voice—"never say that you have accused the lass of . . . ?" His voice trailed off into silence.

"Of being my brother's doxy?" Richard finished for him in a harsh voice. "What the blue blazes do you take me for, David?" he blustered, horrified that his friend's blunt question came so close to the mark. He had done precisely that, he thought with sudden apprehension, and the suspicion that had nagged at him all morning began to take on the shape of reality.

Laughton heaved a sigh and poured them both a second brandy. "I see," he said heavily. "Say no more. No wonder the girl has shaken the dust of Kent from her boots. Cannot say I blame her." He looked at the colonel pityingly. "But then, perhaps that is what you wanted all along, Richard. You really wished to be rid of the girl who reminded you too painfully of Lady Helen. Is that it? You are punishing yourself, and Lady Regina, too, of course, for what happened ten years ago."

"Charles said that—"

"The devil fly away with Charles!" Laughton exclaimed angrily. "Do you wish to lose your wife or not?"

"No," Richard responded with equal force, and knew that he spoke the truth. He wanted his wife back, regardless of what she had or had not done with his brother.

"Then I suggest you get back in the saddle, my dear boy," Laughton drawled, sampling his brandy with relish. "And ride *vent-à-terre* to Wexley Abbey and pray that her ladyship will listen to your apologies. I trust for your sake that she is less birdwitted than you are."

An hour later, mounted on his fastest horse and headed into

Hampshire at a dangerously fast pace, the colonel followed his friend's advice.

He prayed, every step of the way, that Regina would understand and forgive.

"Will you wear the diamonds or the emeralds tonight, milady?"

Regina glanced at the abigail's sour face in the beveled glass of the dressing-table mirror and smiled wryly. Claudette had adamantly opposed their recent escape from Willow Park, and the wild and dangerous journey through the winter darkness in the open curricle. Pure madness, Claudette had called her mistress's latest escapade, and the comforting presence of Burton, who had been cajoled into driving the curricle, had only marginally mollified the testy abigail. Why must they travel in the dead of night like so many heathens? Claudette had wanted to know. It had done no good to point out that the full December moon had turned the countryside into a wonderland of stark whites and deep, mysterious shadows that delighted the eye. Claudette had refused to acknowledge this beauty, her shoulders slumped in disgruntled silence under a double layer of warm cloaks and scarves, and her hands stuffed into one of her mistress's fur muffs.

On any other occasion, Regina would have reveled in the still beauty of the night and the sheer exhilaration of dashing through the snow-covered countryside in the moonlight. Had she not been so heavy-hearted, she would have insisted upon tooling the mettlesome team of bays herself instead of allowing Burton to handle the ribbons. As it was she took little joy in the strange and lovely world through which they drove at breakneck speed. The roads were good, Burton had assured her only yesterday when she had approached him impulsively with her desire to leave before dawn to travel back to Wexley Abbey before the snowstorm that had been threatening for the past two days to dump the season's first heavy snow on Langley made the roads impassable.

The batman had regarded her quizzically, for once his merry blue eyes devoid of laughter. "Should you not ask the colonel to drive you, lass?" he had asked with predictable directness.

"The colonel is not to know about this, Burton," she had insisted, hoping the ex-pugilist would not betray her to Sir Richard. "He is being impossibly odious," she tried to explain, her voice catching in her throat. "I must get away from here, Burton. Whether you consent to drive me or not. I would naturally prefer that you did," she added with a slight smile. "Claudette and I would feel so much safer with you there."

She never knew whether it was the mention of the abigail, whom Burton had chosen as the object of his teasing attentions, or whether he was moved by a sense of duty toward her, but he had reluctantly agreed to have the curricle ready at four o'clock the next morning and to see them safely to Wexley Abbey.

"The diamonds, I think," Regina responded, not really caring which of her jewels she wore that evening for dinner. Richard was not here to admire them, she thought, vaguely unsettled at the notion. It seemed ironic that she had taken such pains to escape from her husband only to be plagued by an odd sense of loss now that she had achieved her purpose. By now her husband surely must have noticed her absence, Regina thought, wondering whether it would matter to him that she had gone, or whether he might at this very instant be sitting down to one of Cook Gibson's hearty dinners with his mother and brother, secretly glad that he had been so easily rid of his unwanted wife.

Regina shuddered at the thought.

"Are you cold, milady?" Claudette asked, some of the frost melting from her tone.

Regina shook her head. The chill she felt could not be remedied with silk shawls or blazing fires, or even drafts of her father's excellent brandy. The chill that assailed her touched the inner depths of her most intimate self in ways she had never experienced before. She felt a singular loneliness that was patently ridiculous, for here she was in the heart of her family, pampered and petted as she had been as a young girl by the most important gentlemen in her life. All but one, of course. All but one.

She sighed and allowed Claudette to drape a feather-light cashmere shawl around her shoulders.

"See if my mother is ready to go down, will you Claudette," she said, observing the vision in dark green velvet that returned her stare from the cheval glass. The bodice of the gown was sprinkled generously with crystal beads that twinkled in the candlelight, echoing the glitter of diamonds on the wide expanse of bosom and in her ears as she moved her head from side to side. The slim skirt with its elegant demi-train showed off her slimness and molded daringly to her limbs as she walked, but the knowledge that she looked her best did nothing to raise Regina's flagging spirits.

She recalled with a glow of brief happiness the warm reception she had received from her four brothers, all of whom had crowded around her when she had burst in upon them as they sat drinking tea with their mother, demanding to know what brought her back to the Abbey so soon. She had managed to fob them off with vague answers until after the tea tray had been removed.

"It is Swinburn, is it not?" Robert had demanded bluntly, as soon as the duchess had gone upstairs to join the duke in their private sitting room. "Either that or you are behaving like a complete ninny again, Gina. Which is it?"

"Do not badger the poor girl," Nevil intervened, his face reflecting his own concern.

Alex had regarded her rather more critically, his gray eyes steady. "I trust you have done nothing bird-witted again, Gina," he said sternly. "Swinburn is not the man to play fast and loose with—"

"Of course, she has," Robert cut in impatiently. "I can see it in her expression. Out with it, Gina," he added with a flicker of his usual impatience. "Tell us what pickle you have got yourself into now."

"I am n-not in any p-pickle," Regina had stammered miserably, knowing that she could not long hold out against the four of them. "Well, p-perhaps only a little one," she lied. "And it is not my fault. This time I am innocent."

"Innocent of what?" Robert wanted to know, in that incisive way he had of getting right to the heart of the matter.

"Don't bully the chit, Robert," Geoffrey had insisted, glaring at his elder brother. "Cannot you see she is overwrought? Come, my dear," he added, placing an arm about Regina's shoulders and giving her a bruising hug. "Tell us who has hurt you, sweetheart, and your big brothers will tear the wretch limb from limb."

"Yes, that's it," Nevil broke in enthusiastically, his eyes sparkling at the mention of a mill. "Tell us the whole, Gina love, and we shall rearrange his teeth for him." He danced around the room on the balls of his feet, feinting fast and furiously at an imaginary opponent.

This unexpectedly belligerent support from her brothers touched Regina deeply and she gave them a wobbly smile. It also frightened her to think that the four of them—particularly Robert, who was known to have knocked Gentleman Jackson himself onto the canvas—were so ready to attack the colonel with so little provocation.

"Tell us what you are innocent of, Gina?" Robert insisted more gently.

Distraught as she was by the events of the day, Regina could not stop the sob that rose in her throat. That was quite sufficient

for Robert, who demanded, in his autocratic manner that reminded Regina of their father, that she tell them the whole.

And so she had told them, between sobs and hiccups and occasional promptings from Robert, about that dreadful scene in the
library the day before. In bits and pieces, with much cajoling and
occasional bullying, her brothers drew all the details of her relationship with the Swinburn brothers out into the open. When she
came to the part about her decision to risk the elements in an open
carriage to escape from their false accusation, Regina was comforted by her brothers' obvious belief in her innocence. That had
been the hard part, she recalled later as she retired to her room to
rest. It had been dreadfully humiliating to tell her brothers that her
husband doubted her innocence.

Nevil had not helped matters by demanding, in his impulsive
way, to know how the colonel could say such a thing when he
must have known since their wedding night how matters stood.

Regina covered her face with her hands and let the tears flow
unimpeded. Through the haze of embarrassment she heard Alex
mutter to his thoughtless brother that anyone with half an ounce
of wit would see that the colonel had not yet exercised his rights.

"And why in Hades not?" Nevil had wanted to know. Doubtless he would have said more, Regina knew, but Robert cut him
off with a curt order to snabble it if he did not wish to have his
daylights darkened.

It was Alex who broke the uneasy silence that followed that
revelation by putting his arm about her and rocking her soothingly. "No doubt Richard has behaved foolishly, Gina, but it
seems obvious that he was misled by his brother's lies," he said
tentatively. "He is very conscious of the pressures that were
brought to bear on you to accept him. He probably wished to give
you time to—"

"No!" Regina heard herself exclaim in a watery voice. "He
truly believes I am some sort of . . . some sort of . . ." She could
not bring herself to say the word. "He does not want me for a
wife, Alex," she wailed disconsolately, pressing her damp face
against her brother's pristine neckcloth.

"The devil take it, Regina, now you are talking like a blathering
ninny!" Robert exploded. He pried her away from Alex's ruined
cravat and held her by the shoulders. "Do stop being such a peagoose, Gina," he said softly, gazing down at her with those mes-
merizing sapphire eyes that had, Regina knew for a fact, been the
ruin of countless females who should have had better sense.
"Here, take this"—he pulled out his handkerchief and handed it to

her—"and dry those lovely eyes, dear. You would not wish the colonel to see you with a wet face when he comes storming over here to get you back, would you?"

Instead of making her feel better, her brother's words brought forth another choked sob. "He w-will not c-come—" she said jerkily.

"Oh, he will," Alex cut in forcefully. "And when we have finished with him, dearest, he will think twice before causing you any more grief, believe me."

"Lay you a pony he will not," Nevil interrupted, introducing a note of levity into the scene that elicited an instant response from his sister.

"How can you say that, Nevil?" Regina demanded crossly.

Her youngest brother stared at her in surprise, his mouth agape. "Why, you said so yourself, you silly goose," he said disgustedly.

"I'll take you up on that, puppy," Robert said with a grim laugh. "I'll lay you a monkey he does come."

"Reduced to taking money from babes, are you, brother?" Geoffrey remarked caustically.

"Done!" Nevil exclaimed heartily.

"Do not worry, love, Richard will come, I guarantee it," Alex murmured in her ear while the others were arguing the odds against the colonel appearing any time soon at Wexley Abbey.

Regina felt a certain amount of relief that her secret pain had been shared with her brothers, but from that moment on, another anxiety invaded her heart. If the colonel did come for her, would her brothers carry out their threat to teach him not to insult their little sister?

"Her Grace is not yet ready to go down, milady." The abigail's voice intruded upon Regina's troubled thoughts and reminded her that before the night was over, she intended to give her father a less damning version of the story she had told her brothers. Although the physician had pronounced the duke out of danger, Regina was reluctant to upset him with tales of marital squabbles. A stronger motivation for keeping the whole sordid truth from her father, she admitted to herself, was her reluctance to destroy the duke's respect for his son-in-law. Of course, if the colonel did not come to claim her, as Robert and Alex seemed so sure he would, she would have to tell her father the whole.

These unhappy musings were interrupted by a loud commotion from the front hall below. The unmistakable sounds of male voices raised in argument made Regina's heart leap into her throat. Although she wanted nothing so much as to rush out onto the landing to discover the cause of the uproar, her limbs seemed to be paralyzed. Claudette suffered no such inhibitions, and after a quick glance over the banister, she rushed back with a worried expression on her plain face.

" 'Tis the master," the abigail whispered in a muted voice. "Come to take us back, 'e 'as," she muttered, relapsing into her rural brogue, a sure sign that she was unusually rattled. "In a rare taking 'e is, too, milady."

Abruptly released from her trance, Regina stepped out onto the landing. The voices had stilled and an ominous silence rose from the lower regions. Unable to resist the urge, she moved to look over the banister. Besides Hobbs, who stood at rigid attention with a look on his face that clearly suggested that he had no part in this unseemly rumpus, there were five gentlemen in the hall below, but Regina had eyes for only one.

Colonel Swinburn appeared huge in his heavy greatcoat, its numerous capes covered with a layer of snow. He had removed his hat and gloves, and now stood, booted feet apart in a clearly challenging stance, glaring at the four men who blocked his way.

Regina gazed in wonder at this tall man who had obviously ridden through the swirling snowstorm she herself had barely missed. The thick white flakes on his shoulders had begun to melt, and his hat, too, was dripping wetness onto the black-and-white tile of the ducal hall. Claudette had been right. The colonel looked extremely annoyed, his square jaw set in a rigid mask, his lips taut and thin. She could not see his eyes, but Regina remembered all too well the slate-gray austerity that had crushed her spirit in the library at Willow Park. A damp lock of dark hair fell over his wide forehead, an incongruously boyish touch of softness to the granite hardness of the man she barely recognized.

Touched by some emotion she could not identify, Regina trembled slightly as she gazed down upon him. This was a side of the colonel she had not experienced before. There was something wild and strong about him, a hint of danger in the way he stood defying the four men who had evidently challenged him. Could this be the same gentle man who had kissed her in the summer house? she wondered, feeling again the warm strength of his hands on her back. She had been astonished and deeply attracted by that unexpected tenderness, but she was frankly seduced by the erotic aura of masculine power that hung about him now. As she stared, unable to drag her eyes away from his imposing figure, Regina felt herself go warm and soft inside. A lethargic sensation relaxed her bones until she sagged against the banister, feeling strangely pliable and in need of support. His support, she thought, suddenly recognizing the dull ache inside her for what it must be. She had never felt it before, this dizzying sensation of physical desire for a man. She drew a deep breath, but it would not go away. She wanted to run down the stairs and throw herself into the colonel's arms. Only the nagging fear that he might, even now, reject her kept her from surrendering to this wild, quite unladylike urge.

The sound of his voice, husky and resonant, curled up from the hall below and seemed to envelop her in his presence.

"I have come to see my wife."

"Not so fast, old man." Robert's voice was cold and cutting, and Regina shivered at the sound of it. "There are a few things that need to be settled before we allow you to upset our sister again."

"If indeed we ever do," Geoffrey cut in belligerently. "And always assuming that Regina wishes to see you."

Nevil pushed forward to glare at the visitor. "Let me have first dibs at him, Robert," he said, evidently relishing the violence that hung in the air around them. The smell of it reached Regina where she stood, a silent spectator to the drama, and she let out an involuntary gasp.

Five pairs of eyes swiveled up at her, but again she was conscious of only the dark, brooding stare of her husband. The shattering revelation that she desired this man as she had never desired any other, not even the dashingly charming Charles, had subtly but irreversibly altered her perception of the colonel.

As their gazes locked, Regina willed him to recognize her newly awakened need for him in her eyes, willed him to see her as the only woman in the world, willed him to return the love she had so recently discovered in her own heart.

CHAPTER THIRTEEN

The Challenge

The huge iron-studded door swung open on the second rap, and Colonel Swinburn stepped into the warmth of the ducal hall, a thick swirl of snowflakes following in his wake. Two footmen quickly slammed the heavy door shut, and the sudden silence struck Richard as faintly ominous after the roar of the storm which had dogged him ever since leaving Petersfield.

"Good evening, Colonel." The butler greeted him as though the arrival of a gentleman in the snow-spattered greatcoat and beaver, tall boots showing signs of rough wear, and thick red scarf covering half his face from the assault of the elements, were nothing out of the ordinary.

"Good evening, Hobbs," the colonel answered levelly, unwinding his scarf and handing it to the butler. "Have someone see to my horse, will you?"

"Right away, sir." The butler nodded at one of the footmen who disappeared into the recesses of the house. The other ran lightly up the curving staircase toward the drawing rooms on the first floor.

The colonel pulled off his damp gloves and removed his tall beaver, wondering if Regina might still be dressing for dinner. It would cause less commotion if he might talk to her in her private rooms before his arrival became known. This was, after all, not a social call, he thought wryly. The notion of accosting his wife in her bedchamber appealed to him. The compelling need to see her glorious green eyes light up at the sight of him had sustained him over those last tedious miles through the chilling wind and snow. Would she be surprised to see him? he wondered. Gratified that he had come after her? Had she expected him to do so? Perhaps even hoped that he would? Or would her eyes reflect once again that haunted expression that had affected him so profoundly that morning in the library?

The memory of that fateful morning disturbed him anew. He knew he had behaved rashly, acted without considering anything but his own revulsion against what had seemed like a second betrayal. A heart-wrenching repetition of the first. Now he was not at all sure of anything anymore. He had been so convinced that he had known his brother, known and loved him in spite of his flaws, his selfishness, his disregard for others. Now he wondered if he had really known Charles at all.

These musings were interrupted by a movement on the landing above. Richard raised his eyes, hoping to see his wife, but the four gentlemen who walked abreast down the wide staircase chased any thought of remaining undetected from his mind. The menacing demeanor of the four Heathercott brothers told him more clearly than words that his sins had become common knowledge. And unless he was mistaken, the four men who advanced toward him were spoiling for a fight. Even Alex, who Richard considered a friend of long standing, had a grim twist to his lips that boded no good for the colonel.

Richard waited until the four men reached the hall and advanced to stand in a threatening half-circle facing him. Dispensing with social niceties, which seemed superfluous in the charged atmosphere of the hall, Richard came straight to the point.

"I have come to see my wife," he said loudly and clearly.

The Marquess of Gresham answered in the cutting tones of the aristocrat accustomed to the power of rank and fortune. "Not so fast, old man," he sneered with cold condescension. "There are a few things that need to be settled before we allow you to upset our sister again."

"If indeed we ever do," one of the others added aggressively.

The colonel felt the hostility of the four men envelop him like the chill of the storm he had moments before left behind him. Richard recognized danger when he encountered it. He had lived with it for the past ten years in the Army. He smelled it now in the vast ducal hall, emanating from the men who stood before him, poised on the balls of their feet. Ready for that invisible sign they would all recognize as the signal for the brawl to begin.

Willing himself to remain perfectly still, Richard wondered which of them would give that primeval signal for combat, a signal as old as man himself, and as unmistakable as other primitive urges that had driven men to follow their instincts since the world began. The urge to survive, the urge to take a woman, the urge to kill.

Richard felt the thrill of the moment drive all else from his mind. Fatigue dropped away miraculously, his blood ran warm again after the bone-chilling cold of the storm, even thoughts of Regina receded to the back of his mind as his body prepared itself for the fight that he knew to be inevitable.

His hackles rose as the youngest of the brothers, brash and impulsive as one of the colonel's junior officers, stepped forward to demand the right to give the first punch. Richard tensed, but he did not move. Instinct told him that the sign would come from one of the elder men, possibly from the marquess, whose sapphire eyes glimmered with suppressed excitement. This was the one to be wary of, Richard knew from his long experience in assessing the enemy. This man was the only one of the four the colonel had any reason to fear. This man, beneath the deceptive mask of fashionable clothes, extravagantly-tied cravat, and skin-tight pantaloons, was a worthy opponent. The others might be handy with their dabblers, but the marquess had the science of the true fighter.

All this flashed through the colonel's mind in an instant as he stood, feet braced apart, muscles taut, and back ramrod straight, waiting for the signal.

The silence was broken by a sound from above, a gasp that diffused some of the tension and caused all heads to swivel upward.

Richard looked straight up into his wife's eyes. Green eyes that were wide with fear, or so he imagined. But as the gaze held for what seemed like a frozen instant in time, Richard saw glimpses of something else that he had never seen, perhaps hoped for but never expected to see, in his wife's eyes. A warmth, coupled with a strange longing, and a distinct plea for something—he knew not what—that he silently swore he would spend the rest of his life if need be, and fight a whole army of Heathercotts, to lay at her feet.

Regina's eyes had fluttered shut under the intensity of the colonel's stare. Time seemed to stand still, and the dizzy sensation persisted. She wanted to run downstairs, but dared not relinquish her hold on the banister.

When at last she ventured to open her eyes, the hall below was empty, quite as though the previous scene had never occurred. Regina stood for a moment, wondering if indeed she had dreamed it all, but then the stocky figure of Burton appeared at the foot of the stairs. The colonel's batman raised his eyes, and she noticed that his visage was grim.

Suddenly released from her paralysis, Regina rushed down the stairs.

"The colonel is here, milady," Burton said briefly, his blue eyes devoid of their twinkle.

"Yes, I know," Regina gasped, winded from her unladylike descent. "Where is he now, Burton? I fear my brothers are planning to harm him."

Burton grinned ghoulishly. "Indeed they are, lass," He replied. "They have taken him to the armory." He indicated the wide hallway with a wave of his hand. "Like as not, they intend to cut him into little pieces and throw him to the dogs."

Regina felt the blood fade from her cheeks and the ground sway under her. Then Burton's huge hand grasped her elbow, and she heard his snorting chuckle.

"Steady, lass," he said bracingly. "I dinna mean that literal like. The colonel will bloody a few noses before they darken his daylights fer him, milady. Never fear. He's a fighting man, lass. Used to being knocked about and taking a few punches."

"Y-you must help him, Burton," Regina stammered through her suddenly chattering teeth. "Please stop them from hurting him, Burton. *Please*."

Without waiting for a reply, Regina wrenched free of the batman's grasp and fled down the hall toward the room that had, over the centuries, collected the outdated weapons wielded by long-dead Heathercotts in defense of king and country. It was a room Regina rarely visited. She had no taste for those bloodthirsty reminders of her family's violent past. Or of their violent present, she thought, recalling the numerous pairs of dueling pistols that had—if the family records could be believed—settled their fair share of recent disputes.

To her surprise, the door was unlocked, and she pushed it open and rushed in, her breath coming in painful gasps. What she saw caused her to utter a moan of sheer terror. The colonel was backed into a corner of the room, divested of his coat. Facing him, her brother Robert had also removed his blue coat of superfine, and was engaged in pulling his fine cambric shirt over his head.

No one paid her the slightest heed.

"No, Robert," she cried, moving forward as if in a trance to lay a trembling hand on her brother's muscular arm. He looked down at her then, eyes hot and savage, and Regina could not repress a shudder. "Please do not do this," she begged, knowing that it was useless. "You are being utterly barbaric, Robert," she added, anger at the recklessness of her brothers' actions overcoming her fright. "Stop it at once!"

"This is men's business, Gina. No place for a female," Robert said abruptly, waving her aside. "Get her out of here, Nevil." He turned away, and Regina felt herself caught in a firm grasp.

She glanced at the colonel and was alarmed at the wild expression in his eyes. His gaze was as hot as her brother's, and she could not be sure that he had recognized her, so intensely was he glaring at his opponent. In the moment before she was thrust unceremoniously from the room, she saw her husband tear his shirt from his tightly fitted breeches and pull it over his head. The last thing she remembered seeing was the red welt of a recent scar tracing its ragged path from under his breeches up across the rippling muscles of his chest toward his right collarbone.

The sight was so unexpected and the implications of the scar so terrifying that Regina could not find the voice to protest as Nevil swung the heavy armory door shut behind her and dragged the iron bar into place, locking her out.

It was a moment before she realized that Burton was standing beside her, supporting her again with his large hand.

"Easy, lass," the batman muttered. " 'Taint no sight for a lady, and that's for sure," he continued, urging her away from the door.

She had taken no more than four or five steps, before she heard the angry voices of her brothers raised in a flurry of accusations, whose tenor she could not make out. In the silence that followed, she clearly heard the colonel make his response, although the words were lost to her. Then there was a crash, followed by shouting, more crashes, and then Nevil's high-pitched yell urging his brother to *Mow the rogue down*.

Suddenly aware that several servants had congregated silently in the hall, Regina frowned. "Go up and request His Grace to come down here this instant," she said to a nearby footman, waving the rest away imperiously. "Burton," she said, gazing up at the colonel's man imploringly, "is there nothing you can do to help him?"

Burton shrugged. "The colonel would not thank me, milady," he said with what Regina considered a distressing nonchalance. "Even if I could batter that door down, which I ain't about to do. There are some things a man has to do on his own, lass," he added more softly. "And this is one of them."

The sounds that issued from behind the locked door soon took on the steady rhythmical sounds of a fight that was destined to continue for some time. The unnerving smack of flesh meeting flesh was occasionally punctuated by the crash of a chair overturned, a vase shattering, and once the unmistakable sound of a picture jarred from the wall and splintering on the ancient wooden floor.

More than once Regina clapped her hands over her ears when one of the men within gave a particularly loud grunt of pain. She found her self praying that the grunts were Robert's, although she feared that they were more likely to be Richard's. She knew that Robert was reputed among the followers of the Fancy to have a punishing right, a term she understood only vaguely, but which sounded ominous.

By the time the duke arrived on the scene, the sounds of battle had diminished to an occasional bone-jarring punch and grunts from both the giver and receiver of the punishment.

"Papa!" Regina exclaimed with a sob of relief, running to fling herself into the arms of the duke as soon as he appeared. "Robert is killing Richard," she explained as her father regarded her in astonishment. "Please stop him, Papa. I shall never forgive—"

"What is going on here?" the Duke of Wexley demanded testily as the sound of a body apparently being thrown against the wall filtered through the armory door. He tried the handle, rattling it imperiously when he found it locked.

After a slight pause, the duke beat an impatient tattoo on the door which met with no immediate response.

"Regina," he said in his authoritative tone, "explain to me, if you please, what all this vulgar ruckus is about."

"My brothers have taken it into their heads that Richard is in need of a lesson, Papa," she responded meekly, wishing that she had not waited this long to inform her parents of the reason behind her sudden return to Wexley Abbey.

The duke frowned, obviously making no sense of his daughter's explanation. "A lesson in what?" he demanded.

"Why, a lesson in pugilistic skills, I would assume, judging from the noise," she murmured. "But I wish you would stop them, Papa. I fear they will do Richard serious damage."

The duke glanced curiously at Burton. "Is this true?" he demanded brusquely.

"Indeed it is, Your Grace," Burton replied instantly.

The duke rapped energetically on the door with his cane. After a considerable pause, during which no further bellicose sounds issued from the closed room, the door was opened by Nevil, who had, Regina could plainly see, a satanic gleam of victory in his eyes. He looked a little nonplussed to see his father standing there.

Without a word, the duke stalked into the room, but when Regina made as if to follow, Nevil blocked her way.

"Oh, no, you don't, Gina," he said sternly. "This is not a sight for a delicate female. Blood everywhere," he added with evident relish.

He had calculated without Burton, however, and when the batman heard these words, he pushed through roughly, giving Regina the chance to slip in under her brother's arm.

No sooner was she in than she wished she had heeded her brother's warning. There was indeed blood everywhere, and the sight of it made her feel rather sick. Robert was slouched in a chair, his head resting on his chest in an attitude of total exhaustion, while Geoffrey and Alex were bending over a still figure on the floor.

With an exclamation of anxiety, and careless of her finery, Regina darted forward, pushing both men aside, and knelt beside the body of the colonel. She saw at once that he had taken a severe beating. His nose was bleeding, the blood splattering down over his bare chest. One eye was puffy and almost closed, and a gash on one cheekbone trickled blood down into his hair. She let out the breath she had been holding when the rise of his chest indicated that he still lived.

"How could you allow this to happen, Alex?" she stormed, glaring up at her brother. "I thought you were one of his *friends*."

"He gave as good as he got, Gina," Alex remarked with incomprehensible male logic. "Only take a look at what he did to poor old Robert."

"Poor old Robert be damned," Regina retorted, quite beside herself at the barbarity of the scene before her. "Robert is an *animal*! You are *all* animals! How can you do this to each other and then gloat over it. You disgust me."

"Regina!" her father said rather more mildly than was his wont. "That is hardly the appropriate language for a lady, my dear!"

Regina whirled on him. "And I suppose this is the appropriate behavior for a gentleman?" She gestured wildly around the blood-splattered room.

None of the gentlemen present seemed to have an answer for that, so Regina turned back to Alex and Geoffrey, who still stood over the colonel.

"Get out of my way," she ordered curtly. "Burton," she called, "where are you?"

"Here, milady." The batman appeared beside her instantly, his blue eyes regaining some of their twinkle.

"We shall carry the colonel up to his room, immediately," she commanded in tones that brooked no argument. "And you"—she pointed imperiously at Alex—"you will help Burton carry him."

"Regina, my love," the duke put in tentatively. "Could not one of the footmen—"

"No, certainly not," Regina snapped, hearing her brothers

flinch collectively at her audacity in talking back to their father as none of them would ever dare to do. "Alex is Richard's *friend*, you see," she said, her voice heavy with sarcasm. "I am sure he would want to make amends. Would you not, Alex?" she added sweetly.

"Hobbs?" she continued, searching the crowded room for the old butler. "Send down to Mrs. Hobbs, if you will. Tell her I shall need warm water, some of her herb ointment, possibly some laudanum, and anything else she can think of. John"—she addressed one of the footmen—"see that there is a good fire in Colonel Swinburn's room, will you? And Steven"—she turned to the second footman—"take the colonel's clothes upstairs for me, and tell Cook that I shall require a dinner tray in about an hour."

The servants disappeared instantly before this barrage of ducal commands, and Regina glared at the five Heathercott men who stood around uneasily, as if daring any of them to question her authority.

When none of them did, Regina motioned to Burton. "Come along," she said shortly, and swept out of the room.

Pausing in her task of washing blood from the patient's chin, Regina lightly traced the red scar on her husband's chest with the tip of one finger. She shivered.

"How did he get this, Burton?"

The batman looked up from his task of removing the colonel's mud-splattered boots and grinned.

"Waterloo," he replied shortly. "French saber," he added when Regina frowned. "He was one of the lucky ones, lass." This last remark was uttered so somberly that Regina shivered again.

Lucky? she thought, appalled at the notion that a man might be considered lucky to carry such a scar on his body for the rest of his life. Naturally, the alternative was even less palatable, she reminded herself. At least the colonel had not fallen on that most gory of battlefields, buried beneath heaps of other dead soldiers. Thousands and thousands of them, Alex had told her. Regina found she could not begin to imagine a thousand dead men all together.

She rinsed out the cloth in the warm, lemon-scented water and gently dabbed at the gash on the colonel's cheekbone. How that saber wound on his chest must have bled, she thought. And it might so easily have been fatal. She repressed yet another shudder, pausing to examine the man on the bed. He was big, she thought. Big and more heavily muscled than Robert. But he was not really as big as he had seemed earlier, standing down in the hall. She had felt a tremor of desire at the sight of him. He had looked so wild, so powerful, so invincible; he had overwhelmed her senses.

But the colonel was not invincible, of course, and the saber scar was proof of it. Now, here he lay unconscious, completely in her power. The notion titillated her. Regina ran the damp cloth down the strong column of his neck and along the sloping shoulder. She was tempted to run her bare fingers over the same path, but Burton had finished removing the ruined boots and had come to stand beside her.

"I think bascilicum powder would be better than ointment for this gash," she said, gently pressing the cloth against the wound, which still bled sluggishly.

Burton handed her the powder, which Regina applied carefully, wondering who had tended the colonel's saber wound.

"Were you wounded at all, Burton?" she demanded suddenly.

The batman gave her a huge grin. "Not me, lass. No Frenchie had the stomach for it. Took one look at me ugly phiz and turned tail like frightened conies they did. Can't say I minded, though."

"That is a Banbury tale if ever I heard one," Regina retorted, quite unable to resist responding to the batman's infectious grin. "Help me to cover the colonel with the eiderdown, Burton, and then you can go on down and have your supper," she said. "Tell Cook I am ready for my tray now, if you will."

After Burton had gone, Regina wrapped her shawl around her shoulders and settled herself in a chair beside the bed. John, the footman, came in to tend to the fire again, which was burning brightly, the flames sending their dancing shadows against the bed curtains. Regina had ordered the curtains drawn around the colonel's bed on three sides to keep any drafts out, and as she gazed at the still form under the covers, she was struck by an unsettling thought. How cozy it must be, she thought wistfully, for a wife to cuddle up to her husband in his bed.

If she focused her imagination on it, Regina found, she could almost transport herself under the covers beside the colonel. With very little effort, she imagined herself touching him, running her hand, as she had wanted to do earlier, across that wide expanse of bare chest, through the thatch of black hair, until her fingers reached the indented ridge of the scar. There she paused, her fingers moving of their own accord down the ridge until they touched the waistband of his breeches. There they stopped, drawn to explore the length of the scar in its downward slant, yet hesitant to take such unspeakable liberties with a man who was still a stranger to her.

She closed her eyes and leaned her head back, smiling at her own unsuspected shamelessness. But why not? she asked herself. It was not as though she were really touching him, was it? She merely imagined that she was. What harm was there in that? Regina had never before imagined quite as vividly the erotic pleasure to be derived from touching a man's body. If doing it in her imagination could produce this delightful tingling in her own, she wondered, how might it feel to do it on a real live man? The palms of her hands prickled with anticipation, and Regina felt her lips part in a slow, sensuous smile.

"What naughty thoughts have provoked that mysterious smile, my lady?"

The words were spoken so softly that for a moment Regina thought she had dreamed them. Then she opened her eyes with a jolt and stared at the man on the bed. The colonel was propped up on one elbow, regarding her with a quizzical gleam in one eye. The other was still half closed and turning decidedly dark with a bruise the size of a saucer.

She bolted to her feet, her face flaming with embarrassment. Had her thoughts been so transparent? Regina wondered, all too conscious of the immodest visions she had allowed to roam freely through her mind.

"Y-you must not get up Colonel," she said unsteadily. "You took a terrible beating, you know."

"How is your brother?" he inquired, ignoring her warning by swinging his legs over the edge of the bed and sitting up. This seemed to cause him considerable pain, for he clapped both hands to his head and groaned.

"I told you not to get up," Regina pointed out accusingly. "And if you must know, Robert thinks you have broken his nose."

"Good," the colonel muttered with considerable relish. "Serves him right for being a bloody fool."

"You are both bloody fools," Regina snapped with fulminating honesty. " 'Tis a miracle he did not break yours. Robert spars with Jackson, you know. So does Nevil, for that matter, but Robert says he is all bluster and no bottom, whatever that means."

"It means he still has a lot to learn," the colonel said, rocking his head in his hands and groaning. "The devil take it, but my head hurts."

"Lie down again, and I shall prepare a potion to cure that," Regina said firmly, and was surprised when the patient obeyed her. Quickly she measured out several drops of laudanum into a glass of water and brought it over to the bed. "Here, drink this, and you will soon feel better."

When he made no move to take the glass, Regina saw no other alternative but to slip her arm under his head and raise it. She was thankful that his eyes were closed.

"Drink this," she repeated, touching the rim of the glass to his lips. He took a long draft and sighed, opening his eyes.

"I feel better already," he murmured, and Regina felt gratified until she realized that his eyes were focused on her neckline, low enough in upright position, but considerably more revealing in her present inclination, half hanging over the bed.

She pressed the glass against his mouth, which twitched in the shadow of a smile. "Drink it all," she said sternly. The colonel obeyed her, but took his own sweet time about it, his eyes never leaving the swell of her breasts.

When he had swallowed the last drop, Regina settled his head rather abruptly back onto the pillow and stood up, glaring down at him, her cheeks burning. She was mortified to see that the smile still lingered on his well-shaped mouth. "When you wake up, you will feel much better," she said, setting the empty glass on the table with a thump. "By that time, Burton will bring you up something to eat."

The colonel widened his eyes. "Burton? So Burton is here then?"

"Where else would he be?" Regina answered sharply, not at all anxious to elaborate on the circumstances leading to the presence of the colonel's batman at Wexley Abbey. "Now, try to sleep."

"Regina," he said after a brief pause, during which he examined her keenly, "there is something I need to say to you."

"Not now," she broke in quickly, her heart hammering uncomfortably at the thought of hearing more recriminations from this man who had come to mean so much to her. "And besides, I think you have said quite enough already," she added, unable to keep the bitterness out of her voice. "I for one do not wish to hear another word about that lying brother of yours."

After a prolonged silence, Regina began to relax, imagining that the opiate had taken effect. Then she heard the colonel mutter quite audibly. "I cannot understand why Charles would lie to me."

Regina bristled. "But you believe that I would, I suppose?" she exclaimed sharply. "Is that what you are insinuating, sir?"

The colonel tried to sit up, but his body would not obey him. "I did not say that, my d-dear," he murmured, his words beginning to slur.

Regina was not to be mollified so easily. "I heard perfectly well what you said," she said bitterly. "You would prefer to believe your precious brother innocent rather than me. How you can be so blind after hearing what those poor females in Brussels had to say about him, I cannot imagine." She glared at him, heedless of the tears forming in her eyes.

"Why d-did you . . ." the colonel began, his head falling forward as sleep invaded his faculties. "Why did you lead me to b-believe . . . to believe you were one of them, Regina?" He jerked his head up and stared her straight in the eye, before slowly sinking back against the pillow.

Regina laughed mockingly, but her heart felt like granite in her breast. Her mistakes were catching up with her, she thought cynically, and it served her right for making such a muddle of her life. Had she been able to see as clearly at twenty-two what she saw today, she might never have imagined herself in love with a charming, lying rogue. She might have encouraged the elder brother instead—for she clearly remembered glimpsing the admiration in his dark eyes before she made it abundantly plain that she preferred the company of the younger man.

Except for that brief interlude in the summer house, the colonel had never again looked at her with admiration. All she had discovered in him was coldness, dislike, perhaps even contempt. Particularly contempt, she thought miserably, if he believed her to be one of his brother's *amourettes*.

"You were quite ready to believe it, if I remember rightly," she could not help reminding him. "But if you must know, I hoped that if you thought me no longer an innocent, you would refuse to wed me," she confessed with brutal honesty.

"Silly chit," the colonel muttered, gazing at her from beneath drooping lids. "I did not believe it at all, but I could not take the chance."

"Chance?" Regina repeated, puzzled at the drift of the colonel's words. "What chance do you mean?"

The man on the bed made another attempt to raise his head, but it flopped back drunkenly. "The chance that my b-brother had dishonored you . . . as he d-did Helen . . . and s-so many others. I h-had to p-protect . . ." His voice faltered and died away.

Regina felt her mouth drop open.

If what she had just heard was correct, then she would have to face the unpleasant and startling fact that the colonel had not agreed to take her to wife because the powerful Duke of Wexley had demanded it of him. In that the dowager had been right. It was not coercion that had forced her son to wed. But the colonel's mother had been wrong to imagine that Sir Richard had embraced matrimony for any tenderer reasons, or because the duke's daughter had reminded him of his former love, the elusive Lady Helen.

No, she thought, feeling the implications of this revelation chase all rational thought from her mind. The colonel had agreed to wed for none of these reasons. He had done it because he had to protect his brother. Had he not just said as much?

Regina shuddered, feeling the chill of despair creep into her very marrow.

She stepped closer to the bed and saw that the colonel had at last fallen into a deep slumber. She gazed down at the strong jaw, the lean cheeks, tanned by the suns and winds of France, the generous mouth, now softly relaxed in sleep, and the rise and fall of his breathing, and nostalgia for what might have been rose up to choke her.

On sudden impulse, Regina reached out to brush a lock of dark hair from the colonel's forehead, and the mere touch of him made her fingers tingle. She straightened her shoulders and told herself firmly not to be a mawkish peagoose. Surely Lady Regina Elizabeth Constance Heathercott would not dream of giving up this easily.

It might well be true that Sir Richard Swinburn had married her for all the wrong reasons. He had not entered parson's mousetrap for the Duke of Wexley, nor for himself, and only incidentally to redeem her reputation. No, the colonel—odious, endearing, stiff-necked, incomprehensible creature that he was—had sacrificed himself for his brother. For Charles, a man who was not worthy to wipe the colonel's boots.

Impulsively Regina leaned forward and placed a soft kiss on her husband's weathered cheek. Her lips lingered sensuously on the rough skin. Without quite knowing what she did, but drawn implacably by some inner need, Regina's lips moved across the curve of his cheek and came to rest beside his mouth. Feeling deliciously wanton, she pressed a kiss tenderly into the corner of his mouth.

No, she told herself, with more assurance this time, a Heathercott did not give up at all. She would make this man hers if she had to spend the rest of her life in the endeavor.

CHAPTER FOURTEEN

Encounter with the Past

Sir Richard came awake slowly in the unaccustomed luxury of a warm room, whose brightly glowing fire had evidently been tended all through the night. The curtains had been closed around three sides of the bed, creating a cozy cocoon of warmth that Richard, accustomed to bivouac in the roughest of accommodations, found rather suffocating. He pushed aside the covers and sat up, enjoying a glow of satisfaction as he recalled the events of the previous evening.

As Lady Regina had pointed out, he must have taken a severe beating, and his bruised knuckles felt stiff and raw with the violence of the punches he had inflicted upon Gresham. He grinned into the dimness of the room. He had enjoyed hitting that handsome face, pounding that aristocratic nose, and punching that clean, sculptured chin, he realized with sudden insight, and the reason appeared all too obvious. The marquess had the same striking blond charm and flawless profile as his brother Charles. Gresham also reminded the colonel of Major Westbrook, another fair-haired bastard who never seemed to have the least trouble attracting any female he fancied. A rogue who had dared to set his sights on Lady Regina in Brighton, Richard recalled. On *his* Regina.

An uncomfortable thought struck him. Had he really enjoyed hitting the marquess so much because of this resemblance to Charles? Richard had never hit his brother, even when they were lads. Not even when he had caught Charles with his hands all over Lady Helen so many years ago. Perhaps he should have done so, he thought wryly. Perhaps he was partially responsible for Charles's irresponsible, selfish, womanizing ways.

Deprived of his father at an early age, Richard had felt the duty of guiding his young brother into manhood fall heavily upon his shoulders. Had he, perhaps unconsciously, resented that responsibility? he wondered. Should he have taken stronger measures when Charles had shown those first signs of the man he was to become? For Lady Helen had not been the first by any means, Richard rememberd with sudden clarity. There had been numerous village girls, fresh-faced country lasses who had caught his eye when he began to notice such things. Some of them had caught more than his eye. At first he had been amused to see his brother, barely fifteen at the time and with the body of a young god, follow in his footsteps.

Yes, Richard mused, his mind reaching back gingerly into areas of the past he had deliberately suppressed. At first he had been amused and perhaps a little flattered that young Charles had approved of his taste in females. That had all suddenly changed with little Sally Crofts, the miller's shy, elfin-like daughter. He had carefully explained to Charles that a gentleman did not force a girl to lie down with him in the poppy-studded fields of rye, or behind the sweet-smelling haystacks. But one afternoon he had come across a distraught Sally, tearstained face pink with shame, trudging home across the back pasture, and had discovered his brother's perfidy.

Charles had, he later found out, promised marriage.

"A gentleman does not deceive a girl with false promises," he had told his brother sternly after a lengthy and decidedly painful interview with Mr. Crofts in the library at Willow Park.

"Oh, she was willing enough," Charles had explained flippantly. "The wench could not bring herself to the sticking point, so I helped her along a little," he added, vastly amused at this vulgar witticism. "She liked it well enough, Dick, take my word for it."

Little Sally Crofts had been packed off to visit her aunt in Cornwall, and the incident, unpleasant though it had been at the time, had been forgotten. Or had he deliberately put it out of his mind? Richard asked himself now. Had he not wished to admit to himself that Charles, his own flesh and blood, had a dishonorable streak in his nature that he did not want to recognize? Perhaps that had been the time to give his brother a sound thrashing. Their father, a stern and proud man, would undoubtedly have done so, Richard admitted wryly. And by failing to do so, had he unwittingly contributed to his brother's long career of irresponsible womanizing? Had he himself been instrumental in the ultimate seduction of Lady Helen?

The notion was an unpleasant one, and the colonel hastily suppressed it. Such a line of logic would inevitably lead to the three young women in Brussels, to their unshakable conviction that Charles would really wed them; it would lead straight to Regina, to her illusion that she was betrothed to a gentleman who would keep his promise to her.

At least that promise had been kept, he mused, gingerly prob-

ing his left eye, still puffy and tender from yesterday's bout of
fisticuffs. By the wrong Swinburn, of course, but kept nevertheless. Richard grimaced as his fingers traced the gash on his cheek.
It was more painful than the battered eye, and he suspected he
would carry the scar for a long time. He wondered if he had left a
lasting mark on the marquess's handsome face. Perhaps the broken nose, if indeed it was broken, might mar the perfect symme-
try of that godlike profile. He hoped so.

This uncharitable thought was interrupted by Burton, who burst
into the room with shaving water and a mug of steaming tea.

"Top o'the morning to ye, Colonel," the batman called out in a
voice that matched his size and girth. The habitual merry twinkle
had returned to his blue eyes, which examined his master's visage
keenly. "Cut bothering ye, is it, sir? Well, her ladyship left some
of that powder she used on ye last night." He set the shaving
water down and handed the colonel his tea.

"Make for a tricky shave this will," Burton remarked, applying
the bascilicum powder liberally to the colonel's raw cheek. "But
it ain't festering and that's a blessing. We have her ladyship to
thank for that, of course. Regular dab at patching up the wounded
she is, and no mistake. We could have used the likes of her at
Waterloo."

The information that Lady Regina had attended him herself
surprised the colonel. Richard had thought sickbed duties would
be beneath her, but apparently he had again misjudged his wife.
Burton's pithy account of Regina's firm control of the situation
brought a smile to his face. So that delightful vision of his wife
leaning over him, her full breasts invitingly close to his face, had
not been a dream after all.

He was not given much time to dwell on such pleasant thoughts
before a sharp knock on the door announced the arrival of Alex
Heathercott, who came to see if the invalid had regained enough
of his energy to go out shooting.

"But I am not an invalid," the colonel protested, glad to return
to this easy camaraderie with one of his few true friends. "Is your
brother to be one of the party?"

"If you mean Robert, then the answer is no," Alex replied with
a laugh. "He looks as though a whole regiment of Lancers has ridden over his face and is not feeling up to anything more strenuous
than lying abed with a cold poultice on his nose. It is not broken,
by the way," he added. "Robert asked me to be sure to set that
rumor to rest."

"Pity." Richard laughed. "Your brother is a very competent

boxer, Alex, but perhaps too controlled for the real world. I'm a street fighter myself. Learned the hard way when I joined the Army."

"Robert was impressed, although he will probably never admit it. I have never seen anyone press him as hard as you did last night, Dick. I hate to think what might have happened had you been rested."

"He has the science and I the endurance," the colonel said pensively. "You might say we are well matched. Regina calls us both bloody fools," he added, then instantly regretted bringing up his wife's name, for his friend's amusement faded.

"From what I hear, you are certainly that," Alex said dryly.

No more was said on the subject until the two men had chosen their guns from the large selection in the armory. Except for a dark, wet stain on the carpet and a missing picture from the wall, the room had returned to normal, and Richard found it difficult to remember the devastation that had reigned here so recently. Even after they had spent a very pleasant three or four hours out in the winter sunlight and bagged a dozen or more fat pigeons and an odd grouse or two did his host bring up the subject Richard had been dreading.

Not until much later, as they returned from the village inn where they had partaken of a hearty country meal and consumed numerous tankards of local ale did Alex mention his sister.

"I know it is none of my business, Dick," he began after clearing his throat several times.

"Perhaps it would be best to leave it that way, then," the colonel cut in dryly, hoping to divert his friend from expressing what was obviously on his mind.

"Gina is my sister, Dick, and I do not like to see her unhappy."

"She is also my wife," the colonel replied stonily. "And I have no wish to make her unhappy."

Alex glanced at him curiously. "That is not what she has told us, lad," he said gently. When the colonel made no move to reply, he continued uneasily. "This business about your brother is the veriest poppycock. He obviously led Gina to believe they were secretly betrothed, and while it was certainly unwise of her to listen to an offer—if indeed Swinburn ever made an offer—without our father's approval, surely you have no reason to believe that she so far forgot herself—"

"Of course, I do not," Richard cut in abruptly, unwilling to hear his previous suspicions put into words. For quite suddenly, he was as certain of Regina's innocence as he was of his own fool-ishness in mistrusting her.

Alex made no further comment about his sister, for which Richard was thankful, and their conversation proceeded along more comfortable lines until they crested the top of the hill that led down through Wexley Park to the front of the house. It was then that the colonel discovered what he should have guessed sooner, that the duchess's Christmas festivities would include a number of guests besides himself.

Even as they crossed the park, a glossy traveling chaise, piled high with trunks made its way up the drive and halted before the big studded door.

"I should go in through the kitchens, I suppose," the colonel said uneasily. "I would not wish to scare off Her Grace's guests with these battle scars." He ran a hand over his left eye, which had lost some of its puffiness but had begun to turn an interesting shade of blue.

"Nonsense, old man," Alex said, his voice betraying his amuse-ment. "I cannot make out the crest from here, but anyone who can allow those four slugs to be hitched to his carriage must surely be insensitive to such minor blemishes as black eyes. Let us greet them, shall we?"

The guests—two ladies and a portly gentleman—were already mounting the steps in the wake of the ducal butler, when the colonel and his host reached the house. One of the ladies, muffled in a fur cloak and an elegant bonnet, turned around at Alex's hearty greeting.

"Aunt Phoebe!" he called and hurried forward to receive that lady's enthusiastic embrace. "Mama mentioned that you might not come to us this year. I am glad that she was wrong."

"So am I, my dear Alex," Lady Egermont replied in her sultry voice. "I am spending Christmas with my niece in Winchester, but the weather was so fine, I prevailed upon Middlemarch to bring us both down here for a short visit."

Middlemarch? The colonel froze in mid-step. He never knew what answer he gave to Lady Egermont's cordial greeting or to her gentle twitting on his colorful eye. His eyes furtively followed the younger lady as she ascended the steps to join the portly gen-tleman, who had turned to examine the newcomers through an or-nate quizzing glass held delicately between his fat thumb and a bejeweled forefinger.

"By George," he said heartily, peering shortsightedly through the gem-studded glass, "I do believe those are two of the Heather-cott boys. Strapping fine fellows, are they not, my love?"

And then the Countess of Middlemarch glanced over her shoulder and Richard found himself looking upon a face he had hoped never to set eyes upon again for the rest of his life.

Regina's step was light that evening as she came down to the drawing room before dinner. She had spent the day helping her mother with preparations for the formal dinner and ball which was a Christmas tradition at Wexley Abbey, and had been for as long as anyone could remember. Then she had offered to assist Cook in the preparation of the seasonal baskets distributed to the tenant families. Since Regina had known her father's tenants all her life, it was no trouble at all to select just the right gift for each child, each elderly retainer, and for every family on the estate.

Next year things would be different, she told herself as she neatly folded a tiny pink woolen cardigan for the Gibsons' latest baby girl. Next year she would be doing this task for the tenants at Willow Park, she thought, vowing that by then she would know the names of every last one of her husband's tenants as a good chatelaine should.

She tucked the baby garment into one of the larger baskets, her fingers lingering on the tiny article. Yes, she mused dreamily, next year she might even have a baby of her own. The notion made her blush, but the prospect of carrying the colonel's child brought a sudden ache to her womb. There were certain hurdles to be overcome first, she reminded herself, the most obvious being the colonel's reluctance to cooperate in the endeavor.

Although Regina was determined to begin the seduction of her reticent husband as soon as possible, she had been vaguely relieved to learn, when she entered the breakfast room that morning, that Alex had taken the colonel off to shoot pigeons. His absence gave her the opportunity to talk to her father, for the duke had made it quite plain that he was entitled to an explanation for the destruction of his gunroom. Regina had given him a suitably tailored version of the truth.

She was also able to talk to the Marquess of Gresham.

"Robert," she exclaimed breathlessly, having run her brother to ground in the stables that afternoon, "I need your advice."

The marquess turned from the horse he was examining and cast her a jaundiced look.

"I trust you have no further quarrel with Swinburn," he remarked dryly. "I doubt I could stomach another mill with that gentleman, at least not until my nose has ceased to feel like a cursed pincushion."

Regina grinned. "Poor Robert," she teased. "Richard turned out to be handier with his fives than you had imagined, is that it?"

"Pray do not resort to cant expressions, Gina," the marquess said wearily, as though he had no hope of being heeded. "And yes, your colonel has more bottom to him than I expected. With a little training, he could match up with the best. I shall suggest it to him."

"You will do nothing of the sort, Robert," Regina exclaimed angrily. "I do not wish to spend the rest of my life patching up his face."

It was her brother's turn to grin. "And what *do* you wish to do with the rest of your life, Gina?" he asked gently, his sapphire eyes glinting with amusement.

"I wish to start a family," Regina blurted out before she lost her nerve.

"Ah! A noble endeavor," the marquess responded with a hint of cynicism. "But a subject upon which I am singularly uninformed, my dear. I advise you to apply to the colonel instead," he added laconically, turning back to his horse.

Regina felt her cheeks burn, but she would not retreat now. "That is precisely the problem, Robert," she said, determination giving her strength to continue this highly improper conversation. "Richard does not appear to be interested in . . . well, in starting his nursery, if you know what I mean." She was mortified when her brother swung around to stare at her, laughter dancing in his sapphire eyes. "I was wondering if you . . . " she hesitated, her eyes on the tip of her half-boot, which nervously shuffled back and forth in the hay.

"If I would what, Gina?"

Regina raised her eyes and saw that the marquess was no longer laughing at her. "If you would show me . . . that is, tell me how to . . ." She took a steadying gulp of air. "Tell me how to make him interested," she concluded in a rush, her cheeks blooming a deeper shade of pink.

There followed a considerable pause, during which her brother seemed to be at a loss for words. Finally, he rubbed a hand across his forehead and smiled at her dubiously. "My dear Regina," he began, in a voice tinged with reproof, "I do not think I am the best person to—"

"Of course you are, Robert," Regina interrupted crossly.

"Everyone knows you have had dozens of mistresses, so you must know what females do to entice you to—"

"That is quite enough, Regina," the marquess cut in hastily. "I do not know what rumors you have been listening to, but they are vastly exaggerated. And if you believe that all men can be enticed—as you call it—in the same way, I regret to inform you, my dear, that you are up the proverbial gum tree."

Regina stared at him for a moment, perplexed. "Are you saying that men are not always willing to . . . well, to jump at the chance to . . ." She floundered, unable to find a suitable word to express her meaning delicately.

"To jump into bed, love? " her brother completed the thought for her, a reluctant smile curving his attractive mouth. "If that is what you mean, you naughty minx, you are wrong again. Some of us are far more particular than others about whom we jump into bed with."

"Oh, dear," Regina murmured self-consciously, her eyes once more riveted on her half-boots.

"And do not ask me any more scandalous questions, Regina," the marquess said sternly. "This whole conversation is vastly improper as you must know."

Regina glanced up, noting that her brother's tone was not echoed in his eyes, which were full of compassion. She smiled shyly and ventured one final question. "Do you suppose the colonel is one of the particular ones?"

"No doubt about it, love," the marquess replied, abruptly turning back to his horse. "He also appears to be an unusually considerate fellow. But I do not think you should fret your lovely head over such matters," he added enigmatically. These things usually take care of themselves, my dear. And that is the last I shall say on the matter."

Her brother's words still rang in Regina's mind as she joined her mother in the Blue Saloon later that evening. If anything, Robert had confused her with his parting remark, and she wished that she could seek her mother's advice, but that was a step Regina had difficulty even imagining, much less acting upon.

Among the guests seated with the duchess, Regina instinctively singled out her beloved aunt, Lady Egermont, and her spirits rose instantly. Here was the very confidante she needed, she thought. Aunt Phoebe would be sure to know how to bring a recalcitrant husband to heel. After greeting several of the local gentry who flocked to the duchess's dinner table during this festive season, Regina sank onto the blue brocade settee beside her aunt.

"My darling Regina,"—Lady Egermont greeted her warmly— "I see that you are as blooming as ever, love." Before Regina could disabuse her, the countess turned to the ethereally fair lady sitting on her other side. "You remember the Countess of Middlemarch, do you not, Regina? My dear sister-in-law's eldest daughter?" she paused to interject, eyeing both younger ladies speculatively.

"Of course," Regina hastened to say, for indeed she remembered the infrequent yet vastly pleasant encounters she had enjoyed with her aunt's pale-haired relative. "I believe the last time we met was at Lady Mansfield's garden party last April, was it not? I remember quite distinctly we talked about your darling little boys. Three of them, if I recall correctly."

Lady Middlemarch's face broke into a dazzling smile at the mention of her children. "Yes, indeed," she replied in her soft, cultivated voice, "Lord Middlemarch prefers country life, so we seldom get up to London, and three small children seem to require more space than the city affords."

The life the countess painted caused Regina to smile rather wistfully.

"Your father has been telling us about his recent successes with his orchids, Regina," Lady Egermont remarked after a few minutes, sipping delicately at her sherry. "I know you share my brother's passion for these exotic plants, Regina, so I am counting on you to give us a tour of the conservatory tomorrow." She waved a bejeweled hand in the direction of the huge hothouse the duke had commissioned years ago adjoining the saloon. "Helen is interested in starting her own collection."

Although Regina would have preferred to hear more about the countess's children, she smiled at her aunt. "Orchids are much easier to grow than is generally supposed," she said. "In fact, they thrive on a minimum of fuss, a characteristic that my father finds vastly endearing." She glanced at the gilded clock on the marble mantle. "There is still time before dinner for a quick tour if you wish. What do you say, Aunt?"

Lady Egermont shook her luxurious curls. "Not for me, dear. I have promised your mother to help with the guests. But by all means take Lady Middlemarch with you. I can see she is all agog to see the orchids."

This was true, Regina discovered, for the young countess had risen to her feet excitedly, her blues eyes shining. "Indeed I am," she affirmed eagerly. "That is if you think we can slip out unnoticed."

"I can assure you we shall hardly be missed," Regina whispered, catching the countess by the hand and leading her swiftly to the towering glass wall that permitted an uninterrupted view of the tangle of greenery in the huge hothouse. She opened one of the many glass doors and ushered her excited guest into the lush warmth of the conservatory.

"It is quite like a jungle," Lady Middlemarch said in an awed voice. "At least what I imagine a jungle must be like, not having been in one myself."

Regina led the way down the damp brick pathways, past masses of fragile-leafed ferns from tropical Africa, pots of oddly shaped, prickly succulents from India, massive clay tubs of flowering shrubs from China, and trailing vines that reached out with curling fingers to brush their gowns, until they reached a far corner of the room. Here she paused, overcome as she always was by the brilliant colors, exotic shapes, and regal elegance of the blooms that had so fascinated the duke that he had made the collection of them a lifelong hobby.

"Papa's collection has been the subject of various articles in horticultural journals," she said proudly. "Only last year, the Royal Horticultural Society arranged a tour of the Wexley Conservatory for its members. Apparently it was an enormous success, for there are plans afoot for a second tour next summer."

"I can quite see why," the countess murmured, obviously dazzled by the display of color. "Are you sure you were not funning when you said they are easy to care for?"

"Absolutely," Regina answered with a laugh. "I am sure it is far more challenging to raise three little boys, as you have, Lady Middlemarch, than to grow a dozen orchids."

The countess smiled and laid a small hand tenderly on her slender figure. "I hope to make that four before the summer is out," she confessed shyly. "I have but recently discovered I am again in that happy state."

A stab of envy so sharp that she almost gasped with the pain of it struck Regina in the region of her heart. "I envy you, my lady," she blurted out before she considered the propriety of her words. She blushed furiously when the countess turned to stare at her.

"Oh, I am sure that when you marry this miracle will happen to you, too," the countess said, her voice soft with compassion.

Regina pulled herself together and smiled. "I see that my dear aunt, sad rattle that she is, has not told you that I am recently wed," she said. "It is not surprising that you have not heard of it, since the wedding took place in Brussels. I married a soldier," she added, the picture of the colonel, severely handsome in his regimentals, flashing through her mind.

Lady Middlemarch's blue eyes looked startled. "Then I must certainly congratulate you on your choice, my dear. And it is only a matter of time before you, too, will be a mother." She clasped Regina's hands and gave them an impulsive squeeze. "You must not despair so soon," she added with an encouraging smile. "I had to wait nearly seven months before I was blessed with my first." She turned away to examine a spray of purple butterfly-like blossoms on a tall, arching stem.

"A soldier, you say? Then I assume that your husband was with the Duke of Wellington at Waterloo?"

"Oh, yes," Regina said. "We were wed shortly before the battle." She saw no reason to enlarge on that basic truth.

"How romantic!" the countess exclaimed, her blue eyes pensive. "I almost married a soldier myself once. All this was long ago, of course," she added hastily, when Regina showed her surprise.

"Colonel Swinburn was on Wellington's staff, so he was in the thick of things," Regina remarked absentmindedly. She wondered if she dared to ask the beautiful countess's advice on enticing a reluctant husband to her bed. Lady Middlemarch obviously excelled at this art, but Regina hesitated to reveal her dilemma to a virtual stranger, however pleasant.

"Swinburn?" Lady Middlemarch spoke with unusual sharpness and Regina glanced at her in surprise. "Did you say Swinburn, my lady?"

"Please call me Regina," she said with a smile. "And yes, my husband is Colonel Swinburn."

The countess had gone pale, Regina noticed in alarm, her translucent complexion taking on a waxen tinge.

"Richard or Charles?"

Regina raised an eyebrow in surprise at this evidence that the countess was acquainted with the Swinburn brothers. "Why, Sir Richard Swinburn, naturally. His brother is a scoundrel of the first stare."

Lady Middlemarch smiled sadly. "I am well aware of that fact, my dear Regina," she murmured, half to herself. "I learned that to my sorrow many years ago. But that is all in the past now," she continued abruptly, evidently determined not to dwell on this painful subject. "And I must congratulate you all over again, my dear," she added with forced gaiety. "Sir Richard is a fine gentleman; I used to know him well. A man to be trusted, which is more than one can say of his brother."

An odd sensation came over Regina as she listened to the countess's words. Was not Richard's old love also a Lady Helen? *Lady Helen*, she repeated to herself. No, this beautiful, gentle creature could not be Richard's Lady Helen, could she? The very female who had betrayed him with his own brother? But if she were, a little voice inside her nagged, was it to be wondered at that he remembered her after all these years? Could he be blamed for still loving this pale beauty with the tragic eyes?

Regina's world suddenly turned bleak and her heart felt like lead, cold and hard, inside her. Could this woman, this mother with three children and another expected soon, be the reason the colonel had no heart to give to his wife? Was it still in thrall to this Lady Helen who had broken it ten years ago?

In a sudden attack of cowardice, Regina wished she could run away again. Her recent determination to make a real marriage out of the awkward patchwork arrangement she had been forced into by fate wavered alarmingly. But where could she run? she wondered, disgusted at this unprecedented missishness. She wanted to run to Richard, to snuggle in his arms as she had that evening in the summer house. If only she could be sure that he wanted her there.

A great yearning came over her, a yearning for some of the fulfillment Lady Helen had found in life, even though she did not have Richard. And who did have him? a defiant little voice spoke suddenly from a bright corner of her mind. Why, Lady Regina Elizabeth Constance Heathercott had him, did she not? Although she was Lady Swinburn now, she mused, the title still uneasy on her tongue. Abruptly she needed to see him, to know that, even though he did not yet desire her, he was indeed hers.

Regina swept a distraught glance through the glass wall into the Blue Saloon and, as if conjured up by her feverish brain, the colonel materialized before her eyes, standing with Alex, both staring at her through the glass.

And then he had pushed open the door and was striding toward her along the damp brick path, his face set in grim lines belied by the concern in his dark eyes.

"Regina," he said sharply, reaching her side in an instant and encircling her waist with his arm. "You looked as though you would swoon. Has something frightened you?"

Comforted beyond words by this show of tenderness from the

very man she had recently despaired of winning, Regina indulged herself by leaning against the bulwark of the colonel's chest and uttering a small sigh. As far as she could determine, her husband had not even glanced at Lady Helen Middlemarch, a circumstance she found vastly comforting.

"Lady Middlemarch and I were admiring Papa's orchids," she said in a low voice. "But it is rather overheated in here, which made me feel a little faint."

Regina had never swooned in her life, but it felt so indescribably pleasant to be supported against a gentleman's chest like this that she judged the dissimulation entirely justified.

"I believe we should remove the ladies to the drawing room immediately," Alex suggested, offering Lady Middlemarch his arm and bearing her off without further argument.

After a moment, Regina reluctantly straightened her shoulders, but she did not move away from the sheltering embrace of that strong arm. She glanced up at the colonel through her lashes, wishing that she had listened more carefully when her Aunt Phoebe had explained the principles of flirting to her. Aunt Phoebe knew all there was to know about flirting, Regina recalled enviously, and if she had paid attention, she would not be standing here like an old ape-leader, without the least notion about how to go on.

"What did she say to upset you so?"

The brusque question was so unexpected that Regina opened her eyes wide. "Who?" she murmured, disconcerted by his hooded gaze.

"Helen," he said coldly. "What did she say to you, Regina?"

"So you do know her," she said, a statement rather than a question.

"Yes. Did she not tell you?"

"She *is* your Lady Helen, then? You do not deny it?"

The colonel looked at her strangely, Regina thought, but he did not answer her question. Instead he took her arm and escorted her out of the hothouse into the drawing room, where Hobbs had just announced that dinner was served.

CHAPTER FIFTEEN

Settling Accounts

At the breakfast table the following morning, Regina had to endure the sight of her husband being monopolized by her brothers as the gentlemen put away substantial servings of York ham, soused herrings, buttered eggs, enormous slabs of rare beef, besides the usual kippers, muffins with strawberry jam, and toast, washed down with indecent quantities of ale. All this amidst a boisterous exchange of masculine talk on subjects as diverse as horses, boxing, the prospects of lasting peace on the Continent, and the quality of ale at the local inn.

On the whole, the spectacle made Regina feel quite ill, and she was pleased to note that Lord Middlemarch, whose girth suggested otherwise, displayed a pleasing moderation in his choice of sustenance. The earl had escorted his wife into the room himself and settled her beside the duchess, who made a point to preside over her own breakfast table. He had, with a tender gallantry entirely new to Regina, selected his wife's meal with his own hands and set the plate before her with a loving smile.

Obviously Lord Middlemarch doted on his wife, and Lady Middlemarch appeared to bask in his open admiration. She demurred at the quantity of food set before her, but when the earl whispered something in her ear, she blushed prettily and smiled up at him with such affection in her blue eyes that Regina felt a lump form in her throat.

As she toyed with her toast, Regina examined Lord Middlemarch more carefully, curious to discover what it might be about this quite ordinary gentleman that had won him the hand of a lady who was undoubtedly a diamond of the first water. The earl was actually quite stout, she noted, and not even tall or broad-shouldered as all the Heathercott men were. And the colonel, too, she mused, her eyes flicking briefly in his direction, only to find him laughing at one of Nevil's scandalous witticisms.

Middlemarch was decidedly finicky about his attire, and dressed in the first stare of fashion, which unfortunately he was not built to show off to the best advantage. His pale yellow pantaloons displayed a pair of thighs more conspicuous for their plumpness than any claim to elegance, and the striped green waistcoat he sported this morning was of a particularly gaudy hue. The earl's face would never be deemed handsome, and while his plump, ruddy cheeks suggested a kindly uncle, there was a merry twinkle in his eyes and a firmness to his jaw that spoke of good humor, strength, and amiability, all qualities that a woman might well covet in a husband.

His wife apparently appreciated him well enough, for Regina intercepted a warm, intimate glance between them that contrasted vividly with the barrenness of her own marriage. The bluff earl suddenly seemed very appealing to her indeed, and she watched wistfully as he adjusted the shawl about his wife's shoulders and motioned for the butler to pour her a cup of tea.

What should a female do to elicit such tenderness in a husband? she wondered, unable to comprehend how she, a duke's daughter who imagined she would have the world handed to her on a silver platter, had achieved none of the romantic dreams of her young girlhood. Actually, she no longer wished for those foolish fantasies, she realized with sudden insight. Fantasies of a charming suitor, eternal love, and happiness. No, the only charmer she knew had turned out to be a complete rotter, and love, even the briefest, most ephemeral kind had proved to be as elusive and unattainable as the man.

Never in her wildest dreams had Regina imagined that one day she would feel so sorry for herself. Or that she would actually envy a woman married to a stout, red-faced, foppish gentleman, who looked more like a farmer than a lover. But who was to say how a lover should look? Regina wondered, astounded by the new direction of her thoughts. All she knew was she had never had one, and the longer she watched Lord Middlemarch's fatuous smile, the more she felt deprived and heartsore at what she was missing.

"What about it, Gina?" Nevil exclaimed loudly from the other end of the table, interrupting her morbid meditations. She glanced at him and saw that all the gentlemen were looking at her expectantly. She had no earthly idea what her brother's question had been and was in no mood for his usual teasing.

"What about what?" she said coolly.

"Nevil has suggested that we should bring in the Yule log this afternoon, dear," her mother explained. "Since the weather is so fine."

"Yes," Nevil added, his blue eyes dancing with natural exuberance. "You always know where the largest ones are to be found, Gina, so you must lead the expedition."

"I have promised to help Mama—"

"Oh, no, dear," her mother intervened quickly. "Your aunt has kindly offered to assist me this afternoon, and I am sure Lady Middlemarch would enjoy a stroll in the woods before she leaves the Abbey. The trees are so lovely at this time of the year," she continued, addressing her guest. "And if the weather holds, it should be very pleasant indeed."

So it was that the younger members of the party found themselves wandering in the woods that afternoon, the gentlemen forging ahead in hopes of scaring up a rabbit or fat grouse, while Regina strolled along beside Lady Middlemarch, who had been delighted to join in the traditional search for the appropriate log.

A light snow had fallen the night before and the pristine contours of the park, dotted with white-capped firs and cedars glittered in the pale winter sunlight. Normally such an outing would have animated Regina to join her youngest brother in the antics he was indulging in, romping with the duke's Irish wolfhound, Ajax, or encouraging the liver-and-white setters to chase the unwary rabbit that dared show his nose above ground. But today her thoughts were on other matters, and she was looking forward to quizzing Lady Middlemarch on the finer points of keeping a husband as happy and attentive as the earl.

These designs came to naught, however, for no sooner had the log been discovered and hitched to the team of dray horses brought along by one of the grooms for that purpose, than Nevil gathered up a handful of snow and hurled at his sister.

The shot went wild, but Regina was not in the mood for frivolity.

"Do stop acting like a child, Nevil," she said in a frosty voice, which elicited a raucous guffaw from her youngest brother.

"Do not say that marriage has made a spoilsport out of you, Gina," he teased, throwing another one that caught her on the shoulder.

Regina was tempted to yell back that marriage had made her nothing but miserable, and retreat to the Abbey to sulk in private, but she knew this was impossible. She glanced at Lady Middlemarch, who showed every sign of wishing to take part in the snow fight that was brewing.

"Tell you what," Nevil shouted eagerly. "There are five of us and two ladies, so I propose we play a version of hit-the-bull's-eye. Robert can be the referee; Alex, Richard, and Lady Middlemarch on one side; me, Geoffrey, and Gina on the other."

Regina felt her spirits rise in spite of herself. "Perhaps you should tell Lady Middlemarch exactly what hit-the-bull's-eye means, Nevil," she suggested, wondering if the countess might not find the game too rough for her taste.

"The ladies are the bull's-eyes naturally," Nevil explained, favoring the countess with a broad wink. "Each team tries to get in as many hits as possible, while protecting their own bull's-eye. The ladies may duck, but they must not run, and the hitters may not come closer than twenty feet to the target."

Regina glanced at the countess. "If you do not care for such childish games, please do not feel obliged to participate," she said.

"Oh, no," Lady Middlemarch replied, her cheeks pink with anticipation. "It does sound like fun, and I shall trust the gentlemen on my team to protect me from getting pelted too heavily."

It was then that Regina realized that her husband had, all unwittingly of course, been placed in the position of defending his former love from the flying snowballs. She caught his eye and saw that a similar thought was going through his mind. She wished they had been on the same team, for she would have enjoyed being defended by him, but he was now committed to hitting her, a role she hoped he would not take too seriously.

She took up a position on the slope of a gentle hill, knowing from past experience that it was more difficult to score a hit at that angle. Lady Middlemarch placed herself in the center of a clearing, and was all too soon the target of several hits by an exuberant Nevil. Regina was adept at ducking and escaped the majority of the missiles aimed at her until she took a direct hit on the left cheek from the colonel, who had circled up the slope for a better position, while Alex tried valiantly to ward off Nevil's enthusiastic barrage.

The blow took her by surprise and she staggered, tripped, and fell full length in the snow. In an instant the colonel was at her side, kneeling over her, his eyes dark with anxiety.

"Forgive me, Regina," he murmured amid gleeful shouts from Alex, who reminded the referee that a target downed was worth ten extra points. "I thought you would duck." He lifted her up effortlessly and steadied her with one arm loosely around her waist. With his handkerchief he gently removed the snow that clung to her cheek and mopped up the water that threatened to run down her neck. He seemed about to say more, but Nevil's impatient urgings to get back to the game forced him to return to the other side to deflect a renewed attack by Regina's team to score a downed target of their own.

Eventually Lady Middlemarch succumbed to Nevil's determined onslaught and sat down in the snow to the accompaniment of squeals of triumph from the opposite team. Regina was glad to see that it was Alex rather than Richard who helped the countess to her feet and dusted off her coat. Before Nevil could call for a resumption of the game, the Earl of Middlemarch hurried into the clearing, accompanied by the duke. The earl would not hear of his wife continuing such a rough game, in fact, Regina suspected he was none too pleased to find her romping in the snow with such abandon.

"Her Grace has sent us to call you all in to tea, my dear," he said after Lady Middlemarch had assured him that no bones were broken and she had suffered no bruises whatsoever. "In your condition, my love, you must take better care of yourself," he said in a serious voice, all the while clasping his wife's hands as though she might shatter into a thousand pieces. He extended his arm and, flanked by the duke, bore his wife off toward the warmth of the duchess's drawing room

The rest of the party straggled along behind, and Regina, despairing of receiving the same attention from her husband, fell in step with Nevil, who began a heated argument about whether or not he was to be trusted with his sister's curricle and four.

"I would be inclined to agree with my wife," the colonel remarked when Nevil demanded his opinion. The novelty of hearing the colonel refer to her as his wife created a chaotic sensation in Regina's breast, and as the two men continued their argument, she allowed herself to wonder when that sweet title would become a reality.

These pleasant ruminations were interrupted as they neared the Abbey by the sight of a smart traveling chaise drawn up before the door.

"That is one of Papa's," Regina remarked excitedly. "I asked him to send over to Langley to fetch your mother," she added, glancing up at the colonel's face to see his reaction. "Lady Swinburn had expressed a desire to accept Mama's invitation, but I knew she would hardly like to drive down to Hampshire by herself."

"That is very thoughtful of you, Regina," he said, a small smile curling his lips and making Regina's heart do strange things.

Her joy was short-lived.

No sooner had they entered the great hall in the wake of the Middlemarches and the duke than Regina heard a charming, faintly flirtatious, and all too familiar voice complimenting Lady Middlemarch on her looks.

"Not a day older than when I saw you last, my dear Helen," Charles murmured with practiced smoothness. "And that must be nearly ten years ago, was it not? No doubt your remember the circumstance as well as I." The smirk that accompanied this cruel remark made Regina's heart falter.

The dowager, who had been exchanging greetings with the duchess, turned around at this. "Helen?" she said, her voice high with shock. "My dearest Helen! How delighted I am to see you again, child." She came forward, arms open, and Lady Middlemarch stepped into her embrace and hugged the dowager with a hint of desperation.

Deprived of his first victim, Charles turned toward Regina, who shrank back against the colonel.

"And our lovely Regina," he purred, an insinuating smile on his perfectly formed lips. "What a pleasant surprise indeed to be surrounded by such lovelies." He sauntered forward a pace, but the colonel stepped in front of Regina to bar his way.

"What in Hades are you doing here?" he growled in a low voice, and Regina could almost feel the hostility radiating from his rigid back.

Charles assumed an air of injured innocence. "Am I to believe that you are not happy to see me, Dick?" he murmured, flicking an imaginary piece of lint from the sleeve of his fashionably-cut coat.

"That is absolutely correct," an icy voice drawled. The Marquess of Gresham stepped forward to stand beside the colonel, and Regina quailed at the look on her brother's face. "Regina," Robert said without taking his eyes from the unwelcome guest, "escort the ladies upstairs if you will. Your husband and I have a little matter to discuss with the captain here."

Regina did not wait to be told twice. By this time the other three Heathercott men had ranged themselves beside their brother and the colonel. All hell was about to break loose, and Regina had no desire to witness another brawl.

Linking her arm through Lady Middlemarch's, she led the way upstairs, leaving her father to escort the duchess to the safety of her sitting room.

The door of the armory closed behind them with a sinister click. Not surprisingly, Richard thought, his brother appeared rather white around the gills, and was having difficulty maintaining the blustering pose he had assumed when they had hustled him away from the front hall. The colonel did not blame him; the grim-faced phalanx of Heathercotts was ominous enough to rattle the most sanguine of men. Memories of his own encounter with the wrath of Regina's brothers was still fresh in his mind, and his knuckles still ached from the punishment he had taken.

Yet he could not find it in his heart to feel sorry for Charles. The very arrogance of his brother's presence at Wexley Abbey told Richard more clearly than any words that Charles had not changed. His cynical words to Helen had, oddly enough, reminded Richard of little Sally Crofts, one of the first of a long list of females to suffer from Charles's selfish pursuit of pleasure. No, he thought with a twinge of regret as the Heathercotts crowded his brother into one corner of the room and relieved him of his coat, Charles had not changed. Would *never* change, if Richard knew anything about the matter.

But Fate had caught up with this philandering, lying charmer, the colonel mused, and for the first time in his life, Richard could not dredge up a single excuse for his brother. Not even when Charles threw him a reproachful glance did the colonel's heart waver. This time Charles had gone too far. The colonel could overlook his brother's unforgivable abuse of shy little Sally; indeed, he had already done so long ago, he realized with a feeling of chagrin at his own youthful callousness. He had also forgiven Charles's betrayal with his former betrothed, a betrayal Richard had, perhaps mistakenly—he was beginning to suspect—laid at Helen's door. But his brother's slanderous lies about Regina, Richard refused to tolerate.

The thought of his wife brought the colonel's attention abruptly back to the present. It had become abundantly clear that if he wished to make his marriage to Regina into a satisfying and lasting relationship, he would have to banish Charles from Willow Park. And Richard knew beyond a shadow of a doubt that he had never wished for anything so ardently in his life. To win his wife's forgiveness and to keep her safe, he was quite prepared to destroy anyone who threatened her happiness.

Charles cleared his throat and adopted, as he had so many times in the past, Richard thought, an air of outraged innocence.

"Are you going to stand there meditating while these thugs dismember me?" he demanded plaintively, cutting his blue eyes in Richard's direction, and letting a pathetic little smile quiver on his lips.

"These are Regina's brothers," the colonel replied flatly. "They are naturally interested in responding to the accusations you recently made against their sister."

Charles's smile faded, and he turned a shade paler. "I know nothing of any accusations, Dick," he blustered, lounging with creditable nonchalance against the wall.

The Heathercotts maintained an ominous silence, and the colonel realized that the situation was increasingly explosive.

After several minutes, Charles straightened his shoulders—Richard grudgingly admired his bravado—and waved one hand languorously at his brother. "You must have misunderstood me, my dear Richard," he said smoothly, his ready smile radiating innocence and goodwill.

Richard heard a low, throaty growl and was startled to find that it came from his own throat. "I seem to remember you gloating about enjoying my wife's favors." There, he thought bleakly, it was out in the open, and what happened next was up to Charles.

Charles's smile faltered. "She was not your wife at the time, old man—" he began, but his words were cut off when the marquess lunged at him, catching him by the cravat in a stranglehold and hoisting him bodily up in the air against the wall.

The captain kicked at his attacker furiously, but he was quickly pinned by Nevil and Alex, who jostled him roughly. He threw an appealing glance at the colonel, but Richard remained aloof, wishing he did not have to do what he knew must be done.

When the captain's face began to turn purple, Gresham let him slide to the floor and released his grip.

"Now I know that you lie," the colonel said softly, "and we are all waiting to hear your apology."

Charles grinned slyly, and for an instant Richard felt a flutter of panic. What if his brother was not lying after all? But as quickly as the thought invaded his mind, he rejected it. He believed in Regina's innocence and would defend her with his last breath.

"And exactly how do you know that, old man?" Charles jeered, his frayed confidence returning.

Richard's jaw became rigid. "Let us just say that I know without a doubt that your accusations are false," he said, forcing himself to meet his brother's gaze with a coolness he was far from feeling.

After an awkward pause, during which Charles's smile became a leer. "So?" he purred, "the citadel has fallen has it? Bravo, brother. For once you have been there before me, you dull dog, you. But do not rest on your laurels, old man," he added with another complacent sneer, "who knows what the future holds?"

What followed after that reckless remark Richard could only vaguely remember as he mounted the stairs, two at a time, intent on settling accounts with his wife as decisively as he had settled them with his brother. He recalled a scalding rage taking hold of him at Charles's unwise boast, and then of its own accord, his fist had lashed out, connecting firmly and crushingly with his brother's elegantly shaped nose. Memories became jumbled after that. The sound of bone against cartilage, the unmistakable crunch of the latter giving way to the former, the quick spurt of blood spattering onto the mangled cravat, the shock in his brother's blue eyes, devoid of all trace of smugness now, staring in disbelief and horror as the blood dripped down his handsome face.

"That one is for little Sally Crofts, you lying, randy bastard," he remembered growling deep in his throat. "This is for Regina," he added, raising his fist again. Luckily the marquess had restrained him, a grim smile on his handsome face.

"Let us take care of this bragging coxcomb for you, Richard," Gresham remarked with a laugh that brought a look of fear to the captain's pale face. " 'Tain't fair that you should have all the fun."

The colonel had been glad to leave the Heathercott brothers to put Charles back on a horse and see him off the premises. After sternly warning his brother that he would no longer be welcome at Willow Park, Richard had left the room.

Oddly, as he made his way up to his wife's sitting room, all Richard could think of was that tantalizing birthmark Regina reminded him he knew nothing about.

But he meant to find out. A smile of anticipation dissipated the dark scowl he had worn for the past half hour. Oh, yes, indeed, he thought. Before his wife was much older, she would not be able to say that her husband did not know her very well indeed.

That was a promise the colonel intended to keep.

"I warned him he might not be welcome here," the dowager murmured in a faltering voice. "But you know what Charles is, he must have his own way in everything." The elder lady sighed, rather piteously Regina thought, wondering how much her mother-in-law really knew or guessed of her youngest son's perversity.

The three ladies had retired to Regina's private sitting room after the marquess had told his sister, in a tone that brooked no argument, to clear the hall for what Regina had imagined would be a monumental brawl. They were now seated comfortably before the fire, enjoying reviving cups of tea and freshly made scones, while the two younger ladies did their best to calm the dowager's fears.

"And much as I love my son," the dowager continued painfully, "I have to admit that the wretch deserves to have his ears pinned back for him after the nasty rumors he has been spreading about our dear Regina." She took one of Regina's hands in hers and patted it reassuringly. "Richard never believed a word of it, you may be sure of that, dear."

"He believed it of *me*," Lady Middlemarch said unexpectedly. "That was ten years ago, of course, and I am glad to see that Richard is definitely wiser now." She turned to her hostess with a sad little smile on her lovely face. "You may not know this, my dear Regina, but I was once betrothed to your husband." She stopped abruptly and turned to gaze at the dancing flames in the hearth, as if the memories were too painful to speak of.

"Yes, indeed," the dowager remarked. Her voice quavered slightly as though she, too, were recalling painful memories. "Charles came between them and ruined everything, just as he is trying to do with you, my dear."

Lady Middlemarch made an impatient gesture. "I was as much to blame as he was," she said firmly.

"You were so very young, my dear Helen," the dowager protested mildly, but Lady Middlemarch waved the excuse aside.

"I was young, 'tis true," she said. "Young and supremely foolish. But I should have known the difference between true worth and false charm. If I allowed myself to be blinded by the glitter, to believe that there was indeed no harm in granting Charles a brotherly kiss, then I deserved what I got. And when Richard walked in on us, I realized that I had been deliberately betrayed into trusting a lying cad."

There was an awkward pause, during which Regina felt a rush of compassion for this lovely creature who had, in that one rash moment of weakness and misplaced trust, lost the man she had loved.

The dowager broke the silence with an audible sigh. "Regina knows all about Charles's lying ways, my dear. He deceived her into believing herself betrothed to him for nearly two years."

"Yes, I was very naive," Regina confirmed with a laugh that had none of its old bitterness. "Along with a dozen other females, if you can believe that. I personally met three of them in Brussels. Two of whom claimed to be carrying a child by him."

The dowager gasped in shock. "I know Charles is a wicked rogue with the ladies, but I find it hard to believe that—"

"There was no mistaking the condition of at least one of those poor girls," Regina interrupted firmly. "I was sadly shocked myself, but the evidence was there before my eyes. Besides, all three of them wore garnet rings similar to the one the wretch had given me two years before."

After a thoughtful pause, she admitted the truth that she had never expected to hear herself say, but which had suddenly become abundantly clear. "It was a lucky coincidence that Charles was not in Brussels at the time."

"Yes, dear," the dowager agreed, setting her empty cup down on the tray. "You were indeed lucky that Richard was there instead. That lad will never give you a moment's worry, my dear," she added with evident affection. "Richard is, if anything, too good to those he loves. Take Charles, for instance. Richard was forever getting him out of scrapes when they were boys, and then he bought him the commission in the Army and provided him with a more than generous allowance. I am not surprised that Richard found it difficult to believe ill of this brother; he doted on him almost like a father."

Another thought that had long bothered her rose to the surface of her mind as Regina listened to the dowager describe her eldest son's protective attitude toward his brother.

"It must be painful for Richard to have to admit that his brother has deliberately deceived him over the years," she murmured, her gaze lingering on Lady Middlemarch's perfect profile. "Especially concerning the breaking of his betrothal to you, Helen."

Lady Middlemarch glanced up with a rueful smile. "I daresay he may have occasionally wondered if I was quite as guilty as I appeared," she said lightly, passing her cup to her hostess to be refilled. "But that is all in the past now and best forgotten. And forgiven," she added after a slight pause.

"Have you forgotten and forgiven him?" Regina could not stop herself from asking. She had to know if the beautiful countess held any lingering feelings for the colonel in her heart.

Lady Middlemarch smiled her sweet smile, and Regina knew what her answer would be. "Oh, yes, indeed," she murmured, her eyes growing soft and dreamy. "You see, I got a second chance at happiness, my dear. My William might not be the handsomest gentleman in England, but he is certainly one of the best husbands a woman could wish for. I would not exchange him for Richard, if that is what you are wondering, dear. And not for a thousand dashingly handsome rogues like Charles."

Regina felt as though a great weight had been lifted from her heart at the countess's words. Now if only Richard might be persuaded to accept the second chance at happiness she was more than willing to give him, her own future promised to be as rosy as Lady Middlemarch's evidently was. She must find a way of breaking down the barrier behind which she knew there lurked the man whose passions she had vowed to arouse.

"I tremble to think what those ferocious brothers of yours are doing downstairs, Regina," the countess remarked, shuddering visibly. "And I have never seen Richard look quite so fierce himself. He must love you very much to be so outraged with Charles. And deeply hurt, I imagine," she added pensively. "He will need your support and understanding to survive this crisis, Regina. And your love, too, of course."

The countess's speculative blue eyes were fixed on Regina, who felt a wave of color suffuse her cheeks. "He already has that," she murmured in a low voice, knowing that she spoke nothing but the truth. She did love the colonel. More than she had, in the innocence of two years ago, imagined it was possible to love a man. She had definitely not felt anything even remotely resembling this intense, almost painful longing for Charles. She had been a romantic fool back then, much as Helen must have been when she succumbed to the temptation of Charles's false kisses. Had she not experienced the same heady euphoria herself? She had been as selfishly concerned with her ephemeral pleasure as Charles must have been, she thought, suddenly seeing her infatuation with her husband's dashing brother with wiser eyes.

There was nothing ephemeral about Regina's feelings for the colonel. His dark, brooding countenance, which once had seemed so remote and cold, and the promise in his eyes, inscrutable yet hinting at hidden passions unknown to her, had aroused her primitive female yearnings. With a sudden tremor, Regina remembered the colonel as he had stood defiantly in the hall the other evening, daring her four brothers to lay a hand on him. He had looked magnificent, irradiating a wild, masculine aura that had melted her very bones. In that precious moment, he had enchanted her. She had gazed upon him with the eyes of a woman in love, and he had filled her with a longing as old as the world itself.

Regina drew a deep, steadying breath to curb the racing of her heart. Soon, she thought. Soon she would break through that stern control he always seemed to maintain in her presence. She would touch him, she mused, run her hand over his face, his neck, and scarred chest, and his dark eyes would warm with the passion she so desperately needed to see in them.

Passion for her.

These erotic musings were interrupted by a sharp knock on the door, which opened immediately to reveal the man who had given rise to them.

The colonel paused on the threshold, his fierce expression relaxing. "I beg your pardon, ladies," he said with a hint of a smile. "I had thought to find my wife alone."

The implications of this blunt remark made Regina's face flame, but any reply she may have made was preempted by the dowager, who took one look at her son and let out a frightened screech. "Y-your shirt, Richard," she stammered nervously. "You are covered with blood. You have not killed him have you?" The tremor in her voice was clearly audible.

The dowager had vastly exaggerated the matter, Regina saw, as the colonel glanced down at his cravat, dotted with spots of what could only be blood.

"I must beg your pardon a second time, ladies," he said calmly, "for bursting in upon you in all my dirt. And to answer your absurd question, Mama, no, Charles is not dead. At least he was not when I left him," he added wryly. His eyes sought Regina's and she was sure that he was amused, a conclusion that was confirmed when he briefly raised one dark eyebrow.

"I shall go and change," he said, speaking directly to her now. "But I would beg a word with you, Regina, before you go down to dinner."

She nodded mutely, physically unable to utter a sound.

And then he was gone, the door closing softly behind him, leaving Regina with the sensation of standing before a painting shrouded with a concealing cloth.

Behind that cloth lay the revelation she had longed for. Was the colonel about to reveal to her a glimpse of the rest of her life? she wondered, conscious of a warm coil of desire spiraling up through her body.

That brief moment when she had gazed into his eyes, hooded but not without a gleam of that hidden passion she had longed to see in them, gave her reason to hope.

Perhaps the chance to touch the man she loved would come sooner than she had expected.

CHAPTER SIXTEEN

A Question of the Heart

A t the sound of the door closing, Regina's blush receded, leaving her slightly breathless. Her eyes met Lady Middlemarch's and the teasing gleam she saw there brought a second wave of color to her cheeks.

"It seems your husband is in dire need of immediate comfort," the countess murmured with a rather saucy twinkle. She rose to her feet and brushed out the creases in her skirt. "I think we should leave you, my dear Regina." Impulsively, and to Regina's astonishment, Lady Middlemarch put her arms about her and gave her an affectionate hug. "I have a feeling you will not have to wait much longer," she whispered conspiratorially, her own cheeks becoming quite pink at the indiscretion.

"I trust you may be right," she said softly, smiling at the irony of her words, whose meaning extended far beyond what the countess had intended. Yes, indeed, she thought, as soon as the two ladies had left to dress for dinner, she would give anything to make sure that Lady Middlemarch's prediction might come true.

Regina looked longingly at the door that led to her husband's bedchamber before turning away to enter her own. She came to a halt before the cherry-wood cheval mirror and stared at her reflection. Was it possible that in six short months she had changed so much? she pondered. Regina suddenly found it difficult to recognize herself as the naive, impulsive, foolish girl who had embarked on that madcap flight to Brussels last June. That innocent, romantic creature had dissolved into the past, and Regina felt no sorrow at her passing. She was a married woman now, she thought, with a woman's needs, and could feel nothing in common with that thoughtless, pampered child who had arrived in Brussels demanding to be wed to a man she had not set eyes on for two years.

Thank God that Colonel Swinburn had been there instead.

She had not seen it at the time, naturally, blinded as she had been by false illusions, but the colonel had saved her from herself. How could she have imagined, even for an instant, that Richard had been the villain in her own private Cheltenham farce, when all the time he had been the hero? How utterly thoughtless and naive of her. And how unspeakably cruel to have openly displayed her disdain and abandoned him on their wedding night. Regina shuddered at the memory of her childish arrogance. Was it any wonder that the colonel had treated her coldly ever since? Or at least most of the time, she corrected herself, recalling the delicious interlude in the summer house when he had given her his first kiss.

Regina shivered again, not with distress at the past this time, but with a bright glow of hope for the future. Abruptly, she knew what she must do. Richard had given her an excuse to go to him, and she must take it. Without waiting an instant longer in case she lost her nerve, she flew into the adjoining sitting room. Pausing only long enough to knock briefly on her husband's door, she pushed it open and stepped inside.

There, she thought, the first step was taken. She hoped those that must follow would be as simple.

The colonel had his back to her and had evidently just stripped his shirt off. He whirled at her entrance and stood, booted feet apart, dark eyes meeting hers inquiringly across the room.

Suddenly shy at the sight of so much masculine flesh—although why she should be Regina could not imagine, having seen it at close quarters once before—she hesitated.

"I-I do beg your pardon," she stammered. "I thought . . . that is, I did not mean to disturb you." The notion of escape passed briefly through her mind, but as though reading her intention, the colonel smiled faintly, and Regina's resolve steadied. She would not run away from this man again, she told herself sternly. Her first flash of fear dissolved, and she returned his smile. Before she could consider what she was doing, she had closed the space between them. Drawn by that same animal magnetism she had felt before, Regina stared up into her husband's dark eyes and caught her breath at the hint of primitive maleness she saw there.

Instead of flinging her arms about him as she felt the insane desire to do, Regina plucked the shirt from his fingers and examined it.

"I trust this blood is not yours," she said, anxiety overriding her sudden shyness.

"No," she heard him say, his husky voice causing her fingers to tremble slightly.

Regina could think of nothing else to say, but when she glanced up, the naked passion she saw in his eyes caused her to lower her own quickly. They came to rest on the pink scar slanting down his chest, and obeying an urge she made no attempt to control, Regina reached up and placed a finger gingerly on the mutilated ridge of the flesh. She distinctly felt him shudder.

"Why did you not tell me of this?" she asked softly, beginning to trace the scar downward with her finger.

She heard him swallow, and his answer when it came was husky with emotion.

"I saw no reason to distress you."

"Perhaps you thought I would not care?" Bravely she raised her eyes to meet his and was surprised at the rueful smile he gave her.

"Perhaps I did not wish my wife to know of my deformity," he said in a low voice.

This notion surprised her, and made her forget her own nervousness. "There are things a wife should know about her husband," she began, her tone lightly scolding until she remembered all the other things she did not know about this man. Her voice faltered then, and her eyes dropped.

"Really?" he said, and Regina was delighted at the wry amusement in his voice. "What things, for instance?"

Regina felt herself blush at the unspoken communication between them. Her husband knew as well as she just which things she did not know about him.

"Well, things like this," she murmured, running her finger down the scar toward his navel. "And your age," she added quickly, glad to find another neutral subject. "I do not know how old you are."

He laughed at that, and Regina felt his chest vibrate beneath her finger with the rumble of it.

"Thirty-four," he said. "I am thirty-four, my dear." His smile abruptly faded as her finger traced the scar downward. "Sweet Jesus, Regina," he groaned, his voice a husky whisper. "You have no idea what you are doing to me, love." Abruptly he grasped both her hands and placed them, palms down, on his chest.

Regina felt his nipples harden, and the sensation rocked her. A sweet intoxication seeped through her and she closed her eyes, focusing all her senses on the touch of this man's warm skin and the heavy beating of his heart beneath her fingers.

Suddenly she felt his breath on her face and his lips brushed her mouth with featherlight strokes. Her whole body seemed to come alive under his touch, but Regina wanted more than a repetition of that tender summer house kiss. Oh, much, much more. She would have it, too, she thought, and with a reckless disregard for modesty, she parted her lips and leaned into him with a little moan of pure pleasure. This man had aroused in her the needs of a woman, Regina thought, and she would not be denied.

What happened next made her wonder briefly if this could be the same cool, controlled man she had married. His mouth abruptly opened over hers, hot and demanding, and she was swallowed up in a maelstrom of such shattering new emotions that her senses reeled, and the room seemed to sway drunkenly around her. There was a ferocious desperation about the colonel's kiss that shocked and thrilled her simultaneously. Never had Regina felt so . . . so possessed by a man as she did in her husband's arms at that moment. Her breasts felt quite flattened against the hardness of his chest, and his arms were two steel bands around her that forced the very breath from her body.

Just as Regina thought she would swoon for lack of air, his kiss gentled, and his hands began to roam over her body with a singular disregard for decorum. But what did decorum matter? she thought with an odd detachment as one of the colonel's hands cupped her derriere and pressed her up against him so intimately that she was left with no doubt as to the direction his thoughts were taking. What did anything matter compared to the excruciatingly sweet knowledge that this man desired her?

Emboldened by this discovery, Regina moved tentatively against him and was rewarded with a growl of pleasure against her neck, before the colonel pulled back to stare hungrily down at her.

"You are a beautiful witch, my love," he murmured huskily, his eyes twin pits of barely controlled passion. "I think the time has come, my sweet, to . . ." He paused to gaze at her intently, a slow smile curling his mouth up at the corners.

Regina's blood pounded in her ears, and she could not bear the suspense. "To what?" she whispered shamelessly, more than ready to hear her husband lay claim to what had been rightfully his for more than six months now.

He grinned, and Regina was momentarily disconcerted. The colonel had never, but never grinned at her before. He was not a grinning type of man, or so she had thought. But he was certainly grinning now, and suddenly she felt unsure of herself.

"Time to do what?" she repeated, a touch of asperity in her voice.

He kissed her again before he murmured against her arched neck. "I think it is high time I took a look at that birthmark you have been bragging about, my dear."

Regina opened her mouth, but the incongruity of his remark deprived her of words.

"After all," he said conversationally, "there are certain things a husband should know about his wife, would you not agree, my pet?"

It took Regina several seconds to realize that the colonel was entirely serious. He meant to look at her birthmark. She blushed hotly, thinking of the intimate position of that butterfly-shaped blemish. "Perhaps later," she murmured, trying to extricate herself from his grasp. "It is not exactly accessible," she added hastily, conjuring up the first excuse that came to mind. "And besides, we must dress for dinner."

With a sharp stab of disappointment, Regina realized that she had done it again. She had tried to run away. To escape from the very experience she had so longed for. What was the matter with her? she wondered, wishing she had never spoken those cowardly words. She glanced up at the colonel and saw with a flash of relief that he was laughing at her. Perhaps he would not let her escape. Regina fervently hoped so.

"Dinner can wait," he said with a hint of his old, dictatorial manner.

There was a time when this masculine tone of authority would have sent her up into the boughs, made her bristle furiously, and respond with one of the many cutting set-downs she had so frequently used on him. The memory of her former intolerance shamed her. For the life of her Regina could not think of a single reason for contradicting the colonel, a circumstance that pleased her inordinately and made her smile. Perhaps she might become a dutiful wife after all, she mused.

"Can it not, Regina?" the colonel insisted gently, quite spoiling the impression of unconscious authority implied in his previous tone by pressing his warm lips against her throat.

"Yes, of course," Regina murmured, without even thinking, so enthralled was she by the flurry of sensations that assailed her as her husband's mouth trailed downward and came to rest on the exposed curve of her breast.

Dinner was irrelevant anyway, Regina mused fuzzily as the colonel's mouth moved lazily across to her other breast. She closed her eyes and gave herself up to the pleasure of the moment. Suddenly she felt fingers in her hair, gently teasing the curls free of the confining pins until they fell in a warm mantle down her back. And then he was kissing her again, fingers twined in her hair, lips demanding her surrender, tongue exploring with erotic intimacy the soft contours of her mouth.

Yes, she thought, dinner and everything else outside the compass of her husband's arms was irrelevant. Regina released a soft sigh of pure contentment and surrendered herself, lips, body, and heart, to the man who had revealed this unexpectedly passionate need for her. To the man who would, very soon now, she hoped, give himself to her with equal abandon.

Regina moaned in protest when the colonel broke the kiss and drew back. "I want to see that birthmark," he insisted huskily.

She did not have to be told that the birthmark was not all he wanted to see. Regina saw the desire in his eyes, but understood without quite knowing how she came by that knowledge that the next move was hers. Richard was waiting for some sign from her. Regina had no idea what it was, never having been quite this close to seduction before. Instincts she never dreamed she had came to her aid, and no sooner had she uttered the words than she knew she had given the man she loved the final surrender he had waited for.

"I shall have to remove my gown," she murmured demurely, her lashes hiding the glow of happiness in her eyes.

Richard laughed low in his throat, and Regina felt a hot wave of desire uncoil within her.

"That will be no trouble at all, my love," he said with obvious relish, his hands already fumbling at the closings of her blue striped lustring gown.

Regina closed her eyes and rested her forehead on his bare chest. All too soon he was pulling the gown gently from her shoulders, and Regina found that it was surprisingly uncomplicated to allow it to slither down her hips and fall in a silken pool at her feet. She felt singularly exposed in her light shift but not embarrassed as he picked her up effortlessly and carried her over to the bed.

He stood there for a long moment, gazing down at her with a warmth in his eyes that Regina had only dreamed of seeing there. She twined an arm around the strong column of his neck and willed her husband to put into words the message she had seen lurking in his gaze.

"I love you, Gina," he said, as if reading her mind. "And I swear to you that I shall protect you so that never again will you be bothered by that brother of—"

Swiftly Regina stopped his lips by pressing a finger firmly against them. "Hush," she chided. "I know you will, my love, but this is neither the time nor place to speak of that. We must forget and forgive the past," she said, consciously echoing the Countess of Middlemarch's advice. "And concentrate on the future."

She smiled with a newly discovered flirtatiousness. "I thought you wanted to see my birthmark."

She held her breath after this daring reminder, but the colonel's response was everything she could have wished.

Much later, after her husband had placed her tenderly on the bed and leisurely removed her stockings, shed his own boots and breeches, and stretched himself on the bed beside her—the better to conduct the search for the elusive birthmark, he explained with a wicked grin—Regina's secret was finally uncovered, and her husband's lips claimed it as his exclusively.

Regina was only too happy to grant it to him.